Mutation Nation:

Tales of Genetic Mishaps, Monsters, and Madness

Edited by Kelly Dunn

Rainstorm Press
PO BOX 391038
Anza, Ca 92539
www.RainstormPress.com

ISBN 10 – 1-937758-02-8
ISBN 13 – 978-1-937758-02-8

Library of Congress: 2011919491

Mutation Nation
Rainstorm Press http://www.RainstormPress.com
Copyright © 2011 by Rainstorm Press
Copyright continues on the Acknowledgments page
All rights reserved.

Interior design by –
The Mad Formatter
www.TheMadFormatter.com

Cover illustration "Kindred Kind" © Audra Phillips 2011
www.AudraPhillips.com

Acknowledgments

Many thanks to Peter Atkins, Ellen Datlow, Dennis Etchison, Maryelizabeth Hart and Jeff Mariotte, Del and Sue Howison, Stephen Jones, Nancy Kilpatrick, Mike and Jodi Lester, Ben Loory, Eunice Magill, Lisa Majewski, Lisa Morton, Lyle Perez-Tinics, and Audra Phillips for their friendship and advice. Thank you also to all the contributors for giving me such marvelous variations on a human theme.

For Richard Matheson
and
George Clayton Johnson:
friends of mutants and survivors of the Twilight Zone

Introduction: This Land Is Their Land

Kelly Dunn

Mutation. Its root word, *mutare*, means, "to change," and at its twisted heart, change is what this collection of short stories is about. Change can be exciting, beneficial, beautiful. But when we think of change in relation to our own DNA, such deviation from the norm can be damaging, frightening, fascinating, and, on rare occasions-- exhilarating.

It seems that most people are curious about others of their kind who, by accident of birth or later-life happenstance, look, live, or are differently abled than the majority. Genetic mutations, with their invisible, often baffling origins, make human variation a terrifying, albeit tantalizing, mystery to be explored.

My own interest in mutations began when, at age eleven, I was given a book entitled *The True History of the Elephant Man: The Definitive Account of the Tragic and Extraordinary Life of Joseph Carey Merrick*, by Peter Ford and Michael Howell. Reading the story of Merrick, the 19th-century Englishman so horribly deformed that he was exhibited as a freak called the "Elephant Man," made my heart ache for this gentle, intelligent person trapped in a body that changed, catastrophically and uncontrollably, all his life. What made Merrick extraordinary was not his unusual appearance or his physical challenges, but rather his ability to maintain his humanity, and his unique view of the world, through all the trials he endured.

The story of Merrick's life informed my thinking as I began to discover fiction written about human beings affected in life-changing ways by their mutations. Some of my favorites have included the "misborn" in Walter M. Miller Jr.'s novel *A Canticle for Leibowitz*, who, ultimately, become a perverse symbol for humanity's renewal; the abused child in Richard Matheson's short story "Born of Man and Woman," heartbreakingly illustrating a mutated family dynamic; and H.P. Lovecraft's "The Shadow Over Innsmouth," which compellingly shows the terror and exultation inherent in human transformation.

And now there is *Mutation Nation*. In this book you will find all manner of mutations: unholy symbiosis, imitations of humanity on the cellular level, the results of radiation, physical changes caused by psychological distress, birth defects, and special gifts of nature—or the supernatural. You'll find lurkers in the backwoods, and sickness in the city. You'll even see where mutation might take humanity in a frightening future.

There is so much power in the idea that we have inside us the ability to change, for better or for worse, on the most primal level. See this power at work. Contemplate the mystery, the miracle, and, *bien sûr*, the horror, as you get to know the very special citizens of *Mutation Nation*.

Table of Contents

Angel and Grace
Ed Kurtz

1.

The deeper he went into the wilds of East Texas, the more Win Leake came to believe there was nothing but pine trees, cotton, and tarpaper shacks for a thousand miles in any direction. He wandered the backwoods for two days, sleeping on pine needles and being chased off by the suspicious locals whenever he asked about the whereabouts of a Mrs. Bryar. He ran for a mile when a colored man took a shot at him through a grease paper window, hollering about white folk always getting up to mischief. He started to worry about bears like the one old Delmont Bryar tried to kill when he killed his own self instead.

Near dusk on the second day, Win caught the scent of freshly cut sawdust and followed his nose to a humble sawmill in the middle of the woods. The sweet perfume of the pine contrasted sharply with the grind of the saws and the incessant cussing of the men who operated them, but Win moseyed right up to them all the same.

"Hullo, fellas," he said by way of greeting. "Seems I'm a damn sight lost."

The two sawyers, browned by the sun and naked to the waist, regarded him and then looked at each other. The taller one shrugged his broad shoulders and the shorter one said, "Whar ye' 'spected t'be?"

"I've come to pay my respects to Mrs. Imogen Bryar, the widow of my dearly departed cousin Mr. Delmont Bryar. Do you fine gentlemen know the Bryars?"

Again the sawyers shot glances at one another, curiously startled glances, and when the taller man resumed sawing as though Win had never spoken at all, the shorter man wiped the sweat from his brow and approached.

"Can't say as I knew Del had him no cousin," he drawled.

"Once removed," Win explained. "I'd been living in Arkansas when I heard the sorrowful news."

Read the sorrowful news, more like. The tidings were revealed in the obits, *Shreveport Times*, which Win had read like it was the racing

9

form.

"Sorrowful," the sawyer parroted, considering the word like a jeweler appraises a gem. He sucked his teeth and sauntered over to a pine stump, upon which a brown jug sat in the shade. He tipped it over his elbow with his thumb in the loop and drank ravenously of what Win presumed to be some kind of white lightning.

"Seeing as you knew my cousin," Win said, "surely you can point me in the right direction."

"Pert near a mile nuth o' here," the sawyer said, stabbing a thumb that way. "Ain't no road. You come to Barney Pott's hog pen you gone too far."

Win thanked the man for his aid and headed north. He felt the sawyer's eyes burning a hole in the back of his head until he was well hidden amongst the dense verdure.

2.

Though he assumed to find a bevy of leaning shacks along the way, Win tramped through the woods for hours with nothing but weakly moonlit pines for company. He no longer worried about determining which shack would house Mrs. Bryar; now he fretted over the utter loneliness of the scarcely inhabited backwoods and whether or not he would ever see another human being again. His stomach thundered and his throat went dry, and when a bank of dark clouds floated cruelly between the moon and the earth and plunged the woods into abject darkness, Win sat down on the ground and waited.

He did not have to wait long. Some twenty minutes into his sit-down, he spotted a faint yellow orb moving lazily between the trees. The light was accompanied by the soft crunching of pine needles and dead leaves. The orb grew in size and flickered, drawing near, and a moment later Win found himself looking up at the business end of a 20-gauge shotgun. The woman who aimed the gun at his head held up a smoky lantern with her other hand, illumining her drawn, deeply lined face. It was not a welcoming face, nor a friendly one. She might have been comely once, Win thought, but the harsh realities of backwoods poverty had seen to that.

"Who're you?" she bellowed.

"Name's Win, ma'am. Win Leake."

"Don't know no Win Leake," she said. "What you want?"

"I'm looking for Imogen Bryar. A sawyer told me I might could find her out this way."

"You found her," the woman said glumly.

"Well, heck," Win said, cracking a smile. "Ain't you just as pretty as old Del told me!"

Imogen wrinkled her nose and knitted her brow, giving her the appearance of an old leather bag. "You knew my Del?"

"Why, sure I did—we was cousins, me and him."

"That ain't right," Imogen said, jabbing the barrel at him. "Del don't got no cousins or any other kin. All Del had was me."

Win gasped dramatically and feigned a stricken look to rival any nickelodeon damsel in distress. "Oh, Del. All these years gone by … I ain't never should have said the things I said to him, but I did and he went away and by God! He really never told you about me? About the times we had when we was knee-high to a rooster?"

"Del never said nothing about no cousins," she reiterated. "On account of he didn't have any."

"I never knew he hated me that bad," Win said, and hung his head. "And now he's gone back to Jesus and I won't never make it right. What a world, Imogen. What a devilish damn world."

Imogen raised one eyebrow and lowered the shotgun so it pointed at Win's legs instead of his face. She cocked her head to one side and said, "Where'd you say you was from?"

The obituary had named Delmont's hometown, along with the especially alluring word "estate"—the word that had driven Win from his flophouse hovel in Shreveport to the Land Office and all the way to these godforsaken East Texas woods.

"Caddo Parish," he said, recalling the name from the obit.

"What part?"

"Y'know, I ain't for certain on account of my family left when I was real young. Went on to Arkansas for a while, though me and old Del kept in touch, writing letters and such."

"Letters! Del couldn't write his own name to save his life."

"Oh, I know that—he just told someone what to write to me and they scribbled it all down."

"That right?"

"Sure, it's right. We was thick as thieves, me and Del."

"Then how come I never heard of you, Win Leake?"

"Like I said, we fell out. I always reckoned we'd make it up sooner

11

or later, but now he's gone. So I come down from El Dorado to pay my respects. It's all I can do, Imogen. I wish I could do more, but I can't."

Now the shotgun drooped all the way to the ground and Imogen sucked in a deep breath.

"You really my Del's cousin?"

"In the flesh, ma'am."

She pursed her lips and glanced up at the sky just as the cloud-bank moved away from the moon. Win studied her more closely in the dim, bluish light, taking in her graying hair and baggy, home-made dress. She sighed heavily and set the lantern on the ground, whereupon she offered her hand to Win.

"I expect you best come to the house, then," she said. "No sense in leaving you out here to get bit up by skeeters all night."

3.

The name, printed in bold type at the head of the obit, was Delmont Bryar; he was just fifty-three years of age when he shuffled off his mortal coil, having aimed his blunderbuss at a brown bear, where-upon the ancient gun blew up in his face. Mr. Bryar was a native of Caddo Parish, it seemed, though lately of East Texas where he left a widow, Mrs. Imogen Bryar, his only kin and therefore the sole inheri-tor of the Bryar estate.

Estate, Win felt, was a fiddly word. It did not indicate worth in and of itself, and could just as easily mean ten dollars as ten thousand. And ten dollars certainly was not worth travelling clear out to the wilds of East Texas for.

Accordingly, Win had ambled down to the Caddo Parish Land Office, where he presented himself as a lawyer representing the Bryar family interests and inquired about any holdings the late Mr. Bryar might have left to his grief-stricken widow. To Win's mind, no man could claim much of an estate unless he had land.

As it turned out, Delmont Bryar had land in spades. This was good, and Win nodded and grunted in the way he imagined a disin-terested lawyer would do. When the clerk next asked whether or not the Widow Bryar would be wanting to speak with the Humble Oil people about leasing the property, Win's disinterest gave way to bulging eyes and gaping mouth. He told the clerk he'd have to get

12

back to him about that.

He all but ran from the Land Office and went directly to the rail yard, where he hopped the first train headed east. Win simply could not wait to make the acquaintance of Mrs. Imogen Bryar.

4.

The house Imogen led him into was a tarpaper shack, of course, though a substantially larger one than Win had yet seen. The shack appeared to have started out simple, just one room like the rest, but numerous additions contributed sections of varying, trapezoidal dimensions and a sagging porch on the front. A length of rusty pipe jutted out of a hole in the drooping roof, spewing a thin stream of wood smoke. A rotting pinewood fence penned in a mud pit on the shack's east side, but there were no animals within. The hatchet lodged into the top of one of the fenceposts suggested there once had been.

Imogen waddled past the fence to the porch, which groaned beneath her weight. The door creaked open when she pushed on it with her shoulder. A grouping of bottles hung with twine clinked noisily when the door knocked into them. She went in and suspended the lantern from a hook in the low ceiling. Win wore a smile when he entered the dim, musty space, even as he took in the clutter of broken handmade furniture, iron pots and skillets, animal pelts, jugs and bottles, tin plates and cups, a pile of filthy quilts in one corner and a wood-burning stove in the other. He noted a scythe with a dull, jagged blade leaned up against a wall and a peculiar baby doll perched on the only remaining arm of a chair. Closer inspection revealed it to be two dolls stitched together, back to back. They were crudely made, like almost everything else in evidence.

"Such a lovely home," he remarked.

"Figgered you was from the Humble when I seen you settin' there in the dirt," Imogen said.

"What, Humble Oil? No, ma'am. Not me." It was the first true thing he had said to her since he'd told her his name.

"You set down," she commanded as she propped the 20-gauge beside the scythe.

He did as he was told, selecting the least rickety-looking of his several choices. Nonetheless, the chair whined like a dying cat when

13

he sat on it.

"I got to tend to the girls," Imogen said, groping for the leather handle to the door in the back wall.

Win presumed she was referring to some old hound dogs or maybe livestock, but the caterwauling that rose up from one of the back rooms put such notions to rest. A pair of distinctively human cries were rocking the shack, which came as no surprise to Imogen Bryar.

"They'll be wanting their supper," she said. "You jest wait here, Win Leake. I'll be back directly."

"Daughters," he said in a whisper. "Why, I didn't know—"

"*I'll be back directly*," she said again.

And with that, she was through the door and gone like a vapor.

The *Times* obit had not said a word about any children. Win sat in the wavering lantern light and wondered why.

5.

In a short time Imogen returned from her motherly duties and inquired about Win's own plans for supper. He answered that he would appreciate anything she was serving, and she pointed him towards the same door from which she had only just come.

"We et in there," she said.

Win eyed the door warily, wondering what he could expect to find on the other side.

"Go on," Imogen urged him. "Have you a set. Won't be a minute."

He nodded and flashed a grin as he rose from the unstable chair and reached for the leather strap. The door came open to reveal a long, narrow room with two pinewood tables, short and square-shaped, situated in the middle. At the end of each table was a wooden chair, and in the middle a roughly hewn bench was placed between. Each table sported a burning candle in a tin cup, which shed enough light for Win to see the dead leaves and pine needles piled up in the corners of the room. He took a seat at the end of the nearest table.

From the front room he heard Imogen clanging about as she worked at the stove with her ironware, and a slight shiver worked its way up his sweat-drenched back. He had waltzed right into some mighty peculiar circumstances, but he'd come this far and he wanted Delmont's land. The alternative was toil by the sweat of his brow, and no amount of peculiarity was likely to set Win Leake on that course.

Presently the lady of the house backed into the room, her arms wrapped around an iron pot. She set the pot on the table and handed Win one of the two tin plates she had tucked into her armpit. No sooner than he accepted it, Imogen set to scooping the contents of the pot onto the plate. The helping was brownish and lumpy, a sort of stew. His stomach convulsed when he caught its vaguely meaty odor. The moment his hostess sat down—in the chair at the other table— he dug into the slop with a broken wooden spoon. It tasted vaguely earthen, as though clay were a primary ingredient, which Win guessed was probably true. He finished it off anyway.

"Met him when he come out here to work for a lumber yard," Imogen spoke up, apropos of nothing. "Guess he got in some kind of trouble back in Louisiana, don't know what kind. Runned off to Texas. Strong as an ox, Del was. Stronger, maybe."

"He was a strong boy, too," Win ventured.

"Well, he was wanting a place to sleep wasn't just the ground, and I let him sleep on the porch for a while. Later he came on inside, paid me five cents a night to stay in the front room there. That was good for a spell, 'til he said he wanted a bed. I gave him half o' mine, and it cost him ten cents."

The candles' flames bounced as though a draft had passed through, but Win had not felt one. His eyes were fixed on Imogen, her worn face framed by the dirty, oddly leaning room. She shoveled a spoonful of brown mire into her mouth and swallowed without bothering to chew.

"After Del got up on me that first time," she went on, "I didn't take no dime from him anymore. Slick as a preacher, that man. Coulda talked me into any ole thing, I expect."

"That was Del," Win said. "Always a smooth talker."

"Yes, he was," she agreed. "Yes sir, he surely was."

"But he gave you some lovely children."

"Del?" Imogen cracked a smile and fell into a peal of laughter. It sounded like a dozen saws at work. "No, no—not my Del. He didn't never put no baby in me, Win Leake."

"Oh," said Win, embarrassed to the point of flushing pink. "I'm sorry, I just assumed—"

"My girls' papa went to his maker long before Delmont Bryar ever darkened my door, the Lord bless him. Hopper Jackson, I mean.

15

Not Del."

Win screwed up his face, working on a smile that did not quite materialize. A soft, childlike moan sounded from somewhere in the mishmash of tarpaper rooms. His shoulders jumped and Mrs. Imogen Bryar smiled sweetly.

"Ain't been a man in the house since Del died," she said. "Ain't been nobody but me and my girls."

Win nodded and scooped a spoonful of slop into his mouth.

"They're making a regular fuss," Imogen went on. "I 'spect they want to see you for themselves."

"I ain't much to look at," Win said.

"You're plenty," she countered.

He swallowed loudly and asked, "What are their names?"

"Angel and Grace."

"Why, that's plain purty, Ms. Imogen."

The small voices cried out again, reaching something like a harmony in the middle as their wavering voices crossed like swords in their hollow desolation. Win furrowed his brow.

"Well," Imogen said as she rose from her chair, "You might as well get acquainted."

Win watched her closely as she took up a candle and waddled over to the farthest corner of the dirty, slanting room. She knelt down and ran the palm of her hand along the floor until her fingertips found purchase in a gap between the jagged floorboards. She dug in and pulled up a section of the floor, revealing a hole big enough to crawl through. The light of the candle illumined a derelict ladder, its steps artlessly nailed into the frame at various jutting angles.

Win gaped.

"They're down there? Angel and Grace?"

"That's right," she answered.

The cries came clear and close from the dark depths beneath the floor. Imogen threw her legs into the hole and, taking the candle in one hand, began her descent. The steps creaked ominously.

Imogen said, "Come on, now. Hurry up." Then she was gone from Win's view.

"*Maaaa*," one of the girls moaned. "*Maaaama.*"

They were either very young or just plain touched in the head, Win decided. Either way, he deemed it unwise to offend the woman when a perfectly good opportunity to impress her was presented to him on a platter. So he rose from the table and went to the hole in the floor and climbed down after Imogen to meet her daughters.

6.

The floor and walls were nothing but dirt, shored up on all sides by rough-hewn lengths of pine. Scraggly roots curled out of the ceiling. There was a small table in one corner, its surface cluttered with grimy tinware, and a pair of iron fireplace tongs leaning against the wall. The tinware itself was cluttered with maggots and flies. On the opposite side of the musty space a pair of shadows lurched just outside the glow of Imogen's candlelight. She cooed at the shapes, kissed at the air and made low, purring sounds. The girls moaned in reply.

"My girls," she muttered. "My babies."

"*Maaaama*," a strained voice said.

Win paused at the bottom of the ladder. His eyes narrowed at the rocking figures in the corner. Several flies abandoned the rotting food on the tinware to circle his head instead. They buzzed noisily in his ears and he swatted at them, cursing beneath his breath.

Imogen moved into the center of the dank, humid space, whereupon Win observed a long, pallid extremity swing into the flickering halo of candlelight. A gnarled, groping hand snatched at the air, its skin taut and riddled with scabs. Imogen took the hand into her own and a voice gurgled wetly. Now the light fully illuminated one of the two girls in the corner. Win gasped.

The unfortunate creature's head appeared twice the size it should have been, the forehead high and angular, while the back of the skull was elongated and lumpy with tumors. The eyes were small and black, wide-set and as soulless as a spider's. There was no nose to speak of—only a puckered pit in the center of its face—and a wide, drooling mouth with infrequent, rotted teeth flapped madly as it babbled. Win saw that the thing was entirely naked, whereby he spied the long vertical wound that ran between two drooping, scabby breasts clear down the length of her abdomen. The wound was red with yellow splotches, badly infected, and swarming with maggots.

Win gagged and looked hurriedly away.

"I want you meet somebody, Angel," Imogen said sweetly. "This here's your cousin Win."

The girl jerked her bony arms and waggled her fingers, of which

17

Win noticed there were only three on each hand. She was seated on a wooden bench, her mangled legs hanging helplessly beneath her. They looked broken in various places, almost jellied. She made a sound he took for a laugh, and it sounded like scraped sandpaper. Win shuddered.

"I reckon she likes you," Imogen said. "That's just fine. Angel was the one I was worried about."

Angel cried out—"*Nyuhh*"—and smashed her hands together.

"Worried?" Win asked, a nervous titter in his voice. "Why ever for?"

"On account of Grace is already married," Imogen said.

She raised the candle then, casting a sickly yellow light over the entire corner. Win stared and his breath hitched in his throat.

Fused to Angel's back in a veiny, knotted mass of twisted flesh was what he presumed to be Grace. She was every bit as disfigured as her sister, though her head was a sagging assortment of black-blue cysts and dripping pustules, and she had no eyes at all. When Angel jerked, Grace bounced feebly behind her. Only when she raised her massive, abscessed head to release a low, plaintive moan did Win realize she was not, in fact, dead.

"Good God," he whispered. "Siamese twins." The moment he spoke, a pitiful cry emanated from the ground at Grace's feet.

"Oh, hush your mouth, Henry," Imogen snarled. "That man, I swear."

"*Henreeeeee*," Grace squealed.

"Huh—help," said a voice in the shadows.

Win sucked a deep breath into his lungs and stared into the darkness until Imogen's light came near enough to reveal the nude, emaciated man shackled to Grace's boneless ankle. He was curled up so that his knobby knees touched his stringy black beard, and his sunken eyes glared solicitously up at Win. He was covered in grime and sweat and not a few poorly healed lacerations. Beneath him, the dirt was turned to mud by the suffering man's own waste.

Both of Henry's arms ended at the elbows, where badly healed stumps squirmed with teeming bugs of every stripe.

"Please," he rasped. "Please help me."

Imogen waddled around the conjoined girls and delivered a sound kick to Henry's ribs. He yelped and cowered, pressing himself as deeply into the foul corner as possible.

18

"I said shut up, Henry!" she screeched.

"Sweet Jesus," Win said. "What the hell is this?"

"This is Henry, my Gracie's husband," Imogen answered. "And I'll thank you to quit all that cussin' in my house, Win Leake."

"He's chained up!"

"A'course he is, you nitwit. We don't want him to get away, now. Them two is bound by the holy bond matrimony, you know, and that can't get unbound by nobody."

Grace convulsed then, pulling her and Angel both to one side and then the other. Her serpentine legs wobbled beneath her, rattling the chain that connected her to Henry.

"But who is he?" Win asked, his voice rising in pitch. "How'd he end up here?"

"Who, dumb ol' Henry? He was my Del's brother. Come round last summer, sniffin' out some land he reckoned on havin' a right to. My little Gracie here, why she was just wild about Henry, wasn't you pumpkin?"

Grace burbled until her burbling turned into a growl. Henry started to weep at her limp feet.

"Just wild," Imogen said. Then, upon turning to touch Win gently on the elbow, she asked, "Are you married, Win Leake?"

7.

Not only was Win well aware of the regularity of shotgun weddings in the rural South, he had actually narrowly avoided one himself. The girl was a mulatto housemaid who passed for white, and it was her employer who directed his outrage at Win for putting the offending bun in her oven. The man jabbed double barrels in Win's belly while a footman ran to fetch a pastor, though by the time the clergyman arrived, all he found was a man with his hand blown off by his own shotgun, hollering bloody murder while Win high-tailed it out of Tennessee for good.

He struggled to recall the girl's name, feeling it was somehow important all of a sudden, while he absent-mindedly pulled at the iron cuff encircling his right ankle. Welded into the cuff was an iron chain that was welded to another cuff on the other end, which was attached to the repulsively squirmy left leg of Angel Jackson. Her heavy head bobbed on her neck as though it floated on water, and her crooked hands worried the long scabby gash that ran the length of her torso. Win did everything possible to ignore her, digging deep into his memory to find that housemaid's name. Occasionally the lump on the back of his head would flare, and he would grimace at the thought of Imogen getting one over on him by pounding that rock against his skull. He could not help but wonder if he would have had so much trouble remembering the mulatto girl's name had he not been struck on the noggin by a three-pound stone.

At length Win snapped his head up and cried out, "Leonora! That was it—Leonora."

Angel groaned and scratched at the air with her twisted fingers. A similar scene unfolded on the other side of the bench, a mirror image of a deformed unfortunate and her unwilling groom. Henry mostly just wept, however, while Grace made moist baby noises and hummed tuneless melodies. Win had already given up all attempts to make conversation with his fellow captive, finding him as poor a conversationalist as Angel and Grace were. Nonetheless, he bellowed the Tennessee housemaid's name at the sobbing man like a call to arms:

"Leonora, you blubbering bastard! Leonora!"

Angel hissed.

"Oh, you hush up," Win snapped back.

Presently the panel at the top of the ladder shifted and clattered away. A shaft of weak, dusty light poured down as Imogen descended, her bare feet black on the bottoms. From one hand a tin pot dangled by the handle, its contents sloshing from side to side.

"Supper time," she said cheerfully.

"Glory be," Win grumped.

"Now, you best eat it up, Win Leake. You don't eat any more than a bird and you got to get your strength up. You're fixin' to get hitched in case you went and forgot."

"How on God's Jesus green earth could I? I'm chained up in a hole in the goddamn ground, for Christ's sakes!"

Imogen's brow furrowed, darkening her face.

"I told you about that cussin', now," she said low. She set the pot down on the little table near the ladder and retrieved the fireplace tongs from the corner. Win's eyes bulged as he considered the woman's intentions.

"God, no," he said. "Not that."

"If you're to be my Angel's husband, you'd best start acting right,

20

Win Leake. This'll teach you. Might could take a turn or two, but it'll teach you."

"Imogen, Imogen please ..."

She stepped in front of the lantern, transforming into a backlit shadow of a woman who wrapped her fingers around the handles of the tongs and snapped them closed. Win flinched and squeezed his eyes shut at her approach. A small whimper roiled out of his throat. His face flushed hot and tears spilled down his dirty cheeks.

"Jesus Christ, what's wrong with you people?" he muttered.

"Wrong?" Imogen exclaimed. "There's nothing *wrong* with family, Win Leake. You happen to part of this one and you ought to start acting like it."

"I ain't your family."

"Don't be stupid. You're Del's cousin and that makes you kin to us."

"But I ain't, Imogen. I ain't nothing to Del, never was. I never even laid eyes on the man, I swear it."

"You stop that, now," she barked, stabbing the flat tip of the tongs at Angel. The latter shrieked, which elicited a cry from Win. "You men will say anything to get your way. Any old thing at all."

The end of the tongs pressed up against the crusty wound in Angel's abdomen, and she flailed her crooked hands at it, kicking up a flurry of white maggots. The response did her no good: with a little exertion, Imogen pushed the lipped iron into the wound with an audible crunch. Angel tossed her huge, lumpy head back and screamed loud enough to shake dirt loose from above. Grace followed suit, absorbing her sister's anguish and unleashing a jarring screech of her own. Imogen clicked her tongue against her teeth and said, "Land's sakes."

With that, she gave the tongs another sharp thrust and then wrenched the handles apart. Angel's trunk split down the middle, sending her drooping breasts careening into her armpits. White foam frothed out of her gaping mouth as she screamed and whipped her head back and forth. Win scrambled for the wall behind him, pulling the chain taut. He had begun to hyperventilate. He was vaguely aware that Angel's black insect eyes were fixed on him.

"That's a girl," Imogen cooed as she tensed her shoulders to hold the massive wound open. "That's a *good* girl."

Win tried to look away, but the slick red mass bubbling out of the

21

opening transfixed him. His mind reeled—he was dizzy with the insanity of Imogen capturing him to forcibly marry her malformed daughter, only to murder said daughter in the worst way imaginable. The poor creature's guts were boiling out of her torso, all slippery and wet and befouling the already fetid air. Win felt his gorge rise, bile burning a path up his throat. Frozen with fear and revulsion, he simply vomited where he crouched, most of it washing over him even as he stared at the gruesome tableau Imogen made of Angel.

The mother grunted under the strain of holding the girl's trunk open; the girl keened mournfully at the roots hanging down from above. Win moaned with fright as Angel's voice receded, melting back into her. She was dying, he was sure of it. Angel was dying and her mother was killing her and Win's brain pulsed with fear-induced madness, horrified at the limitless possibilities of Imogen's senseless plans for him.

"Don't," he rasped. "Imogen, stop ..."

Then the voice grew again, built in intensity and rage. The scream filled Angel, filled the hole in the earth beneath the tarpaper compound. The girl's twisted body shook and her face went slack. Behind her, Grace babbled an endless stream of nonsense, her voice getting higher and more manic as she went on. Henry shrieked.

Imogen said, "Come on, now. It's all right, baby girl. Come on out."

The red mass shifted in the shadows of Angel's split torso, and the keening voice erupted from within. Win's shrieks eclipsed Henry's, pierced the dank air like a thousand hot needles, tore out of him until his raw throat bled. Even after his vocal chords gave out and the only sound to escape his lips was a scratchy whistling, Win kept screaming his silent scream at the dripping claws that unraveled from Angel's guts.

They were pincers, like a crab's, with saw-toothed edges that wrenched open and clapped shut with stunning rapidity. The pincers spun around madly, driven by the ropy tendrils Win mistook for entrails. They snapped at him and he flattened against the hard packed dirt, his eyes bulging out of their sockets. He swatted a hand at them, a reflexive action, and a pincer clamped down on his fingers, holding tight. The bones in his fingers crunched apart as something in the girl's gaping cavity hissed.

"There you are, you shy thing," Imogen said. There were tears in

22

her eyes.

Between the red, writhing ropes of flesh that lashed from Angel's open chest came a wailing mouth, a gummy black tongue undulating past double rows of jagged white teeth. The mouth pressed forth, bringing the rest of the face into view like a baby emerging from its mother's womb. In sharp contrast to Angel's tiny obsidian eyes, the creature stared with enormous crystalline orbs, blue as the ocean and wiggling about as they took in their surroundings. Its small, round head was the same blood red as the writhing arms that preceded it, deeply wrinkled like a bloody prune. A prominent ridge jutted from the center of the crown. It had no nose and no ears. It bawled at Win, setting its gaze on him as the claw retracted, tugging his destroyed hand towards the slavering mouth.

"No!" Win gasped. "Christ, no!" Win jerked, tried to pull his hand back, but the thing's hunger was more powerful.

"It's just a taste, you big baby," Imogen scolded him. "She ain't fixin' to kill you or nothin'. Henry's still here, ain't he?"

By way of response, Henry whimpered.

And then the creature inside Angel bit down on Win's thumb, severing it between grinding teeth and moaning with pleasure as it chewed the digit to pulp. The claw released his broken, bleeding hand and he retreated to the wall, the chain at his ankle clattering loudly. The monstrous thing swallowed, smacked its blubbery red lips and sighed with satisfaction.

"Goooood," Angel groaned.

Imogen eased the tongs out and dropped them to the ground as the snapping pincers wound back into Angel's trunk and the grotesque face sank into the throbbing crimson network of her entrails.

"Such a good girl," said the mother. "Been ages since she et, poor thing. Not since she finished off our Del."

Angel slowly lowered her head, made a soft burbling noise and used her upper arms to close the flesh over her body as though she were putting on a coat. Her face turned to Win and he gave a violent shudder, certain that she was grinning at him.

"You're gonna make a fine husband, Win Leake," Imogen said proudly. "One of the best my baby ever did have."

A jet of red-black blood spurted from the stump where his thumb had been. It was Win's last sensation before the cellar went black.

8.

Henry died in August after a long week of incessant convulsions. By then the creatures inside Angel and Grace had grown considerably, and came out on their own to feed whenever they wanted. The larger they grew, the worse the sisters got; their pallid skin turned an ashy gray and they fell silent and still. Win found himself strangely unfazed by the regular appearance of the hellish red things, even welcoming. For the most part they were the only company available to him, his sole contact with anything beyond his own lonely thoughts. And, in the dark, damp hole beneath the tarpaper shack above, Win had gradually come to accept Imogen's understanding of what it meant to be part of a family.

Angel took Win's hands and feet, his arms and legs. Imogen bandaged him up, but Angel always came back for more. Soon he fell ill, weak and unable to keep food or water down. For a time Imogen kept him secured to Angel by way of a leather harness around his ribs, but his failing health rendered it unnecessary. He could do nothing but lie still on the dirt floor and watch as Angel and Grace gradually withered away while the devils inside of them grew strong.

In time the cutting claws rotted off and the girls breathed their last, a development ostensibly expected by their mother, who came down the ladder to help the slippery creatures slough the dead sisters off like a snake sheds its skin. They too were conjoined at their backs, and as the blood dried and the twins continued to grow, Win came to realize that Imogen had every reason to call them by her dead children's names. They had not merely replaced Angel and Grace, whose remains were taken away as one takes out the garbage: they *were* Angel and Grace, born anew. And though their misshapen heads and gnarled hands belied the same pitiful abnormalities of their predecessors, Win was sure they were getting better. Less deformed. More intelligent.

The night the drifter came down after a hot meal in the dining room above, Win knew Grace finally had a new beau. The man hollered and shouted at the emergence of the snapping claws and mewling face, of course, and Win would have told him not to bother if he had had any voice left in him. But he didn't, and the drifter—name of Adlai—kept right on bellowing to the high heavens while Grace's parasite gobbled him up, piece by piece, gathering its strength to become her. A better Grace, new and improved in nearly every way.

Someday, Win figured, she might even transform into a comely girl of gentle manners and a beguiling smile. They both would, she and Angel. Lovely girls to make a lucky pair of fellows proud. The belles of the ball. Queens of East Texas.

Tears scored paths through the dirt on his cheeks as he privately acknowledged that he would not live to see them thrive. But Win was overcome with a deep satisfaction that he was a contributing factor to their coming out, however small his contribution was, and he died feeling he would always be with them, his perfect little Angel in particular. It was madness and grief that stoked the embers of his adoration, and he would not be the last to die in love with a monster in the ground beneath a tarpaper shack deep in the pinewoods.

Love was cruel that way.

Queen of Hearts

Helen E. Davis

Jenna lay awake in her bed, listening to her heart. For the first twenty-eight years of her life it had beat steadily, sometimes faster and sometimes slower, but always with the same *ba-dump, ba-dump, ba-dump*. After the viral infection, her heart wheezed like an old man. Months passed as the wheezing grew to gasps and she started to drown in her own blood. Her new heart solved all that, returning her to an active life with a steady *ba-dump, ba-dump* rhythm.

But now it sounded like an out-of-whack steam engine: *ba-dump, dump, bump, dump, bump.*

She frowned, feeling the cold disk of the stethoscope between her fingers. Was that a new *bump*, tacked on at the end? Yes. The rhythm now was *ba-dump, dump, bump, dump, bump-bump*, with each new chamber adding its own little beat.

She moved the stethoscope down her right side to where the other heartbeat was. Two years earlier a doctor had thought she was pregnant, based on that abdominal heartbeat, but it was only a second heart growing where her appendix should have been. When she asked doctors about the extra heart, they would all shrug in puzzlement— and point out that as long as it didn't interfere with the functioning of her body, she should leave it alone.

Where else was she growing spare hearts? There were flutters in her arm, her calf, and her back, and on the days that she had a pounding headache, she worried that a heart was inside her skull, crushing her brain with every squeeze.

She moved to put away the stethoscope, and her fingers brushed against a small, scaled patch at her waist. *Better get that checked by the dermatologist*, she thought. *Another doctor, another expense.*

* * *

"Here's another one like you."

Jenna looked up from her work and frowned at her gum-cracking, purple- and pink-haired co-worker. Other than the hair, all of Aimee's accessories were black: clothes, lipstick, dark raccoon circles that made targets of her eyes. Instead of earrings, the girl wore mismatched safety pins. Jenna asked, "One like me, how?"

Aimee tapped her screen with a long, black fingernail, then cracked her gum loudly. "Kidneys everywhere. It's on *Odd News Today.*"

And she thinks I'm the freak, Jenna thought. Still, she pushed back her chair and walked over to Aimee's computer. There, tucked between ads for leather underwear and fake-fur fetishes, she saw a photo of a young, dark-skinned man and a grainy ultrasound. Scattered among the organs she recognized were grape-like clusters, each with a thin white line snaking down to a kiwi fruit-shaped bladder. They were labeled, "Kidney Globules."

"And how is this like me?"

Snap went the Juicy Fruit. "Kidneys growing everywhere. Small, working kidneys."

"He didn't have a kidney transplant, did he?"

"Yeah, but it turned cancerous, so they took it out. You don't think it's some sort of virus, do you? Like the one that turns people into zombies?" Aimee leaned away from Jenna.

"That's a video game," Jenna said dryly. She looked again at the man, and felt the faint brush of remembrance. Had she known him before? "Send me the link to that page. I've got to find him."

* * *

They come from all corners, those who attend. Walking, swimming, scrunching, flying; on two feet, on four, on six, on none at all. It is a time of gathering, of sharing, of communicating. Part play, part work, all games of dominance. Who is better? Who is worse? Who will take the highest honors? With each one so different from the next, there is only one way to compete.

* * *

All Jenna's hearts pounded as she sat on a bench by the park pond, waiting. Children dashed on the far side, yelling to each other, oblivious to the strangers near them. One child could disappear and the others might not even notice, so involved were they in their game. On Jenna's side of the pond, a flock of geese watched the kids' play with disdain, then marched in the opposite direction. They paused at a bench where a young man in a suit ate from a paper sack, and loudly demanded his lunch.

Entitled beggars, Jenna thought. *If he fed them rat poison, they'd never know the difference.*

"Jenna McClain?"

The man startled her. He wore jeans and scruffy sneakers, a dark hoodie pulled over his head, and a nervous expression on his thin, dark face. Yes, she did know him. Had known him, and not just from a photo on the Internet. But where?

Tubes. White gauze. Green curtains swaying in the wake of someone walking by.

"Do you know me?" she blurted out.

"I'm Dajoun Pierce. You asked to meet me here. You said we had a common interest." He perched on the far end of the bench, like a pigeon ready to fly.

"Yes, yes. We do. But—I think we've met before." Nausea hit her like a truck, pushed her away from him. She scooted to the other end of the bench. "I'm sorry."

Dajoun's face twisted in a grimace that matched her own twisting gut. "Something—something in the air? Let's go somewhere else."

No one else seemed affected, and when he stood up her nausea eased. Fresh air, scented with roses, blew across the bench. "Stay here. It's another bit of the oddness."

"Oddness?" His forehead wrinkled, the deep furrows speckled with small scaled spots. "You have too many kidneys?"

"Hearts. I'm the Queen of Hearts."

"When—when did this happen?"

"I had a heart transplant."

"Kidney. When?"

"Four years ago."

"Four years, three months, and nine days."

"Yeah." Jenna quickly calculated. "Four years, three months, and twelve days. Where did you go for it?"

Dajoun frowned. "Odd, that. I can't quite remember. I knew it, wrote checks to it, told my family and friends all about it. But when I try to remember, it just slips away."

She tried to remember her own clinic. It was—a surge of bile burned the back of her throat. "Ugh."

29

"That, too."

Maybe there *was* something in the air. Something odorless, just in this area. Jenna started to rise.

"Sand," Dajoun stated.

Jenna sat back down. "What?"

"Sand outside my window. Not the beach, though. I saw cacti, too."

"Stars at night," Jenna added. Idly, she scratched the patch of rough skin that now encircled her wrist like a snakeskin bracelet. "So bright, so many. The Milky Way ..."

"Washed across the sea like a pail of spilt milk. You *said* that." He stared at the soft grass, lush despite the dry California fall, as he spoke.

"When?"

"You were looking out the window. I remember that."

Jenna looked hard at Dajoun, then suddenly dry heaved. Remembering Dajoun, remembering the name of the facility—that brought on the nausea. But—"Green curtains waving."

"Between the beds. There were, others. Other patients." Dajoun frowned, then gagged.

We're not to think of them. We're not to meet them, or speak of them. Yet—the curtain dragged out another scrap of memory, a voice beyond the curtain. A happy voice, accented with drawn-out vowels and clipped consonants. "Take care of those lungs. Made them myself, made them special."

"The orderly," Jenna said.

Dajoun didn't seem to hear. "Six, ten others. At least."

Others who might be afflicted with the same strange condition. "How do we find them?"

Turning, Dajoun gave Jenna his attention, then whipped back and heaved over the grass. "It's getting stronger."

She felt it as well, a clamp around her chest. Her hearts pounded; her gut threatened an explosion. She slapped down her business card. "Email me."

* * *

"Found seven obituaries," read the subject of the email waiting for Jenna that evening. Dajoun certainly worked fast. She clicked it open.

30

In the email she found the particulars. All had been patients who had received new organs approximately four years and three months earlier, at an unnamed clinic, and all had suffered from a cancer related to the transplanted organ. One, a knee transplant patient, had died when great bony shafts had grown through her body and pierced her internal organs. In another, a pancreas transplant patient, the out-of-control growth had carried the patient away with insulin shock. A third man, who had received testicles, had died of heart failure brought on by too much testosterone. Three patients had died from surgical complications after multiple attempts to remove the wayward organs. And one woman had killed herself.

The email ended with a statement from Dajoun. "I guess we're the lucky ones."

Only for now, Jenna thought. The pounding had started inside her skull again: *bump, bump, bump, ba-dump, bu-dump.*

* * *

There are always posters at these things, great displays of numbers and graphs. Numbers, for numbers are based on physical reality, and graphs, because a graph is just a set of numbers in relation to another set of numbers. Illustrations are common, yes, but dependent on the attendees, and what they can sense. The media may be electrons in gas or scribbles baked into clay, but there are always posters and always numbers. Numbers representing living beings, sacrificial laboratory animals.

* * *

"You're looking for something," stated the woman seated at the table in the diner.

Jenna turned to look at her. The woman wore large sunglasses, very dark, and a flowery scarf hid the rest of her face. A loose cloak hid her figure; but her voice ...

Jenna swallowed fast. "I'm sorry."

"There's no need to be," the woman said. She stared at Jenna now. "You were looking for something. I interrupted you."

Jenna stared down at her lunch. "Mustard. Pickle relish."

"Over by the wall." The woman gestured without freeing her

31

hand from the cloak. Her scarf gaped open, allowing a glimpse of pustule-draped cheeks.

Bile burned the back of Jenna's throat. The woman's stench, she thought, as she grabbed packets at random and hurried to the door.

But there was no stench. The place smelled only of hot dogs and relishes, potato chips and grease. Facing away from the woman, Jenna felt no sickness.

Just as with Dajoun.

Bracing herself, Jenna turned back. She asked the woman, "Do I make you feel ill?"

"Oh, honey," the woman spoke gently. "I broke that suggestion long ago. I'm a stubborn cuss—I wouldn't let them muck with my brain."

"Did you have an organ transplant four years ago?"

"I did." Her hand eased out from beneath the cloak. It was covered in blue scales like a fitted glove. Fingers, far too many, twisted bonelessly like the arms of a squid. One curled towards the rash on Jenna's wrist. "And honey, so did you."

* * *

"Just keep telling yourself that the repulsion is not real." The woman's soft Georgia accent purred in Jenna's ears. Her name was Luella Bates, and she had been a nurse before diabetes had taken her sight. All she had wanted was her sight back. No conventional treatments helped. Then one day she was offered an experimental transplant.

Jenna remembered that. She also had been too weak for a normal transplant, wouldn't survive the anti-rejection drugs, but if she were willing to try an experimental therapy ...

"But it worked," she said out loud.

"Keep your eyes closed," Luella said sharply, firmly; the tone of a woman who was used to regulating the lives of others. "You're not ready to look with your eyes. You have to master your mind first, 'cause that's where they mucked with you."

"Who?" Jenna touched the hot dog on her plate, still uneaten and getting cold. She would get a fresh one when she went back to the office. New packets of mustard and relish. A soda.

"Them," Luella stated. "The transplant—not people. Creatures. The Transplanters."

"What? What do Transplanters have to do with hot dogs?" She envisioned people planting hot dogs in the park, the hot dog bushes growing, then geese running gobbling the still-green hot dog fruits. There would also be a mustard and relish plant, with rosettes of packets for flowers.

"Don't let your mind wander!" Luella snapped, then sighed. "That's another of their tricks. Distraction and repulsion."

"Magnets?"

"Honey, open your eyes."

Jenna did. She saw the woman sitting across from her. Her scarf had pulled away just enough for Jenna to see the small white orbs dotting her cheeks, orbs with a dark pupil in each one. Turning away quickly, she searched for a wastebasket, glad to have the reaction to cover her disgust. "I have to go. I simply have to go."

"But we need to talk."

"Yes." Jenna opened her purse and grabbed a business card. "Email me!"

* * *

Using a hand mirror to see the wall mirror behind her, Jenna examined her back. She could see a cluster of small blue spots in the gap between her left shoulder blade and her spine. There were three more at her waist, on the right side. And they were scaly like the ones on her wrist. And like Luella's tentacle fingers.

A swaying curtain, the sharp smell of disinfectant. A hiss from the ventilator, the dull thud of a pump, somewhere beyond the curtain. A window, square, with stars behind the upright arms of a saguaro cactus.

She tried to think of more, but the pounding of her hearts pushed the memory away.

* * *

There are always lab coats at these things, though the definition of a lab coat changes with the form. Sometimes the coat is a protective device, a sheath worn over other coverings. Sometimes it is an array of sensors testing for toxic substances. For a few individuals, the coats are symbolic regalia, as these few have nothing physical to protect. Always, though, there are lab coats, for such things are nothing

33

less than a mark of wisdom, a call for respect. A promise of life, if one is ill. Take the pill that the one in the lab coat offers and hope that this is not the pill that does nothing—or perhaps the pill that does worse.

* * *

"Where was the transplant clinic?" Jenna typed in an email to Dajoun. "What was it called?"

"Oregon," Dajoun emailed back. "Or Wyoming. Someplace with a desert."

Those states sounded right. Except ... It *had* to be one of the two, she could almost remember which one. But ...

Saguaro cacti in Oregon? Or Wyoming?

Maybe the clinic was in Texas. Yes, that sounded right. It had to be in Texas. She would have flown there, of course, then rented a car. Of course.

But how could she have driven when she was so sick and gasping for breath? She remembered those days—and suddenly saw herself struggling to climb the steps of a small bus. A white bus with a green stripe along the side. She had leaned on the railing and stared at the stripe, gasping, as a strangely accented voice scratched behind her. "Up you go, I have new heart, just for you."

How could they have driven all the way?

And didn't the saguaro cactus only grow in the Sonoran Desert?

No. She cut the thought off and stared at the wall above her computer monitor. If she *knew* the clinic was in Texas, or Wyoming, that was where it had to be. She had to accept that.

Shutting off her computer, she went to get ready for bed. She brushed her teeth, combed her hair, and collected her stethoscope for her nightly heart count. On her way to bed, she dropped a new toothbrush and a sample-sized toothpaste into her purse, just in case, for no reason at all, she happened to be away from home the next day.

* * *

The next day, for no reason, Jenna called in sick and went for a drive. She should go east, she told herself, and look for the clinic. No, she needed a break from hearts, from people stranger than herself, from

34

Transplanters who weren't people. She was just going for a drive, nowhere in particular. *No-where.*

She took the road that ran by her house, following it until it ended on a major street. There she turned east, towards the mountains. No reason; she was just driving out of the city. When the major street ended at another, she again turned towards the mountains. Always towards the mountains, just driving. She had no other goal.

By midmorning she was in the mountains, working her way from one rural road to the next, winding up and down the slopes. She found a pass, cut for a wide divided highway, and took the highway just long enough to get through the peaks. There she curved off and faced a two-lane road which disappeared into the pine forest on either side.

Go north, whispered a voice in her mind. *North to Wyoming.*

I'm just out for a drive, she told herself as she turned south into the feeling of wrongness.

She stopped at a diner perched on a cliff, a river curving far below. The clapboard siding, the green-shingled roof, the way the shutters hung, slightly crooked: It seemed perfect, like a photo in a book, or a painting in an art gallery. But there needed to be grimy white smears on the ground, the grainy dredges of a long-past snowfall, and splashes of blue, yellow, and green by the front door. Tulips.

An early-turning leaf blew past her face as she pushed open the door and walked inside. There she found square brown tables, as they ought to be, and stiff-backed chairs. She sat down at the right one.

The waitress, hard-faced and middle-aged, came up with her notepad. "The usual?"

Jenna wondered what the usual was. "I guess so."

"Been awhile. What happened to you all?"

Jenna shrugged. "We lost touch."

"Sorry to hear that. You all were such a close group."

We were? But who were we?

At the first hint of nausea she reminded herself that it really didn't matter. She was out for a drive, nothing more.

* * *

That afternoon, while driving east on a road that felt very wrong, she watched the land change. The pine trees abruptly became shorter,

35

sparser, and then disappeared altogether, all in the space of a quarter-mile. In her rearview mirror she could see the tall pines crowding up to an invisible line. The rain shadow of the mountains, where clouds dumped the moisture they had been hoarding from the desert to the east, someone had once told her. Who?

To the nausea and overwhelming wrongness she replied, *No one important.*

Sand blew over Jenna's car. Regretfully wishing that she had thought to bring extra water, just in case her journey might take her someplace dry, she went on.

* * *

Dinner was at a truck stop where a trio of Native Americans sat around a table in the back nursing beers while a leggy blonde picked over the collection of audiobooks by the counter. As Jenna ate a limp sandwich wrapped in cellophane and drank lukewarm coffee, she watched the woman pay for her selection and leave to climb into the driver's side of an idling semi. The Native Americans took an interest in a handheld device that one had brought. Then, and only then, the counterman sidled over to Jenna and said in a low voice, "You know where you're going, right?"

"I'm not going anywhere."

"Yeah, that's right. There's no cell phone service out there, and even the GPS don't know it exists. Just a big white spot on the map."

"Nowhere in particular," she repeated.

"You got that right." He winked, then handed her a bulky radio. "That there is a shortwave, and it's tuned to the one here. You get in trouble, you just turn it on and yell."

"Why? Why do you think there'll be trouble?"

He shrugged. "Your kind goes out there, you don't come back."

"My kind?"

"Yeah." He looked up suddenly at the door, just before Jenna heard the tinkle of the attached bells. She turned and saw a state trooper walking in.

As if he had never been talking to her, the counterman hurried away.

* * *

Delving deeper into the increasing wrongness, Jenna found herself driving down what might have been a road or perhaps only a dry rain gully. At the bottom she found a rusted metal building, its front door hanging from a single hinge and tied shut with a rag. Even with her car windows shut, she could hear the screams of siding bending in the wind.

She should leave. This was a dangerous place, and there was nowhere for her to sleep or eat. She couldn't step out to relieve herself without putting herself in danger from wild animals. Scorpions–there were poisonous scorpions in the desert, weren't there?

She dug out the flashlight from the glove compartment. She got out.

There was nothing here, just an empty building, abandoned for years. Filled with spiders. Big, hairy, poisonous spiders.

Jenna untied the door. Beyond she saw a small sitting room, bathed in a miasma that made her retch.

Closing her eyes, she smelled nothing but dust.

Fake, she told herself, and steeled herself to ignore it. When she opened her eyes, the stench skittered away like a roach in daylight.

That's what Luella was trying to teach me. I'll have to thank her.

She played the flashlight beam around the room. It had the feel of a long-abandoned place, but she saw hints of housekeeping. Dirt covered the windows, but there were no rodent droppings in the corners. The vinyl couch cushions had been ripped, but then mended with duct tape. Cobwebs lurked in the high corners, but only there, and she saw no sign of the spiders that had made them. A coffee maker on the counter had cold coffee in the pot, not sludge.

Standing very still, she listened, heard nothing but the soft passage of air through the ducts. Still, that meant that the central air was running—and who would remember to turn off the lights, but not the air conditioner?

To her right she found a door where it ought to be. Beyond, there were beds, the stained mattresses stripped of sheets. Curtains hung between the beds, billowing softly in the air currents.

A curtain, a voice beyond it. A hand slipping around the cloth to pull it aside. No, not a hand. A cluster of blue-scaled tentacles. "Your lucky day, see what I have?"

Sheer panic flooded out the memory. *Run!* screamed every fiber of

37

Jenna's being. *Leave now!*

"Fake," she muttered, and forced herself forward. All her hearts pounded furiously, even a brand-new one in her left heel.

Behind the ward she found a large operating room, the shining surfaces dotted with rust. To the side of that was a storeroom, its mostly empty shelves littered with upturned bottles and ripped boxes. And that was it. The building *was* a small one, out in the desert. No space for anything else.

So that was it. She needed to go. To go back to her home, to live her life as she always had. Everything would be fine. She turned the flashlight back through the door and let the beam play along the curtains into the ward. She should go back home, just like they wanted her to.

Right.

Where did they cook our food? Where did they do the laundry? Where did the staff sleep?

Again she stood very still and listened. Voices, faint enough to be ghosts, muttered in the air. A TV, from the regular cadence. Or perhaps a radio.

She flipped off the flashlight and stood in a darkness so thick it pressed on her face.

Still the voices continued. And after a time Jenna found that she could just make out the shapes of things around her. In the back of the storeroom, around what she thought had been the door to a broom closet, glimmered a thin rectangle of light.

* * *

There are always speakers at these things, though the definition of speech may change from one to the next. Still, they are the ones who explain the posters and answer questions. They wear lab coats and communicate with authority. They tell jokes and pass out treats if they need to attract a curious audience. Those who are good at changing their physical form may even go so far as to imitate their subjects, but none of them have ever been able to imitate their specimens at the most basic level. That is, none before today.

* * *

The door was locked, but it was a simple lock, picked easily with a credit card. As silently as she could, Jenna slipped through the door and made her way down the stairs to a clean, shimmering sub-level. She stood in a hallway that stretched far in either direction, much farther than the original building. What was down here was immense.

Her temple pounded. She felt real fear now, real anxiety. The only thing that kept her moving towards the sounds of life and conversation was her practice with the implanted fear and loathing. She found the door, and felt the cool wood beneath her palm as she pushed it open.

And then she screamed.

* * *

With just two upper limbs, two lower limbs, and his sensory organs clustered on a cerebral lump, the speaker looks absurd. His audience laughs. But then his associate, who looks like an unshaped lump with eyes and touch sensors growing everywhere, opens his robe to show what is beneath the translucent skin of his chest. Alien, beating, alive.

"... at the cellular level," the speaker says emphatically. "These can even replace and function as their own body parts. We can imitate them at the cellular level, and the imitations will be indistinguishable from the originals in all ways."

* * *

Six creatures stared at Jenna. They were covered with blue scales and rags, human clothing ripped to accommodate the multitude of limbs that grew from their lumpish bodies. Mouths and eyes seemed randomly placed on bulging heads; tentacles sprouted in disordered clumps. One had something that beat like a heart on its chest.

On her right, a creature heaved up on a trio of limbs and waved tentacles in her direction. Slowly it opened a sideways mouth and rumbled, "Come to us! Join with us!"

Jenna pressed back against the doorframe.

Two others stood, one lifting limbs with too many joints, and the other surging forward on a single, slug-like foot. "Join us! Join us!"

"For God's sake," snapped another, eyestalks swiveling from one to the next. "Leave off! Can't you see the poor thing's frightened out of her wits?"

39

The three sank back into their seats.

"Now." The eyestalks turned to Jenna. "What the hell are you doing here?"

"I'm, I'm Jen, Jenna. I came for answers."

"Answers, huh?" The creature, who appeared to be female, pulled a cigarette from a pack in her pocket. "Are you a reporter? Come to do a story on the aliens in the sandpit?"

"No. I think, I think this is where I got my new heart. But I keep growing more." The pulse behind her eye was enough to jar her vision. *How much longer do I have before it kills me?*

"A heart, huh?" The speaker lit her cigarette, then exhaled a puff of blue smoke. "You growing scales?"

Jenna pushed up her sleeve to show the band on her wrist.

"Well, there's plenty of space here. You can take whatever room you wish, as long as it's empty."

"Move in—with you?"

"We all had transplants here," said another, a small one in the back. "Those damn things either grow out of control or they change you. We're the lucky ones, you see. Our families think we joined a commune."

"We beg them to send us food and money," said the one with three legs. "They usually do. We get by."

"And you hide here?"

The small one rippled, as if trying to shrug shoulders that were no longer there. "No one to see us when we walk in the desert. And we got each other."

"We're a family," said the one with three legs. "Come join us. We always want fresh meat."

"I don't think I'm changing. My hearts are growing out of control. I'm going to die." Jenna put her hand to her head.

* * *

"Your specimens," flutes one member of the audience. "When you implant these organs into their bodies, do they have the ability to control them? Can your subjects keep these organs in their operative forms?"

The other members of the audience look at her as if she has asked if rocks are soft.

40

"There have been problems in that regard, of course," the speaker chirps. "But that's not the focus of our research. We set out to imitate the specimens at the cellular level—and we did. That's the important thing, you understand."

* * *

"You've lasted this long," the smoking one said. "You never know what will happen. Join us."

Jenna wasn't listening to her. She was thinking about the shortwave radio in the car, and how it wouldn't be used. How the man at the truck stop would think that yet another had fallen prey to the monsters in the desert, monsters long gone. Luella and Dajoun might come out here to join her. Everyone else she had known, every-thing else, would have to be abandoned. For under her fingers, be-neath her scaly skin, beneath a flexible, leathery skull, she felt the outline of a beating heart. Surrounding the bulge in a stubby ring, pencil-thick bumps wiggled on their own.

* * *

As they usually do at these things, the audience applauded.

Swanson

Jarret Keene

For Geoff Schumacher

The headhunters lured the six of us away from our non-union casino jobs at the quiet end of the Strip. We were picked because we were young and we looked good in clean white shirts. We accepted because a good paycheck was something we had never known. The first rule of business, we were told, was never to mention the Old Man's name or point him out while we were working. From the moment we started training, we felt his approach, his unusual presence and strong personality. We chalked up his eccentricities as byproducts of moneymaking genius. We believed that good times were here, that our troubles were now in the past.

The Old Man had wanted the best view of the Strip: the top penthouse floor of the Dunes. However, when he learned that directly over that penthouse a dance club blasted loud rock 'n' roll every night until dawn, he instead set up shop in the palatial suites of the Desert Inn. All summer we prepared his rooms. We learned what he liked and what he didn't.

The Old Man loathed rock music, thought the Beatles sounded like dumb teenagers. He preferred the schmaltz of Hollywood composers like Victor Young, a Chicago boy the Old Man had hired to score his own movie, *The Conqueror*, about Genghis Khan. It had starred John Wayne. The movie stank. Nearly everyone involved, including the Duke, died of cancer. The set, deep in a canyon of southern Utah, had been irradiated from the bombs going off at the neighboring Nevada Test Site.

Radiation is the reason why the Old Man created the Caretaker 3000. For a while the U.S. military had been in the market for a combat mechanism that could thrive in the aftermath of an atomic war. They turned to the Old Man, a billionaire businessman, movie producer, and the Pentagon's de facto R&D guy. He manufactured a prototype, a titanium humanoid on treads instead of legs, For three, maybe four, years—in the late '50s—the robot's funding was limitless. But once Khrushchev amassed an apocalyptic arsenal, there was no longer any point. Soon the 3000's primary duty consisted of fetch-

43

ing the Old Man his nightly meal: a Swanson TV turkey dinner (white meat only) with apple cobbler. Which is why we rechristened the Caretaker 3000 "Swanson." Sadly, or so we initially thought, the Old Man considered the robot to be just another appliance.

* * *

When the Old Man wasn't passed out on a concoction of Valium and codeine, he sat completely naked in a lounge chair, sifting through stacks of newspapers and magazines piled around him. He read by lamplight, towels obscuring the windows. He would summon us by flicking a brown paper bag with his fingers. He grew an unruly white beard and his skin began to yellow. His vocabulary mostly consisted of grunts and the occasional one-word command. He collected his urine in Mason jars, looking for signs of poisoning, organ failure. We dismissed him as crazy and kept cashing our fat paychecks. Because we did the Old Man's dirty work, we nicknamed ourselves the Dirty Half-Dozen.

Although he loved taking the military's money for continued research, the Old Man wanted, more than anything, to stop the atomic tests in the nearby desert—tests that he felt were slowly killing him. Only the *Las Vegas Herald*, a local newspaper, bucked the Old Man, consistently running editorials in favor of increased testing, citing the Cold War with the Soviets. The year was 1966, the aftertaste of the Cuban Missile Crisis still on our collective breath. After a few weeks of absorbing this pro-nuke propaganda, the Old Man did what he always did when faced with a problem. He purchased the *Herald's* parent company and soon the editorials did an about-face, arguing for a worldwide testing ban. The first anti-nuke article appeared on a Wednesday. It was one of the first times we saw him smile, his yellow teeth worked up into a grin, when the paper, sheathed in a sterilized plastic bag, was delivered to his room.

* * *

It was Dale, a slot-machine tech who'd seen a lot of sci-fi movies, who'd reprogrammed Swanson from a military prototype into a TV dinner-preparing automaton. Dale was the only one of us with an engineering background, and he seemed to sincerely know what he was talking about. Back in the late '50s, when he was called the Caretaker, Swanson's mission was, in the case of atomic conflict with the Soviets, to defend whatever Americans were still alive after a nuclear attack by eradicating any and all invading armies. Dale erased Swanson's aggressive responses and substituted care and concern, making the robot an invaluable part of our team.

Whenever the Old Man got a wild hair up his ass, one of us, usually Guido, would jump on the telephone and, for example, call the Baskin-Robbins ice cream company and get them to take a special order for the Old Man's favorite flavor, banana nut. Or somebody, usually Seth, a limo driver, would jump in the car to pick up an Arby's roast beef sandwich after the Old Man saw a commercial on TV. Or the smartest guy on duty would dust off the typewriter and postmark a letter to the governor of Nevada, demanding he halt a test blast due to the wind.

But gradually we dumped every one of our responsibilities on Swanson. Dale outfitted him with a crude but effective voice box for phone conversations and installed some new circuits to enable him to type. Driving was actually possible, too, since the Desert Inn was centrally located on the Strip, with plenty of convenient fast-food joints nearby. A trench coat and hat were usually enough to get him through a late-night drive-thru without being spotted for what he was. Behind the wheel, the five-foot-tall, goggle-eyed Swanson resembled a little old lady wearing thick spectacles who could barely see the road. Towards the end, Swanson did everything but earn a fat paycheck every two weeks and become modestly wealthy. We handled that much.

Through the windows, we'd watch the sun rusting down into the hills. Some nights we'd dope up the Old Man with drugs, eat the ice cream Swanson brought us, and fall asleep, dreaming of what our lives might have been like if we hadn't signed on with the Old Man.

Eventually, the Old Man settled into a pattern of watching Westerns on TV. No problem, as it made our jobs easier. But he had moments when anger sparked up within him for seemingly no reason. He threw a cup of coffee against the wall because it was too cold. Another time he demanded we all write letters to the governor because a little ghost town on the edge of the Nevada Test Site called Lockhart had defied his wishes. The residents had sold their uranium mine to a rival company from California for a great deal of money. The Old

Man had wanted the mine for years, and he'd come close, only to lose it at the last minute when his dummy corporation, which had made the initial offer, was accidentally unmasked by a goofy *Herald* reporter researching a totally unrelated story.

"Should've carpet-bombed those Lockhart cocksuckers with my F-22!" the Old Man screamed. Apparently he had tested aircraft at Lockhart's nearby lakebed years before. At least one of the planes had crashed, though the Old Man had walked away without a scratch. "It's not too late. It shall be done!"

We yawned, exhausted from listening to a maniac, and shot him full of heroin.

* * *

He raved like this for weeks. And then Swanson arrived one afternoon with a severed hand—prominent silver skull ring on the middle digit, calloused, dirt under the fingernails—placing it in the hotel freezer with 350 gallons of Baskin-Robbins banana nut ice cream.

Visibly distraught, the Desert Inn restaurant chef came up to the penthouse to alert us. None of us had law-enforcement contacts and there was really no easy way of determining who had been mutilated and if Swanson was in fact the culprit. Certainly the robot had the strength necessary to rip a guy's hand clean from his body, but Dale assured us this was highly unlikely. We looked at Swanson's own four-fingered (with opposable thumb) metallic mitts, their pincer-like appearance, and we could sense a shiver run down the spine of Kimball the Mormon. When Kimball questioned the effectiveness of Swanson's reprogramming, Dale reminded us that the Old Man's military subsidiary, American Tool Company, had never inputted any arm-ripping directive into Swanson's circuit mind. According to Dale, The Caretaker 3000 was equipped with primitive armor and weapons, and was really nothing more than a glorified blast door with arms, legs, a head full of sensors, and twin .50 caliber machine guns mounted on its shoulders. Oh, and a nuclear warhead that would self-destruct when necessary. But it had been neutralized.

So what in the hell did Swanson need with a severed human hand? And where was the handless victim?

* * *

It was agreed upon that Dale was the best person to interrogate Swanson. He did so for hours in one of the empty rooms on the eighth floor that we rented as a noise buffer. He came out looking tired, despite having drained several pots of coffee. Swanson had revealed nothing, Dale told us. The robot acted as if the incident had never happened, that he hadn't brought a severed hand into the hotel. Swanson didn't have a have a face capable of humanesque expression, so all we had to work with was his eerie synthetic voice. Emotionless. And yet it was *wrong* somehow. Charged with something nefarious.

Ignoring Dale's advice to let it go, the rest of us presented the mystery mitt—packed in ice inside an Igloo cooler—to our contacts in what was then considered the Mob at an Italian joint on Sahara and Valley View. We asked if anyone in their crew was missing something important and, oh by the way, did they recognize this ring? Something about the whole thing must have irritated Esposito, one of the New York Mob's top "advance men" and a bona fide gangster, because he started yelling, going off about how if any of his people were missing five fingers he'd be coming to us for answers and not the other way around. Then he threatened to detach our cocks and shove them into our mothers' asses. So we thought: Now might be a good time to exit.

We left the hand with his men, naturally.

* * *

We took the issue back to Dale, who suggested that Swanson had merely found the hand lying in the desert somewhere and brought it back to the Desert Inn to ensure none of us were injured. We nodded. Or maybe Swanson brought the hand to the Old Man the way a dog fetches the morning paper.

When we asked what Swanson was doing roving the desert all by himself, Dale suddenly revealed that our errand boy had taken to conducting early-morning strolls through Red Rock Canyon on the very western edge of the valley, where the fiery rock formations could take your breath away. Swanson let the cool night air saturate his overheated circuitry in preparation for another day of laboring for us, the Old Man's inner circle.

News to us. Dale said Swanson revealed this during another, more recent interrogation. We would've probed the robot ourselves, but there was a big part of us that wanted to simply let Dale deal with this aspect. We couldn't determine if Swanson was lying. We didn't know how to approach a conniving military prototype. Dale alone did.

We believed and trusted Dale absolutely. He had a degree from MIT. The only time we looked at him askance was when he complained of headaches, which got so bad Dale sometimes described them as feeling like an alien presence in his mind. We urged him to stop working so hard, take some time off. But we knew he wouldn't, couldn't. He was our sole conduit between us and the ongoing mystery of Swanson.

We had figured Swanson parked himself in the empty eighth floor every evening, plugged himself into the wall socket for a good night's charge, and counted electric sheep. Instead he was out wandering the desert, feeling crushed under an existential weight that robots must feel. Bravo for him, we thought. Even robots need to carve out a little personal time.

That's what we told ourselves—until the evening Swanson showed up with a sackful of Arby's roast beef sandwiches and an off-the-chart Geiger reading that woke the Old Man from his slumber, nearly causing him to hyperventilate, his emaciated body twitching like a lunatic undergoing shock.

"Get him out of here!" he rasped through a thick haze of prescription narcotics.

* * *

Among his magazines and urine containers, the Old Man had had us install Geiger counters all over the place and in all the rooms, the kind found at the Nevada Test Site, in the event strong winds should blow radioactive dust into Vegas. They'd never gone off before, but something really hot had affixed itself upon the shell of our iron companion. The clacking of the machines was enough to make us believe the apocalypse was finally here.

The idea that Swanson had been out humping atomic bombs actually crossed our minds. Did he realize he was contaminated? Where did he go to get so severely irradiated? He looked at us innocently, the blank stare of a lifeless mechanical doll, albeit steel-reinforced and tank-treaded.

48

"The test site," said Dale. He had a faraway look in his eyes, Swanson's betrayal at once definite yet beyond his understanding. The Old Man had saved the robot from the scrap pile and this is how Swanson repaid him? By trying to poison a man who feared radiation more than anything?

The possibility chilled our blood as we, wearing protective suits the Old Man had provided each of us on our first day at work, took turns scrubbing down Swanson inside a "survival center" warehouse on Industrial Parkway. We left him there for several nights, trying to figure out what the hell had happened to him.

* * *

Even cleaned up, Swanson continued to register low-level radiation. Dale wasn't sure why. He figured it had something to do with the new counter's sensitivity. It was an expensive and highly sophisticated instrument, and perhaps *too* efficient.

We decided to observe Swanson twenty-four hours a day. One of us tailed him wherever he went. He wasn't allowed to see the Old Man anymore and his home base was now the warehouse, so we watched to see what he did with all his newfound free time. If we had to pee, we used our walkie-talkies to have someone cover for us. If we noticed erratic behavior, we were to call Dale right away and have him approach Swanson and determine what, if anything, was wrong. Dale knew how to talk robot-ese, we joked.

One night, a few of us monitored Swanson as he rested his gears and servos in the darkened warehouse. But those of us stationed outside must have fallen asleep for a significant length of time.

A lapse that would cost us dearly.

We can't recall who heard Swanson first. His directional lights suddenly came on, his motor whizzing in preparation for movement. He quietly made his way out of Industrial Parkway and towards the rows of apartment complexes of what was then known as Naked City for the many showgirls who sunbathed topless poolside and partied late at night on the roofs of the more fashionable and luxurious buildings.

Swanson ignored the festivities. He broke into and hotwired a Cadillac parked on Florida and, tires screeching, got on the I-15. He went the speed limit, careful not to draw attention.

49

Jarret Keene

The six of us, the complete Dirty Half-Dozen, tailed him for what seemed like forever.

* * *

When we pulled up to a town in the middle of nowhere, we scratched our heads. Why would Swanson come here? Before we could even ponder an answer, he emerged from the car and, clumsy from the dust, churned his way down the road's cracked pavement and into the dead main street. The sun came up.

There in the center of town was the blackened, burned-out shell of one of the Old Man's F-22 fighter jets. Could it be the prototype version—the plane the Old Man had crash-landed into a desert lakebed decades ago?

Dale sat in back seat of our car, fidgeting. We sensed him rifling through the possible reasons for all this. He took a deep breath, wiped the sweat from his brow with a handkerchief.

For at least a minute nothing happened. Finally we got out and walked, our dress-shoe heels crushing the desert sand.

"Catch the name of this place?" said Dale.

We shook our heads.

"Lockhart," he said.

This was the ghost town the Old Man had screamed about obliterating.

* * *

We stopped in our tracks when we saw them. A dozen misshapen figures dressed in dirty rags. Vaguely human. Sporting massive, basketball-sized goiters and growths on their heads, necks and shoulders, tumors that no doubt challenged their balance. Limbs either swollen or attenuated. Patches of hair sprouted from sunburned, flaking scalps. They resembled monstrously rendered characters from the pages of an EC horror comic book, a juvenile delinquent's gruesome hallucination. They stumbled out of the shadows, but with eerie confidence, calmly, as if they'd waited years for us to arrive, for this terrible moment when they'd finally confront us.

One particularly ugly creature with no legs used his arms to ambulate. He wasn't any shorter because his arms were extended and bent, a fleshy, upright variation on a grasshopper's femur and tibia. He progressed faster than the others and rushed out to greet us. Or maybe slay us. We couldn't be sure. The creature's distorted face was twisted, grooved, pockmarked, a grotesque mound with moist, glistening raisins for eyes. No eyebrows or lashes, so he didn't blink at all. Those eyes simply glared at us, emanating evil and promising focused insanity and rage.

Dale inexpertly pulled a .38 from his lab coat, an act that failed to summon our courage. We stared across from each other, the Old Man's flunkies squaring off against a gang of ghost-town misfits, a mere football's throw apart. Swanson stood with them, albeit quietly, motionless. There were six of us, all men, but being outnumbered lacerated our stomachs.

The worst part, though, was when the creature spoke. He turned our hearts to ice, mainly because he didn't rely on his vocal cords. He instead used his terrifying mind.

"Oh God," Barron whimpered aloud.

"Did ... did whatever *that* is just say something?" Luis stuttered in disbelief. "Inside *your* brains, too, I mean?"

"Telepathy," Dale suggested.

Magic, the creature corrected. *The Bombs give us magic and our powers grow stronger. We want the Bombs to come back. We will make them return with the Old Man's death.*

We didn't know how to respond to this, so the creature continued.

Again, my name is Alter. And these are the people of the town of Lockhart. We—

"You're downwinders," Dale interrupted. "That's what you are."

Yes! Alter scuttled closer, waddling like a mutilated crustacean. *It's true. We were caught in the black ash of weapons. But we do not begrudge the government like other towns. The U.S. military and its scientists have blessed us. We are happy! Happy for the gift of magic.*

"Not magic, I'm afraid to say," Dale countered. "It has to be a rare genetic alteration, an unusual malformation somewhere in your frontal lobe that's allowing for ... for thought transference."

The thing called Alter found this deeply amusing. His chuckling boomed and reverberated inside our skulls. Confused, we covered our ears with our hands, which only increased the volume.

The gun suddenly yanked itself free from Dale's grip and hovered in the air like a hummingbird, barrel swiveling until it pointed directly at Kimball—and discharged.

Kimball instantly clutched his chest with both hands. Glasses sliding off, he collapsed to the ground, blood leaking in the dust. Poor guy. The revolver then went flying, a rocket shooting across the desert. A puff of sand hundreds of yards away confirmed it: no matter how far we were to run from Alter, he'd touch us, eliminate us.

"Psychokinesis," Dale mumbled, barely audible.

Only five of us remained. Alter's shabby apostles gathered before us, groaning perversely, as if achieving a simultaneous and shared orgasm. The sound filled us with loathing, nausea.

See? said Alter, slathering our minds with the ripe sensation of senseless murder. *Magic. Now get back into your car. The Old Man's end is near.*

"How do you mean?" Dale replied. The color had drained from his face, but what he said next belied his obvious fear. "You bunch of freaks will never make it to Las Vegas!"

Laughter like stabbing icicles again. Alter raised an insectoid arm, gesturing behind us. We fought the urge to flee, to shit our pants, to curl up and die right then and there. Instead we turned around to watch as the lid of our car trunk popped open with a sickening click. Alter was bending our reality to his every nightmarish whim.

* * *

Swanson came alive at once, tearing off towards the vehicle. Rotors whirring, he leaned into the trunk and carefully, almost gingerly, lifted out what looked like a body wrapped in cellophane.

We didn't unanimously gasp because the shock almost caused us to faint, knees buckling, legs giving way. Someone dropped to the ground in prayer or astonishment. Another vomited.

It was the Old Man, still alive, stripped naked, bound and gagged. As Swanson made his way back, we could discern the Old Man's sweaty, greenish complexion, his intense suffering. No doubt he longed for the needle; we'd been gone from the hotel for many hours.

Drugs do a nice job of keeping out our voices, yes. But drugs take their own toll. He couldn't escape our attacks forever.

It dawned on us then. Alter and his sideshow siblings had gotten us to bring the Old Man to them. All we could do was observe the horror, watch as Swanson unwrapped the Old Man and began doing

52

the unspeakable. We wanted to run, sure, but something—a residual sense of duty or a guilty understanding that we had failed our boss on a colossal level—kept us rooted.

With a hammer and metal shards, he crucified the Old Man to the broken husk of his airplane.

The sound of steel hitting steel rattled our spines. The Old Man's screams were absolutely soul-ripping, the guttural shrieks of an animal being slowly eaten alive, bit by bit. He hung like a bloody, nude, anorexic Santa Claus, white beard fluttering in the desert wind. Still, we didn't move, *couldn't* move, caught in the headlights of imminent and rapidly accelerating death.

Last time, warned Alter. *Go.*

We went. Just before we reached the vehicle, Dale said something jaw-dropping: "I know why Swanson is registering low-level radiation."

Swanson was primed, explained Dale. The robot, which to our ire had never demonstrated a capacity for collaboration before, had worked with Alter to figure out how to reactivate Swanson's internal warhead. He'd gone from meals on wheels to silver-plated doom.

Guido found the testicles to wonder: "Um, you never took out the warhead?"

"It's called pit-stuffing," sighed Dale. "You basically cram the tritium tube, which is inside the plutonium hollow, with a whole bunch of wires. The only way to get the weapon to work again is to dismantle it, remove the pit, cut the pit open, remove the wire, remanufacture the pit, and reassemble the weapon. It's a very long, very costly process."

Barron offered the obvious: "These weirdos seem to have plenty of time on their hands and a tidy profit from selling their uranium mine."

Dale opened his mouth as if he might say something, closed it. Then he said: "You'd need the right tools. And I'm afraid—"

That you provided those tools yourself? Alter said, piercing our minds again. *In your workshop perhaps? Why, yes. Yes, you did. You made it so easy for us. And sifting through your unlocked head for the activation process was a cakewalk.*

Dale's headaches. The presence he'd described as alien. Goddamn it.

Standing by the car, we were much farther away from the mutant horde at this point, maybe fifty yards. But we could still make out

53

what happened next. To our amazement, one of the mutants raised his arm, which was clearly missing a hand. But then the creature grinned with his razored rictus, an anglerfish haunting a dried-up ocean floor. We looked on as a disembodied hand with a distinctive silver skull ring on the middle finger—God, it was the very same hand Swanson had brought to the Desert Inn, wasn't it?—crawled up from the dust and onto his leg and along his radiation-ravaged frame until settling and fitting perfectly at the end of what had been, just moments earlier, a mitt-less stump.

Christ, we'd been played for fools by the mutant-gimp inhabitants of a Nevada ghost town.

You helped us. We're grateful. The town folk of Lockhart thank you. Now leave and let the good citizens of Las Vegas know that the Children of the Bomb are coming. That soon we shall inherit the Earth, and humanity shall return to dust.

We all stood stock-still, blank-eyed, in utter silence, waiting for someone to open a door on the vehicle so we could all pile in and peel off, leaving our master to die. Las Vegas would be incinerated by an atomic bomb Dale had failed to defuse inside a robot that was supposed to protect human life, not snuff it out like a cheap party candle. There was no chance we'd ever get away. In Vegas, we'd be sitting ducks, a stupid move.

Our thoughts raced. No more bountiful checks for doing little to no work. No more of the good life in Sin City. No more blowjobs from beautiful call girls, no more mountains of shrimp and lobster, no more golf with the buddies, no more betting on the Packers, no more all-night-and-all-morning blackjack games, no more treating our families to everything they wanted—movie tickets, faster cars, bigger homes, fancier dinners, sweet-sixteen parties, *mitzvahs*, college degrees. No more Swanson serving us ice cream.

No more anything, period.

Those fucking bastards had ruined us.

Finally, Dale shrugged. "Maybe the Old Man has a safe word that shuts down Swanson."

We all knew that a safe word, thanks to our doctor shopping, would be impossible to find, even if we could have talked to the Old Man at this point. Which we couldn't. Any such shut-off was lost in the Old Man's shattered mind, sealed off in his traumatized body, locked in his oozing heart.

54

Lockhart.

Dale coughed into his fist, lab coat flapping like a flag of surrender. He looked exhausted, ill. On impulse, he reached in through the car's open window and turned the ignition key. We were paralyzed. Or we were trying to think up a plan of action. Or a course of action had already been decided for us.

"A Hard Day's Night" came on the radio. Someone cranked the volume knob and we sang along, in unison, with the bittersweet chorus:

So why on earth should I moan
'Cause when I get you alone
You know I feel okay
Magic.

* * *

After that, no one said anything—not a fucking word. Past caring about our puny selves, we had a plan to fight back one last time. We lifted every nearby rock and stone we could find, tossing them into the trunk. Rather absurdly, Luis threw in a Gila monster that had been hiding in a hole, grabbing it by the tail. Then we all jumped into the car, hoping that our combined weight would be enough to thwart Alter's psychokinetic powers. We wanted to drench the fender in his blood, the blood of all the bad citizens of Lockhart, Nevada, where testing had unleashed pure evil. Where testing had unearthed unlikely, preposterous heroes.

Dale stomped the gas pedal, hurtling us towards the mass of mutant gimps with minds like razors and hands that could be severed and reattached at will. Alter's psychic screams all but decapitated everyone in the car. First, Guido's skull caved in, a rotten pumpkin yielding to an invisible sledgehammer's wallop. Barron's head imploded seconds later.

Windshield fractured, dashboard and back seat wet with gore and bone fragments, the vehicle rushed on. Tires hissed. Radiator crumpled, releasing steam as it impacted the first few bodies.

The final image we took to our graves? Swanson on fire, heading right at us.

And as we knew would happen: white light swallowed everything.

Compatible Donor

JT Rowland

Mark handed the surgeon an ice pick. "It's the only way that I don't suffer."

"That's insane. We just want a strip of your scalp to harvest some follicles."

"Look, I've tried everything. Local anesthesia, general anesthesia, booze, heroin—whatever. None of that works. Just do it."

"No," said the surgeon.

"I'm here because the right people, including the recipient of my follicles, know about me and what I have to offer. You may have heard some unbelievable things concerning my services. Let me save us some time and tell you that they are all true."

"But why this ..."

"Thalamus," Mark interrupted, "Switchboard of the brain. Pierce it and I'm out like a light. Simple, effective, and I don't feel a thing."

The surgeon exhaled a deep breath as he thumbed the end of the long ice pick. Mark could see the surgeon chewing his lips underneath the surgical mask. Before Mark could say another word, a steely resolve entered the surgeon's eyes. In a single motion the surgeon raised the ice pick over his head and stabbed it down into the crown of Mark's skull. Mark switched off.

* * *

Food tasted so damn good after each surgery. Hunger was always the first sensation Mark felt after the ice pick was removed from his head. With something simple to grow back, like hair follicles, his body would let him off easy with a cheeseburger and some fries. But next week he would be selling his liver. Regenerating that would take a lot more nourishment. A whole turkey, a couple of steaks, and a few pounds of potatoes might not be enough to satisfy the hunger. The client would just have to make sure he got enough to eat.

Mark sold his organs on the black market for a very good living. The miracle of healing he had was only half of what made his organs special. The other half was that his organs were always a perfect donor match, every time, regardless of the client's blood or tissue type.

No exceptions. No immunosuppressive medication or therapy needed for the lucky recipient. He was a walking set of replacement parts for whoever could afford to pay for them.

The money was good, so good that to pursue any other means of making a living didn't make sense to Mark. A trip to Beijing, a layover in Panama, and a long weekend in Rio de Janeiro gave Mark the kind of cash most households didn't see in five years. To think an act of kindness like donating a kidney to someone in need could lead to such a lucrative lifestyle.

That's what this was, after all, a lifestyle. Mark didn't kid himself about that. But he exchanged any semblance of a normal life for his black-market wealth. And he felt weird about what he was doing. Strange. Mark would always feel this way. Every time he sold a piece of his body he felt that he lost something of himself. Not in anything quantifiable, like a simple piece of his physical being, but a part of his—soul. But the money was good, too good. Mark thought that maybe someday he'd acquire enough wealth that he'd be able to retire like an overused whore who had defied fate and won the lottery.

All through Mark's childhood, there had been hints that he was a little different from everyone around him. He never got sick, and all of the minor bumps and scrapes of childhood seemed to have made an exception with him. He was fifteen years old when he learned for certain that he was born with something special.

The game was called Mercy. You intertwined your fingers with your opponent's, and then you torqued your wrists and clenched your fingers in such a way as to cause each other pain until one of you called, "Mercy." Mark was playing this game with Paul, a friend from down the block.

"Mercy. You for it?" said Mark. Paul was in the process of unwrapping a stick of fruit gum. It was a warm summer day and the two boys were bored.

"What do I get if I win?"

"You're not going to win, but if you do …" Mark thought for a moment. "… I'll let you ride my bike for a week."

"Deal." They gripped each other's fingers, but before Mark was ready, Paul yelled, "Go!"

Paul got the jump on him. He had Mark dead to rights. Mark should have called "Mercy," but this wasn't about winning the game anymore. Paul had employed one of Mark's best strategies, the surprise "Go!" and Mark took it personally. Mark gripped his fingers even tighter and flexed his wrists hard. There was an audible pop. Mark felt a bone snap in the ring finger of his right hand. He cried out in pain.

A panicked look came to Paul's eyes, and he released his grip. "Oh wow. Are you okay?"

The finger bent at an odd angle, causing it to touch the outside middle knuckle of his middle finger. Without thinking about it, Mark gripped his crooked digit and repositioned it. He kept waiting for the pain to strike again; instead it gradually subsided. He flexed his hand, made a tight fist, and then shook it out. "I think I'm all right."

"Maybe it was just dislocated?"

Mark knew that wasn't the case. The moist carrot snap of the finger was still fresh in his mind.

"Hey. You let go first," said Mark, grinning at Paul. "I win."

* * *

The overripe smell of humanity greeted Mark as he stepped out onto the Chinatown streets in Honolulu, Hawaii. The streets were lined with exotic fruit stands, Asian grocery stores, restaurants, and an assortment of clothing and cosmetic boutiques, all interwoven with crowds of window-shopping tourists and locals.

Crowds made Mark nervous. He felt like a wounded gazelle lost in the tall grass of lion country. Dealing with backroom medical practitioners and black-market auctioneers was often fraught with other characters of the unsavory type. Many who, unlike the follicle surgeon, would have few qualms about plunging a sharp instrument into Mark's head. Mark carried a concealed handgun on his hip, and had a man floating around in the crowd keeping an eye on him. Despite these precautions, he felt dizzy with apprehension. He ducked into a nearby bar.

Mark had known for a long time that he was unable to get drunk. It didn't matter how much or how fast he drank. His body was able to metabolize alcohol very quickly. Once he had chugged a bottle of tequila in two breaths. He only felt the faintest ghost of a buzz before his body flushed the intoxicant from his blood. He had used this ability to his advantage in college, hustling friends and classmates out of pocket money by challenging them to drinking games.

59

The bar's interior felt cool, dark, and secure. Every surface was swathed in maroon velvet. Elvis's crooning over the cheap speaker system comforted Mark. The seats were empty save for two stools at the end that were occupied by two elderly locals. They spoke in easy-going pidgin that brought a smile to Mark's sweat-misted face. He seated himself at the bar and ordered a beer.

"How's it?" asked the bartender as he popped the cap off a bottle and placed it in front of Mark.

"All right. Good." Mark didn't feel up to much conversation. Sensing Mark's discomfort, the bartender distanced himself by polishing a bourbon glass as he walked towards the elderly men at the end of the bar.

The last rays of the day's sunlight briefly sprang forth, then receded as the tavern's door opened and a gorgeous hapa woman entered. A mixture of Caucasian and Asian blood formed the exotic beauty of her face. She sat two seats away from Mark at the bar. She pulled a pack of cigarettes from a small black purse and lit one with a green Bic lighter. She exhaled smoke in an irritated way, looking up towards the ceiling as if trying to locate an annoying buzzing insect.

"What has Elvis ever done to you?" asked Mark.

The woman paused in the motion of fingering a lock of hair behind her ear. A quick flick of her eyes assessed Mark's face, another flick measured his shoulders, and the third locked her stare with his. She smiled. "He doesn't do it for me."

"Who does—do it for you?"

"Justin Bieber," she said with a straight face.

"Uh, that's great. I guess." He took a swallow of his beer.

Her dark eyes glinted, amused. "Bon Jovi, Ozzie, Alice Cooper. Stuff like that." She tapped an ash from the cigarette into an empty glass. The bartender picked the glass up and replaced it with an ashtray.

"I'm Mark." He waited for a reply. She let him sit in silence, and just when he was about to accept his rejection, she answered.

"Akela. Nice to meet you." She spoke with a pidgin-inflected accent born of the islands. It was understated and sublime. Mark heard several people enter the bar. Four conservatively dressed *mahu*, drag queens, seated themselves in a booth centered on a wall. Akela spoke softly. "But my name can be whatever you want it to be."

Mark's gaze went back to the woman's face. She nodded "yes" to

60

his question before he could ask it. He smiled. He had just been paid, and she was far too beautiful to pass up. Stupid. It was so obvious. Later, in the embrace of her sex, he barely registered the impact as something sank into his skull and everything switched off.

* * *

"Hello, Mark. What you last name?" An old overweight Asian man stood before him. He spoke with a Korean accent. Thick hemp rope bound Mark to an upended bed frame. Mark gasped. The basement was bare, with walls of moldy, water-damaged concrete slabs. Several tainted yellow bare light bulbs illuminated the area. Mark couldn't think of a single place on the island with a basement. How long had he been out? His stomach sank.

"I don't have a last name."

The old man scrunched his thick white eyebrows. He punched Mark's nose with unfathomable strength. The pain was immediate and intense.

"Now let's see." he said. Dismissing his earlier inquiry, the old man stepped closer. Through his ruined nose, Mark could smell stale smoke and sour fermentation on the old man's breath. The old man grabbed Mark's chin and pivoted it back and forth sideways. He held Mark's chin up and looked down his long face at Mark's nose. Mark could see several blackened fillings in the old man's mouth. "Yes. Yes, so it's true."

Mark's nose had already knitted back together. The only evidence of its damage was in the blood quickly drying on his lips.

"What else can you do?" said the old man, more to himself than to Mark. The old man focused his attention on a steel cart situated against a wall. Mark whimpered, pushing against his restraints. He could hear the individual fibers of the ropes creak with his efforts, but they didn't break. He tried sliding his wrists out from under the ropes, but the knots were very tight. His fingertips tingled with the meager amount of circulation allotted them. There was a clatter of metal tools as the old man sifted through them.

"I wonder ..." The old man faced Mark. He had a large pair of heavy-gauge cable cutters in his hand.

"Wait. What do you want? Wait," cried Mark. The old man seemed to be humming along with an unheard tune and didn't hear

Mark's confused plea. He grabbed Mark's left hand. Mark gripped it into a tight fist. "Stop. Please stop!"

Mark was once again surprised by the strength of the old man's liver-spotted hands. He wrangled Mark's hand like an uncooperative chicken about to have its head cut off and peeled Mark's pinky away. He cut it off at the base.

Mark screamed. In the back of his mind the curious realization surfaced that the pain of the amputation had lagged by a handful of seconds. "Handful?" Hilarious. The cutter was efficient. Mark thought of chicken bones, chicken wings, chicken bones. The old man stood with his hands behind his back as he leaned forward to examine the bloody stump.

"Mmm. Bleeding stop already." A tingling sensation that felt like a clump of ants enveloped the wound. A tiny splinter of bone sprouted, then elongated, separating into jointed segments. A bloody foam followed, solidifying into sinew and muscle and veins. The skin from the base of the wound crept up over the raw flesh and ended at the nail of the newly born finger.

The old man picked up the former pinky from the dusty floor. He massaged it and rolled it around the palms of his hands, lost in thought. Mark sniffed futilely at the stream of mucus flowing from his nose, caused by his terror-drenched weeping.

"Roughly ten minutes that took. Ten minutes. How long for whole hand? Whole arm ..." He turned once again to the steel cart. The whir of an electric motor loosened Mark's bladder. The old man turned around to reveal a battery powered reciprocating saw. He took a few more experimental squeezes of its trigger.

"Please put me out." The hapa from the bar had known how to render Mark unconscious. Mark felt sure the old bastard would know as well. "Can't you just put me out? Do what you got to do but just put me out." Mark's lip trembled with a life of its own.

The old man looked up in surprise, broken from his reverie. He glanced at the cart, then back at Mark. Without a word he retrieved a large screwdriver and stabbed Mark on top of his head. The dull flat tip of the screwdriver glanced off, leaving a jagged cut beneath the mat of Mark's hair. The old man stabbed again, ineffectually. He paused and considered Mark for a moment. Then he grabbed Mark by the hair and rammed the tool through Mark's eye socket, finally bringing blissful oblivion.

There were no dreams while Mark was out. No sensations or stray thoughts existed. All that was Mark became caught in a single moment of thought stretched out beyond all eternity: a single frame of memory paused.

"Why no heal?"

"What?" Mark tried to blink the ruin of his eye into focus. He checked himself over and saw that his right leg had been removed. A half-formed shard of bone protruded from the stump. "I need to eat." His stomach grumbled to accentuate the point.

"How much food?"

"For a whole leg? A lot."

The old man nodded, and then reinserted the screwdriver.

When Mark awoke, he saw that he had been strapped to a metal chair with buckled leather straps. The chair sat in front of a large metal table. His hands were cuffed by iron shackles and secured to the table with long chains. A large tub of plain white rice and browned ground meat sat before him.

"Eat." The old man stood behind Mark.

"What are you going to do with me?"

The old man struck Mark on the side of his head with the screwdriver's handle, the other end of it caked with Mark's dried gore. "Eat!"

There wasn't any silverware, so Mark shoveled a handful of the meat into his mouth and chewed. It was as bland as the rice. The old man picked up another chair and positioned it to watch the marvel of Mark's healing leg. Mark could feel the reassuring prickling through the cloud of pain that his eye and leg made as they regenerated.

Mark consumed the food, but despite there being five pounds or more of it, his leg hadn't even grown to the knee yet. His stomach rumbled.

"Cook the rest of it." The old man didn't take his eyes off Mark's leg.

Mark looked at the old man, puzzled. From behind his captor, a great bulk grunted as it hefted itself up. A fat, balding man lumbered into Mark's view and opened a freezer chest. What Mark saw caused him to gag. He summoned every shred of his will not to vomit. The brute had retrieved the rest of Mark's amputated leg. The calf muscle had been carved off.

The brute looked at Mark. They met each other's eyes. The brute shrugged. Noncommittal.

"Why are you doing this to me?" Mark asked the old man. Vomit stung the back of his throat as he willfully coaxed it not to erupt. The old man didn't seem to have heard Mark.

"To see," said the brute, pausing in thought, "What there is to see."

"Help me," Mark pleaded. He looked at the old man, who hadn't taken his eyes off Mark's leg. The brute shrugged again and disappeared behind Mark. Mark could hear the clatter of aluminum pots and pans being shuffled around. He wept.

The old man reinserted the screwdriver after Mark finished his meal.

Mark felt an odd sensation. He was still strapped to the chair, but he could feel the dusty floor with his right hand. He could also feel the cool metal of the table on his left calf.

Mark's hair stood on end. When he opened his eyes, what he saw didn't make sense. He blinked a few times. He felt cotton-headed, weird. He was looking at his foot in front of him and trying to decipher why it didn't look right. He felt as though he shouldn't be seeing his foot, but there it was sitting on the table in front of him, attached to the end of his arm—only that wasn't right. The foot was attached to his leg.

Everything clicked. Darkness enveloped his vision as he felt his consciousness waning. His arm and leg had been swapped. Mark shook his head and deliberately blinked some more. This wasn't right. It wasn't, but it was. Before he passed out he saw an ear, an eye, and a very blue pinky sitting in a bowl on the table.

The basement was dark. Although there weren't any windows, at least in his line of sight, Mark knew it was some time during the night. It was too quiet; settled. A low light came from behind Mark beyond his vision, white, maybe slightly blue. A plate of boiled chicken sat on the table untouched. He flexed his right hand. He wiggled the toes of his misplaced foot. His limbs seemed to be functional despite their placement. This wasn't a nightmare, oh how he wished it was, but he knew it wasn't. He bent his right arm, now in place of his left leg, and placed his hand on his left knee, which had now replaced his right elbow. He pinched the scrotal-like skin of it. Full sensation. He tried to picture how the joints of his hip and shoulder must have knitted together, but couldn't. In all his life he never ventured to even

64

imagine that his body was capable of ... this.

He heard a snuffle, followed by the sound of someone scratching at his day-old growth of beard. The brute was sitting in the dark in the far corner. Watching him?

"Hey," Mark whispered. The brute didn't respond. He appeared not to have heard. "Hey!" Mark said, more loudly.

The brute stood and walked slowly over to him and sat in the chair the old man had occupied earlier—*today*? He peered at Mark.

"What?" The deep clarity of the brute's nondescript North American accent startled Mark.

"How long have I been here?"

"Couple weeks." The brute had one hand resting in the other as he settled forward, leaning his elbows on the table.

"What's your name?" The brute didn't respond. "Okay. My name is ..."

"Mark, yeah, I don't care."

"What are you going to do with me?"

"Me? Nothing." The brute leaned back into the chair and crossed his arms.

"The old man?" asked Mark. The brute nodded. "I've got a lot of money ..."

"How much?"

"A lot, more than you'll see in your lifetime." The brute was clearly interested now. "Just get me out of here."

"Not going to be easy. The old man isn't alone upstairs," said the brute. "Guns," he added with finality. "Maybe I can sneak you out."

"Yeah. Sneak me out and I'll pay you a lot of money."

"We'll see if I can think of something." The brute gazed around in the darkness, stood up, then returned to his seat in the far corner. Mark didn't dare to sleep that night.

* * *

"What happen I cut your head off?" asked the old man. Mark had been allowed to relieve himself in a small green tiled latrine. It was odd trying to walk with his new handicap.

"I'd die. How could I eat to regenerate a whole body if I don't have a body that could receive food?"

The old man licked his lips. "What about I cut you perfectly half-

65

half? I have two of you?" There was madness in the old man's look as he did a chopping motion into his palm.

"Same problem. I wouldn't be able to eat."

The old man laughed and waved at Mark as if he had just told a good joke. Abruptly, he inserted a steel chopstick into Mark's eye.

When Mark revived, his limbs were back in their rightful places. The metal cart with the old man's tools had been removed. A large plate of white rice, boiled chicken, and several fried eggs sat before him. Mark was very hungry. As he ate, Mark realized that he had been bathed and given a change of clothes. He lifted his shirt, and what he saw made him drop his fork. There was a large sutured X crossing his entire torso. One or several of his organs must have been taken. The sutures itched.

"More?" asked the brute. There was a set of stairs that Mark was finally able to see behind him. He was now only shackled to the table and had a little more mobility.

"I think I'm going to need a lot more."

The brute seemed to have anticipated this. He placed several more plates of food on the table. He took a bite out of a piece of chicken as he sat with Mark.

"I don't need these anymore," Mark said as he picked at the sutures. "Do I want to ask what he took from me?"

"I may have a way of getting you out of here," said the brute as he retrieved a pair of fine-tipped surgical scissors. He snipped at each individual suture while Mark ate.

"What's the plan?"

"No plan, really. Just need to keep an eye out for a sizable opportunity." Mark was going to press the brute further to elaborate further when he continued, "I have to figure out a way to get you past all the kids up front. There are always a few there."

"Kids?"

The brute gave a dismissive wave in response.

"What do you all do here?" asked Mark. The brute sniffed, briefly probed the back of his teeth with his tongue, then licked his lips. He leveled his gaze on Mark. He pointed the greasy chicken bone he was gnawing on at what was left of the sutures in Mark's torso. Mark understood immediately.

"What will you pay me to give up all this?" The brute leaned back and spread his arms as if presenting a grand kingdom.

66

"A lot. So much that your life would never be the same again."

"How will you pay me?" The brute peered at Mark, smirking. "Will I take you on a couple hundred trips to the nearest ATM? Right. There wasn't a wallet on you when we took you, so that's out. So unless you got raw cash stacked up somewhere ..."

Mark sighed, defeated.

"Or how about I give you my address and trust you're a man of your word." The brute seemed to enjoy the exchange.

"There has got to be a way ..."

"There isn't. But if it makes you feel any better, if either I or you can think of a way for me to be paid without a single chance of you fucking me—well, then we can work something out."

Mark was at a loss for words. He sat staring at the brute for a moment. Then he picked up his fork and continued to eat. The brute savored his meal.

Months went by. It could have been a year, for all Mark knew. He was constantly being knocked out, and he always awoke to find that another part of his body had been stripped from him and sold off. There was always plenty to eat, though. The food actually got better as time went on. His keepers even upgraded him to being chained to a cot instead of the table. Business must be good.

Mark fantasized about acquiring a rusty hatchet or something blunt like a crowbar and ripping the old man and the brute apart in a blood-soaked rampaging ecstasy, but he was always shackled, and whenever they needed to move him they always knocked him out.

He couldn't think of a way to pay the brute. When he was first captured, Mark would have taken any opportunity to slip away and do whatever he could to have these people apprehended. But the longer he sat shackled in this basement with the smell of dust, laundry detergent, incense, dried herbs and other earthy and bodily fragrances, the more he wished he could just pay up and get out. Not look back or even think about retribution. He couldn't think of a way to convince the brute of that.

He didn't have to.

This terrifying world was starting to become routine. Mark was marveling at just how much the human body—and soul—could adapt to when the brute came to him in the middle of the night.

"It's time to go." In the still, quiet darkness, Mark saw the glint of steel before something pierced his "off" switch.

When he came to, he found himself in a proper bed with clean sheets. Several more beds trailed away from either side of him, and another row of them lined the wall in front of him. To his horror, he found that both his legs and arms were missing; what remained were short stunted spears of bone, stuck in a futile attempt at regeneration, bound in bandages.

"Hello? Can someone please speak to me?" The room was vacant. The sound of medical equipment and the building's ventilation system were the only things breaking the silence. A moment later, Mark a heard a bump and felt a curtain of air as a double door was pushed open by the brute. He was pushing a cart, a cart very much like the one the old man used, into the room. The smell of curried meat and spicy pickled vegetables followed.

"You did it," said Mark. "How? What happened to me?"

"I smuggled you out. I had to make you fit into something inconspicuous." The brute lifted his chin at something beside the bed. A thick brown denim backpack sat beside medical equipment on the floor. Mark swallowed a lump in his throat.

"Thank you. I will pay you. You don't have to worry about me or anything else ever again." Mark tried to smile, but his weeping was uncontrollable.

"Don't thank me," said the brute as he departed.

It took the better part of two months for Mark's limbs to completely regenerate. The hospital staff was cordial, and the food was very good, a fusion of East Asian and Pacific Island delectables.

From a handful of conversations with the nurses who tended him, Mark found out he was in Singapore. He tried to map out the logistics of his abduction from Oahu. Hawaii was a string of tiny little islands in the middle of the Pacific, a place of infinite coastline. Maybe it hadn't been all that hard. He had been missing for nearly a year. Probably no one had shown any real concern regarding his whereabouts. The few family members he had, he wasn't very close with. Contact with them consisted of a handful of phone calls here and there throughout the year, and the nature of how he earned his living had him on the move too much to really lay down any roots. Mark felt a familiar sadness weighing at his heart when he realized that he had no one to call; no one who needed concerns about him relieved.

He didn't dare try to contact the authorities. The brute hadn't left an arrangement for payment, so Mark had to assume he had something in place for later down the road. Mark did not know what relationship the brute had with the hospital, but it couldn't be good. Several other patients occupied Mark's ward from time to time, but they were severely injured and always unconscious. Mostly, Mark had the place to himself.

The hospital staff never asked Mark how he had received his injuries. Never so much as asked for his last name and didn't relinquish their names when asked. He would have to try and slip away when he was able.

Never again would Mark sleep without his dreams being tormented with nightmares, but these would soon become preferable to his waking hours.

"I bet you're ready to leave," said a pretty hapa in a white lab coat as she carted a wheelchair next to his bed. She was smiling, yet there was a strange contradicting look in her eyes that Mark couldn't completely ignore.

"You have no idea. What's with the wheelchair?"

"Hospital policy."

Mark sat in the wheelchair. She was quick. Mark didn't see what kind of instrument she sank into his head.

Mark woke with a ball gag in his mouth. He tried to spit it out, but it was firmly secured with leather straps buckled behind his head. He was strapped to a wooden table that consisted of a center thick plank with separate planks for each of his limbs. Leather restraints protruded from holes in each plank, holding him so tightly that his hands prickled. A bloodstained sheet covered him.

He shook his head, trying to dislodge its harness, to no avail. He looked about the room. It was large, with vaulted ceilings. An upper level encircled the lower area, giving Mark the feeling he was at the bottom of a pit or dog-fighting arena. He could smell dry hay and wood smoke and cooking meat. He craned his neck and was able to see a steady flow of smoke from the upper level behind him being drawn through a vent in the domed ceiling.

A door opened at the foot of the room. A woman entered wearing an elegant white gi, secured at the waist with a rustic belt. Overhead, several more doors opened, and Mark could hear a lot of footsteps as men and women encircled the area looking down on him. Mark tried to plead through his gag for help. He could see them now. There were curious glances at him, and hushed whispers. They looked like

69

normal people of various different ethnic backgrounds.

"Ladies and gentlemen," said the woman in white, "At no other place in the world can you satisfy your epicurean taste for long pork like you can with us." She lifted the sheet off Mark with a showman's flourish. "I have prepared for you several delectable cuts to sample." The smell of cooking meat took on a new significance.

There was a gasp from her audience, followed by applause.

Ever since the game of Mercy that one summer day, Mark had felt that things simply happened to him, that because of his special ability he had become just a stray leaf bouncing around in the current of the world. A compatible donor, a living meat market. He had never felt more like that than he did now. The meat of his limbs had been cleanly carved off, as had various selections from his torso. Just enough of him was left to regenerate. Bloody foam bubbled at each exposed wound.

His stomach grumbled.

Chrysalis
Roberta Lannes

The bed creaked as Dan stretched. Aileen beside him, facing away, breathed deeply, fast asleep. Grazing her spine, his wrist caused a crackling sound, as if he'd run his hand over brittle, peeling paint. He tensed, but she didn't move. *I'm in a dream,* he thought.

Inside the dream, he saw himself standing by the door in their Portland home, helpless to stop his impending loss: Aileen's suitcases packed, Aileen red-faced, about to walk out on him. Done shouting, she whispered between gritted teeth that she hoped he'd wake up. See the truth. Understand. There were no tears, but he sensed her agony, the anger and disappointment. Heartache rushed back at him, a tsunami of hurt.

He was lost, confused. "Wake up," she told him. "I've been here all the time, but you stopped seeing me. I flew at you like a dumb bird into a big window, bashed against you, and even then, you turned away. But you'll see me now. Just wake. *Up.*"

Jolted from sleep, his eyes flicked open. Dawn cast a fiery light through the cabin's gauze curtains, turning everything a burnt orange. He looked at Aileen and smiled. He glanced over to her suitcases, still packed, lined up where she'd left them when she'd appeared. The same suitcases she'd left with over a year ago. At that time, he'd dared not fantasize he'd see Aileen again, *arriving* instead of leaving, let alone asleep beside him.

He wouldn't wake her. After he'd crawled into bed for the night, she'd stayed up to mull over their talk. She called it "processing"— something she'd learned from counseling during their fifteen months apart. Dan recognized her "processing." He called it *analyzing things to death.* He wouldn't say that to her now that she was here to work things through. That was the old Dan. Selfish Dan. The asshole. But that's what she wanted to do. Complicate things, then spend their next week together picking the confusion apart.

What had gone wrong seemed quite simple to him.

First, he'd taken her for granted. When he'd felt like a fishing trip at the cabin, he'd gone. Without her. Poker night with the guys?

Sure, and he'd arrive home in the early morning hours saturated with cigar smoke and alcohol. Her problem. No matter what, he'd expected her home, meals on the table, everything clean, clothes pressed, and happy faces when he got there. She'd had everything she'd ever wanted. He'd made sure of that. Everything except his love. Attention. Appreciation. Devotion.

Secondly, he'd cheated. Once the post-baby weight had obscured the figure of his once model-thin wife, she'd no longer turned him on. So, he'd screwed around. A lot. Also, once Aileen became a mother, she'd no longer felt like a wife to him. Wives didn't slip into bed beside their husbands smelling of baby puke, or sit beside them watching TV while pumping breast milk into snorting, ascetic, plastic contraptions. A wife cared about her appearance, took time to make her husband feel like a man. Special. Necessary. As Aileen had the first year they were married. So he'd treated her less and less like a wife. More like a wet nurse. Housekeeper. Roommate. For Dan, warm regard grew into contempt, then indifference. And sadly, back then, he'd had no idea how Aileen felt. Nor cared.

Aileen had told Dan, before she'd threatened to leave him, that without Eric and Emma she'd have starved emotionally. With the two kids both in college, there was really nothing to keep her with him. He'd never believed her threats, her needy turns filled with hysterical pleading. She'd lived far too well on the good money he made. She might be starving emotionally, but no way was she going to give up the good life.

Served him right, her leaving. He'd been a complete and utter fool.

Simple. Yeah.

Aileen shifted under the comforter. Dan leaned in close to smell her hair. Once, at the start, he'd relished all her scents—the sweet smell her fruity shampoo left on her head, the crisp aloe and moss of her deodorant, the peach of her skin, even her slightly metallic morning breath. It surprised him a bit that he remembered these scents, realized he'd missed them. But this morning, her hair smelled like sun-bleached wood. Her skin had a woody, pulpy scent he remembered from when Aileen had taught the kids how to make paper. There was no denying she'd changed. Perhaps she'd gone native, given up fragrances and scented baths. Did that mean there had been no men in her life over the last fifteen months? Or that there *had* been

72

one? A man who preferred his women without artificial perfumes? His throat tightened.

No matter. She was here, beside *him*, now.

He knew this reunion wasn't a guarantee of reconciliation. Aileen had been careful to explain she was coming up to the cabin to be with him for no more than a week. A seven-day "test." She'd said it straight out. "I want to see if all your pronouncements are true—that you've changed, that you're dealing with your issues, not running away from what went wrong. I have to see promising behavior. As you put it in the letter, putting me first. That you're doing the walk now, not just the talk.

"I've taken this time to get my old self back. Grow beyond your shadow. I don't need you anymore, so we're sort of starting from a different place. Both of us."

He'd nodded. "We have a long road ahead of us if there's anything left to rekindle." *Please let there be enough*, he'd thought.

Dan had sent Aileen a list of amends he intended making to her. That list had probably been what had prompted her call to set up the week at the cabin. Smart move. After Aileen left him, Dan had ended up in Codependents Anonymous, CODA, working a twelve-step program for people who are bad at relationships. In Dan's case, he discovered, he'd become unconsciously yet profoundly emotionally reliant on Aileen's dependency on him. Addicted to control, his sponsor told him.

He'd never heard of AA programs for anything but alcohol or drugs. He'd learned about CODA from his ex-girlfriend, Teri, who'd joined after Dan dumped her. She got help to heal the wounds from their illicit affair, and three years later, after she got married, they'd become friends. When Aileen left, Dan shared his anguish and misery with Teri, who then dragged him to a meeting. For months he went to daily meetings to "humor" Teri, but eventually, the program clicked with him. As he learned the twelve steps, he took responsibility for being the cliché of a neglectful, abusive husband, then acknowledged he needed to understand and evolve by working the steps. There were days he got on his knees and prayed for divine guidance because he felt so lost.

Dan saw his breath clouding in the air. The fire had gone out after Aileen had taken off her clothes and gotten into bed. He slid carefully out from under the comforter, padded to the pile of logs by the fireplace, and started another fire. He turned to see if he'd roused her, but she was still as stone. As the flame caught and the room warmed, he thought about making coffee, maybe breakfast, surprising her. She'd loved surprises once.

Kneeling bedside, he studied her, her hair scrunched on the pillow, the growing light casting deep lines in her face. For a moment, he wondered if the bliss of her return had blinded him to how much she'd aged in the year she'd been away from him, or perhaps during their marriage he hadn't noticed her growing old at all. Selfish, asshole Dan. He reached out and touched her cheek. Her skin felt different than it had last night when he'd lightly caressed her soft, silky face. Today, it looked and felt like tracing paper. Thin, pale, fragile, tight, and dry.

"Aileen, I love you." He didn't truly know how he felt about her, but he wanted to hold her, kiss her, *show* her that he was serious about cleaning up the mess he'd made of their marriage. His affection for her felt enormous, eclipsing the fear that he'd fail, that she might have a purpose in this he hadn't considered. Doubt trickled beneath his ardor. She opened her eyes.

Dan grinned at his wife. "Hi. I didn't want to wake you, but I'm just so damned happy you're here."

Aileen blinked and yawned. The taut, blanched skin around her eyes, over her cheeks, and around her mouth tore a bit, like once-sunburned skin beginning to rend before sloughing. Dan heard muted twig-snapping, crackling sounds, her body shuddering and jerking as she moved onto her back, throwing the comforter aside. Patches of skin the size of matchbooks peeled away from her shoulders and back, drifting about, and settling onto the sheet. He'd mistaken the sounds of the shedding skin for the burning wood on the fire.

Dan gaped, sucked in air with a gasp, then tried to hide—with a dramatic yawn—his reaction to Aileen's naked body molting like a crêpe-paper snake. But his intense glare compelled her to put her hands to her face. As her fingers slid over the skin, Aileen realized that something was drastically wrong, that the crisp pop and snap was her skin coming off in flakes, coating her fingers and falling like enormous dust motes through the air to the bed and wood floor. She furrowed her brow with recognition, and more skin split and separated on her forehead, like a moist creek bed suddenly baked in desert sun, the mud going hard, separating into irregular tiles of earth. The

74

horror struck her fully, and she opened her mouth and screamed. Panicked, she scrabbled to sit up, but each movement caused more crackling and snapping—larger patches of skin, like torn shreds of paper, coming off her breasts, ribs, and arms. She fell back, rigid, against the down pillows.

"Danny! What's happening to me? My skin!" Her voice, early-morning gruff, escalated to shrill.

Dan stared, speechless. In the night, her pale pink skin had turned dry, brittle, more husk than dermis. Her lush, ever-so-slightly graying auburn hair was today somehow dusty-looking, more wire-gray than reddish brown. Her eyes were unchanged—clear blue, piercing. Inside her open mouth, her tongue moved moist and rosy over her teeth. Dan thought her vagina must also be rubicund and wet, then blushed with shame.

Aileen's eyes jittered from him to her hands, her body, back to him; the panic in them spoke volumes. She licked her dry lips, and for a moment their natural, soft ruddy color returned. Taking a deep breath, she exhaled heavily, the sound reminding Dan of the way leaves on the lawn in autumn shushed under his rake. She grabbed at her chest and the skin, dry and shaped like crumbling dead leaves, lifted and fell back onto her in pearl gray shards. A wail came from deep inside her and filled the cabin. A sound worse than when she'd given birth to Eric and Emma.

Dan fell back onto his ass. "What can I do? Does it hurt? My God. Oh, my *God!*"

When her wailing subsided, her jaw appeared locked open. Her tongue arched and squirmed against itself to make words, half-said, strangled. He could make out some of them.

"I'm scared." Sounded like "aired."

Dan wanted to embrace her, but she looked too fragile. The ancient, boundless care he'd once felt for her surfaced, seeking purchase. Since he could not touch her, words were the only comfort he could offer.

"Where does it hurt?"

Aileen shut her eyes, testing her body with small, deliberate movements. She opened her eyes, turning her head slightly towards him. "Doesn't hurt. Just terrified. What's happening to me? Please. Tell me s'not as bad as it looks."

He spread his arms out over her. "How could ... this ... not hurt?"

75

She stared up at him. "Why is this happening? Now?" Dan thought, *now*, when they had a real chance to be better together. Resurrected.

Her speech grew odder. It reminded Dan of when Eric had tried ventriloquism. He could only managed stilted, awkward forms of words if his teeth and lips didn't move. Dan had laughed at him. Hurt him. He couldn't believe he was thinking about where Eric's damned ventriloquist's dummy was now, a dozen years later. Was he checking out like he used to, thinking about anything but what was right in front of him?

"For once, I've got nothing. Ai, if only … I just don't … know." Dan looked around the walls of the bedroom as if the solution hung there, if only he knew where to look. "Should I go for help? We're so far from everything. It'll take a while, but we can't stay here with you like this." Dan ran his fingers through his hair. "No. Wait. Moving you would be a mistake. Hell. Maybe we should wait. See if this'll pass."

He wondered if he were still dreaming. Stuck in a nightmare.

Aileen closed her eyes again, then struggled to open them. She licked at her teeth, swallowed. "It's the cabin's revenge." She laughed then, though her face remained expressionless, her mouth locked open. A chesty, cackling cough of a laugh.

To his amazement, Dan laughed, too. The old joke. When they'd bought the cabin, it had been nearly derelict. Over three summers, they'd hauled up wood, pipes, hardware, and fixed everything they could until they'd had to hire an electrician, plumber, and contractor. It was as if the cabin hadn't wanted a new life. It had nearly burned down twice. The roof had collapsed right after it was redone, and it creaked eerily, seemingly growling at them to "get out" as the cabin settled each night. But Dan's determination and Aileen's love had annealed the place into their dream house on the lake.

It was there in the cabin during one of their stays that Aileen had gotten pregnant. Two years after Eric was born and Aileen was pregnant with Emma, Dan had started coming up to the cabin without Aileen, staying longer each time. Away from the drain of needy kids and their tantrums, the hectoring of his wife, and the constant anxieties tied to his business, Dan found sanctuary at the lake. He'd forged a connection with the elements, enjoyed the freedom of gliding along the icy water's glassine surface in his boat, sitting in the open air, sun on his shoulders, his mind on one thing: catching fish. Gradually, he grew to love fishing more than running a business, being a father, or acting like a husband.

How many broken promises had there been? "Just the weekend" trips that lingered into a week, two weeks, leaving Aileen with the kids, the big house, and keeping all of it up, especially the appearance to the world that all was well with their lives. "We forced this damned shack into order, didn't we? Man, what an achievement." True, but the cabin was another of his many familial exploitations. "I'm *so* sorry for using this place against you. I want to make it up to you. I want to …"

Aileen moaned. "Stop. I know. Not the cabin." She coughed, not laughing. "It's me. I cursed us." Her eyes fluttered and tears fell, transparent pearls, one at a time, making rivulets, leaving darkening trails through the dust and feathery scraps left on her face. The delicate papery surface was ruined, exposing many spots and crevices of jaundiced, puckered skin beneath. Dan thought of the first snow up at the cabin. An inch, maybe, over the thick green grass, but heavy enough to flatten the plants. Aileen had stepped into the snow and without lifting her feet, had dragged them through the white to reveal the grass beneath, making a huge heart. Her tears were like her feet in the snow, but far more disturbing, leaving disorderly paths.

Dan felt tears welling and clutched at his eyes. He shook his head, took a deep breath. "You cursed? That's ridiculous. You're a saint. You deserve far better than you got with me. I owe you …"

Aileen shivered. The skin left on her arms crackled, like the sound of gift wrap being crumpled in a distant room, as the wood in the fireplace hissed and spat.

"Stop. I came back to tell you. You're not the only one to blame." Her speech grew worse. Back was "ack;" blame came out "lame."

Dan wrung his hands. "What should I do, Ai? Get help? God, if I knew what was happening, I'd …"

"Freak out?" Chesty, cackling cough of a laugh. Dan's "freaking out" took the form of rage, followed by escape.

"No. Not now. I'm staying." He gently stroked her hair. She gave him a wry grin.

She closed her eyes and sighed, her jaw slackened and her lips met. The tension in her body was loosening. He thought of the cell phone in his jacket pocket hanging by the front door, knowing service by the lake was non-existent. He'd disconnected the phone in the cabin when Aileen left him. How could he have known what was to come? Dialing 9-1-1 wasn't an option.

Maybe this panic turning his gut into a volcanic pit, ready to spill over the top, was linked to his guilt. Yeah. That could be it. After all, he'd had an eleven-page list of amends and the contrition to go with it. Perhaps he should be thinking that if Aileen were making a joke, she had to be okay. Not indifferent, but in her usual measured, patient, determined way, she saw an end ahead. So, have fun with it. Yeah.

After a minute, two, she didn't move, or take a breath. Dan watched for the rise and fall of her chest. Nothing. He shouted her name over and over, his heart slamming away. No response. Was she gone? A cry began to slither up his throat. But she opened her eyes just enough that he could see she was there, alive. Then she smiled. The movement caused the last patches of skin around her mouth to flake off, leaving a bluish, silver gray layer of membrane beneath. It wasn't quite opaque, and Dan thought he could see fluid coursing behind it.

For an instant, he felt like bolting. Getting his things, climbing into the car, and driving away. Leaving her with whatever drama was happening to her. But he remembered how unbearable the pain had been when she'd walked out on him. What anguish he'd put her through. His cruelties. She'd endured decades of pain. He wouldn't inflict any more on her.

"Oh, *baby*." He hadn't called her "baby" in twenty-two years. In the beginning, whenever she'd been hurting or scared, comforting her had made him feel manly, strong. He'd forgotten. Whatever Aileen's condition, she was bringing out the better Dan.

She gave him a sidelong glance, shut her eyes, and began breathing slowly, surely. Then parting her lips slightly, she said, "S'weird, I don't know why, but the fear is going away. Just stay with me. I feel … okay. I think something good is happening."

"Good? This? How can you know that, Ai?" He barked at her, incredulous at her composure. "Like when your father had his stroke and seemed to get well really fast and he and your mom went on that cruise? He was dead before they reached the first destination!" Dan grabbed his T-shirt over his heart and twisted the cotton jersey into a ball. "I don't want to lose you again!" All the work he'd done to im-

78

prove, take responsibility … for nothing? No way.

She moaned, exasperated. "No. Not dying."

"How the hell do you *know*? This ever happen to you before? No. So don't tell me you know anything!" He realized he was yelling. "Ai …"

"Shut up." The barking laughter, again. "Have faith. Do the walk." She shut her eyes again.

Dan stood up, realizing he was still in his underwear. How long had he been on his knees? He looked for his jeans. Once found, he pulled them on hastily, his knees creaking, aching, then his thick Irish fisherman's sweater, and stuffed his feet into his shearling boots.

"Are you cold?" he asked.

"No." She seemed surprised. "Feel fine. Good, even. Go eat. Come back. Talk to me."

Dan rubbed his ice-cold hands over his eyes and held them there. When he drew his hands over his cheeks, he stared down at her. The thin papery flakes were giving way to the ashy blue-gray and silver membrane, which was yellowing like an old bruise where the new "skin" had been exposed the longest. Dan's thoughts made wayward jaunts through fascination, forayed into disgust, slammed against wariness, and landed in despair. Aileen was asking him, in her way, to trust her, which he'd never done. Not really. Here the opportunity presented itself. He doubted he'd be up to the task, but if he didn't try, he'd fail.

Okay, he thought. Let Aileen be the one controlling this madness. She said she was fine. What did he know? Could she have a hand in this? Know more than she's saying? Some mean trick. Penance? This was all a waking nightmare, anyway.

What time was it? Dan glanced at the clock in the hall. Half a day had passed! She'd said he should eat. But his belly felt taut with fear. No putting food in there. Maybe coffee. Or brandy with coffee in it. He headed for the wet bar.

* * *

It was shitty of him to waste the rest of the day getting drunk, yet he did it with a boldness and determination. The old asshole Dan. But somewhere between finding his newly restored wife turning into medical spectacle, panicking that he was losing her again as she lay

79

there beatific, decomposing like a lacquered paper maché mannequin, he resigned himself to trusting her. Trusting that she knew what was becoming of her. He just had to wait. But he couldn't do it sober.

Staggering as he went, he hauled the overstuffed leather chair from the main room into the bedroom, slid the bedside table next to the chair, and set a bottle of 80-proof Russian vodka, an ice bucket with ice, a glass, and an unlit cigar on top.

The room filled with late afternoon light, the lake below casting wavering scythes of pale yellow on the putty colored walls. Aileen made an occasional noise, barked a rare laugh at Dan's reflective and self-incriminating monologues. But she no longer spoke.

"I should probably call the kids. They'd want to know we're together. No, cancel that thought. Bad idea. Eric still hates me. He knew before you did. D'you know that? I think he was seven. I was sitting in the car, supposedly taking Karen the babysitter home; instead, when he knocked on the car window, her head was in my lap. I think he had a crush on her. He wouldn't talk to me for a week. You thought it was because I got him a radio-controlled plane for his birthday instead of the telescope he wanted. He loved that plane in the end. Maybe that bought his silence. 'Cause he knew. He watched me, waited for me to be stupid again.

"And Emma ... she told me I'd screwed her up for good. She picks guys who treat her like crap, like I treated you. Said she always hoped I'd get a head injury, have some sense knocked into me, so I could be what you deserved. Hell! She's too young to remember how it was in the beginning. I was up here once a month by the time she was a year old. I missed so much. Both of them ... growing up. You."

Dan slapped his knee, nearly spilling his drink. "What a total shit! I can't think why you'd come back, why you'd want to talk. I know you heard what I was like after you left. How I lost forty-five pounds 'cause I couldn't eat. I got depressed, couldn't see then how I drove you away. Then one day I saw the asshole in the mirror.

"Know who I saw right there with me? My dad. Yeah, King Jerkwad who showed me how to be a husband, a dad. A man!

"Remember when I introduced you and he pulled me aside? I was what, twenty-four, five? He said, "Danny, if you don't fuck her, I will." That makes me sick now, but back then, I felt like a million bucks. I got a girl my dad wanted to screw, look at me! I can't believe how stupid I was!"

80

Chrysalis

Dan sat there, bleary-eyed, exhausted from avoiding what was happening in front of him. He wondered if Aileen had been listening since she'd gone quiet. Maybe she was asleep. He was glad she didn't seem to be in pain.

* * *

Dan woke suddenly from a dreamless sleep to a dark room. A very cold, dark room. He leaned towards where the bedside table had been the day before to turn on the lamp, forgetting he'd moved it next to his chair on the opposite side. He fell onto the throw rug and swore. He found the lamp on the floor and switched it on. Now halfway to sober, he shrieked at the sight of Aileen. He noticed first that the blue gray membrane that had become her new skin was now subsumed by a thick, cream-colored casing, shaped more or less like an Egyptian mummy's sarcophagus. There was no definition of chin, nose, arms or legs.

"Ai!" Compelled to free her face so she might breathe, he grabbed at the rough casing, finding the crisp substance crumbling at his touch. It was thicker than the previous papery layer; more like shirt board from the dry cleaners in weight. The more he scrabbled at it, the larger the pieces that came off the thing, like patches of burned wood on a log in the fire, falling into the ash. He saw a nose, not Aileen's. Smaller. He put his fingers under the nostrils, feeling for air moving in and out, and when he felt her breath, he paused. How could she have breathed inside that stuff? Then he looked in to see the pale gray blue membrane. It had darkened slightly—looked moist, healthy for whatever it was. Again it occurred to him that this could all be an allergic effect, a medical reaction to something she ate. Perhaps her nerves. Coming to the cabin had to have filled her with just as much trepidation and apprehension as it did Dan, maybe more.

He was dizzy from hyperventilating. He told himself to "get it together" over and over. That's what Aileen expected of him, what he'd never been able to deliver. Now it was time he did.

Close up, the newly exposed membrane pulsed with life. He tentatively reached out a fingertip and touched it. Cool, smooth, reptilian, he thought. He'd torn away the casing from the middle of her face, upper lip, nose, and brow. For just a moment, he thought this face was Aileen's from when she was five; innocent, smooth and young. He

81

and Aileen had often compared Emma's baby pictures to Aileen's, remarking on the similarity between mother and daughter at the same age. Was this process about aging? It would explain Aileen's blithe attitude. This awareness did little to assuage his thrumming angst.

Tears welled. This horror was exactly what he deserved, but it was happening to Aileen, not him. He was a helpless bystander, watching his wife disappear before his eyes. Of all the people in the world, Aileen deserved it least. Tender, gentle Aileen. This—whatever it was—should be happening to him.

But he would never *allow* this to happen to him. Aileen had always suffered with "nervous illnesses," her doctor said. Psoriasis, eczema, fibromyalgia. If this was a manifestation of her mental state, then as insane as it appeared, this bizarre transformation of her skin could make sense. Yes! Finally, a thought that mollified his distress.

Right. He checked again that she was breathing, guessed she was sleeping or resting deeply, pulled the comforter up to where her shoulders hid beneath the casing, and made himself another drink. He built a new fire, got it roaring, then settled into the big chair with the two comforters from the kids' old beds. He listened for sounds of her breathing, shifting, moving, but all he heard was the spitting of wood in the fire, still too wet to burn cleanly.

* * *

The next morning, Dan's head throbbed and his eyes hurt as he woke and looked out the bedroom windows to gray skies. He got up, cleaned the grate, built another fire, then went to shower. He stank. Or something did. But he longed for the streaming hot water to warm his bones. Wash away the strangeness.

In the shower, he realized he'd avoided looking at Aileen. Or what had once been her. He imagined she might be nothing but crumbled husk under the comforter, and the thought gripped him in the solar plexus. He went down on his knees and wept. Hard. Only the water going cold stopped his crying.

As he dressed, his face and gut ached from sobbing. He reckoned he was hungry. He made coffee and buttered toast. He ate without tasting, his thoughts dodging the grave scene in the bedroom. The coffee sharpened his mind, so he filled the mug with brandy. There was no more avoiding it, facing her; what she was becoming or disappearing into. He returned to their bed.

"Aileen, if you can still hear me, I am scared. I'm sharing my feelings like the men you've always admired and I thought were wusses. What's destroying you is killing me. I stopped being me when you left, and I know I'm not someone worth loving now that you're here. You were always the strong one, the better of us. This … whatever it is … it should be me!"

Rain smashed down on the shingled roof, tapped at the windows. The cabin slowly went dark, though it was morning. Dan went from room to room turning on lamps, lighting another fire in the living-room fireplace. He remembered how much Aileen had loved the smell of fires and the earth when it rained. She'd loved to swim in the lake when it rained in the summer. She'd learned to cook fish at the cabin. The city girl who got her nails done every week, met her high-fashion girlfriends for gossip-fest lunches, and thought of gardening as pots of herbs on the kitchen windowsill, soon gutted fish, grew tomatoes, potatoes, corn, and peas. She'd gotten dirty, sweaty, and trimmed her nails short so they wouldn't break. He'd loved her so fiercely then!

He went back in the bedroom and stood by the window, staring out at the sheets of rain, smelling the ripe, slightly rotting scent of dead skin mixed with sweat. The fire glowed in the fireplace, its heat intensifying the pungency of the stench. The window was sheltered under the cabin's eaves. Dan opened the window just enough to let in some air and dissipate the odors. He took a deep breath and smelled fresh, wet green things and lake water tinged with a sour note he couldn't place. He turned back to the bed. The comforter no longer rose gently up and down over Aileen's body.

He peeled the comforter back, fearing he'd find a shriveled mass in the shape of her. Instead there was a tough-looking covering colored and textured like a golden onion's skin, resurfaced where he had torn away the casing over her face. Dan considered the thing, dismay and horror circling his core, yet held at bay by a sliver of buoying hope. He had no reference for what he saw; what if Aileen *did* know what was happening to her, strange as it seemed to him? The covering kept repairing itself, thickening, protecting her. So, as she'd said, it was a good thing. Maybe. He allowed that this change in his feelings might be nothing more than his usual sense of denial, but the pulse of anticipation felt as real as the terror.

Then he was struck by the silence. The rain had stopped. Light had begun to etch through the clouds, reaching through the windows to swathe the walls, the bed, Aileen—the Aileen *thing*. He had to get outside.

Dan hurried to the front door, opened it, and stepped outside. The shock of fresh air, the assault of wet, wild scents, invigorated him. He walked out onto the veranda and looked down to the pier where his fishing boat, with its outboard motor and pull-up canopy, sat bobbing in the steel gray water. Pine, scrub, damp loam smells filled his nostrils. This is where he felt most at peace. Elemental.

He shook the water off the Adirondack chair Emma had painted when she was twelve and plopped down. He wrapped his arms around himself and let the sun warm his face. The wet soaking through his jeans brought back more memories. In his head, Emma was there, telling him not to sit in the chair; it was still wet. And Eric, that day he had just wanted to hike anyplace away from Dan and the tension he sensed between his father and mother. Aileen stood in the doorway behind him, admonishing Eric for running off yet again. Dinner would be ready soon; couldn't he smell the chicken casserole? Dan realized he'd had so much, the promise of true happiness all around him, and had just sat there thinking only of himself and what he'd rather be doing.

He dozed off. The chill wind whipping across the water woke him. The sun was going down, and the sky was a kaleidoscope of colors, smudged and burnished. Must be nearly six o'clock, he thought. Then the panic over Aileen clutched at his gut, and he bolted from the chair into the cabin, back to the bedroom.

No change. Was she hungry? Asleep? Comfortable? Alive?

"Aileen. I'm here. I was just on the porch in one of the Adirondack chairs, dreaming …" A profound sense of sadness made him reach out. They'd both come there to talk, begin to work through the maze made of his mistakes and her bitterness. But there was something more impenetrable than his fear hindering that plan.

The encapsulating husk was stiff and hard now. Hard as fiberglass. Was Aileen still trapped inside this thing? He gave it a quick shove and heard a rustling inside. Not frantic, not a startled movement, but like a creature stirring, roused from sleep. Curiosity flared. He wanted to break through the shell, or covering, or whatever it was. He tapped at it with his knuckles, tentatively at first, then hard-

84

er. It remained tough, resilient.

What if he'd hurt her, it, by fussing with this heavy fibrous casket? *Casket*. Damn. Not the term he wanted to use, but there the word danced in his head. Damn it! He pushed the word away. Tried out "pod." Yes. Better. Damn. *Damn.*

The rustling inside the pod-thing continued, became intermittent, and then stopped. He'd wait. That was easier at this point. Too many possibilities for him to do harm and set back their plans. He'd done enough damage to his wife already. Safer to do nothing.

He sat down in the big chair, looked at the unlit cigar, and thought about how much he wanted to light it, puff away, bring back the sense of control he felt with a drink in his hand, his friends around him, cocksure. Aileen was locked away and probably wouldn't smell what she'd once called "the stink of rotting beggars in Calcutta being burned." But he had to put her needs before his now. And he guessed it would be stupid to use a flame so close to whatever lay in their bed. In their cabin.

He drank the rest of the half-full bottle of vodka, lusting after the cigar, while he waited. For what? He dared not think about it.

* * *

Sometime around midnight, after he ate a steak selected from the groceries he'd brought to the cabin, he opened the bottle of Chianti Aileen had gotten for them. Red, thick—what he'd always preferred to her Zinfandels and Chardonnays. Thoughtful Aileen. He'd have one glass before he got back in the overstuffed chair to sleep beside his Aileen thing. He'd begun to think of it as a thing that held her safe. He couldn't fathom what he might find inside; his brain wouldn't let him. Which comforted him.

The wine was amazing. He saw two more bottles in Aileen's canvas satchel, and wedged between the bottles, a manila envelope. He touched the envelope, and his panic reinvented itself as hot lead in his veins. Divorce papers? Evidence from her private investigator of his many infidelities, his financial misdirections? The envelope was thin. He pulled it out and set it on the kitchen counter.

He had another glass of wine, then another, and finished the bottle. When the warm fuzziness dampened his fear, he slipped the packet open, looked inside. Letters. Maybe a dozen, the folds flattened from storage. They weren't from him. The handwriting was only vaguely familiar. He slid them out and let them sit, his gaze going to them, then away.

The nausea came without warning, and he turned to the sink just in time to vomit. The heaving came and went as he hung on to the edge of the counter. The realization the letters had been written by Aileen, that they weren't to him, vied for his attention, but his gut refused.

He knew he'd read them eventually. After all, why had she brought the letters and left them in such an accessible place? She wanted him to know. Maybe they held clues as to why his wife was now trapped inside a strange skin, silent and unreachable.

* * *

Dan was still awake when the sun rose the next morning, the letters in a pile on the floor beside the big chair. He'd been staring at the Aileen thing so long that his eyes stung when he blinked. His shouting and weeping, the blaming and hurtled slurs over what he'd read, had worn Dan out. It had occurred to him during his tirades that it had once been the other way around; Aileen screaming at him for all his various abuses while he sat inert in his smoking chair holding a cigar that had long ago gone out. Her words bouncing off him, his bulletproof detachment like a titanium carapace.

At one point during the very early morning hours, he'd slammed his fist into the bed and jostled the Aileen thing. The sound the thing made had shut him up. Like something strangling, choking inside.

Now, it was quiet. He was quiet, spent. He apologized to the thing, curled himself up in the chair, and slept.

* * *

The sound of the bed, creaking with movement, woke him. A quaking. He sat up, reflexively pulling the kids' comforters up around him. The Aileen thing rocked back and forth. Like an egg hatching.

He watched it with a combination of curiosity, suppressed rage, fear, and a smattering of anticipation. The golden pod had turned a beetle-brown in the night and smoothed out into a lustrous shell. Then the Aileen thing made a loud crack and snapped open as an arm

86

pushed through.

It was Aileen's arm, with her same delicate wrist, but the skin's surface reminded Dan of a rainbow trout, almost metallic, with tiny spotting and like an oil slick in the sunlight, undulating auras across the spectrum. The fingers were delicately webbed, translucent. Beautiful. The hand grasped at the casing's hard crust and pushed as the other arm burst through on the opposite side. Her knees came up and burst through, knocking the top of the pod off the bed.

As she freed herself, her head remained cloaked. Dan took in the perfection of her body, the model-thin perfection he'd known in their youth. It was Aileen as she had been when he'd fallen in love with her. The high rounded breasts, the crisp curve of her hipbone. Then he noticed that her navel had disappeared. In its place was a bony ridge that flared up and spread tines, with webbing joining the tines together.

Finally, she broke the casing from around her head, pushed it aside, and sat up. He stared into her strange new eyes. They were larger, without eyelids, eyelashes, or eyebrows. Still clear blue, but with a thin film tracing over her eyeballs. Her nose had flattened and spread, almost aboriginal, and nothing like the long straight nose Aileen had struggled to accept all her life. Her mouth was smaller, her lips full. Instead of Aileen's wide grin, this mouth was set in a sensual "Oh!" shape. The jaw had thinned down almost to a point, giving her face a teardrop appearance. When she arched her neck, Dan saw what looked like cuts, and worried she'd been injured from one his attempts to break through the covering. He reached out to touch the slits, and they undulated like gills. Gills! Where Aileen had become soft, plump, over the decades, this Aileen was lean, muscled, like a triathlon winner. Her hair, her amazing auburn hair, had turned completely silver, now damp and pressed against her head. He couldn't wrap his brain around what he was seeing, but he didn't want to.

The miraculous thing that had been Aileen stared back at him with Aileen's youthful, winsome innocence. If he could have remade his wife into everything he'd ever dreamed, she would look just like this Aileen. She, it, *was* Aileen, and something more, unique, and the most wonderful being he'd ever seen. The aquatic coloring and grace in motion made Dan think of a mermaid, a sea nymph. She licked her lips, and drew her long fingers over her erect nipples as if discovering them for the first time. A high-pitched giggle came from deep within her. She lay back on her pillow, moving her hands over her body as she stretched and experimented with movement she'd been unable to make for over two days. One hand slid between her legs, parting her hairless labia, where her finger disappeared inside her. She gasped.

Instead of disgust or terror, Dan felt an enormous wave of affection and erotic interest. The vitriol of the night's vigil gone. There was only love. Desire. She opened her arms to him, and he undressed just a little less quickly than he had on their honeymoon.

Her skin felt oily, moist, and supple. She pressed her cool voluptuous pout to his warm lips, and he felt unaccountably filled with rapture. He moved onto her, the slick surface of her skin allowing him to slide effortlessly into her. She acted like a woman, tasted like a woman, but moved like a water-born creature. Her arms wrapped around him, holding him tightly as he moved inside her. With each thrust, he felt thick ribbed walls that robbed him of his will, his control. When he made love to her, he knew she was Aileen, reborn, and so he, too, was made new.

* * *

Aileen purred into his ear as he held her and she tried her land legs. With her webbed toes and long feet, she continually faltered, fell into him, to the floor; so he carried her to the shower. He couldn't resist making love to her again and again beneath the water's spray. She acquiesced each time, yielding to him completely. This ardent being was not his old Aileen. His thoughts brushed against apprehension, tiptoed past doubts, to embrace their newfound union, their bliss. With only guttural moans and sighs, Aileen expressed her love, her glee.

From the shower, he lifted her in his arms, walked to the open door, and stepped out onto the deck. He grinned at the birdsong, turned so his face and hers were to the sun; let the soft breeze dry them both. He would never be away from this Aileen again. As he carried her down the rise to the pier, he marveled at the perfection of her, her passion. His own.

He stood at the end of the pier holding her, recalling how she'd felt beneath him, welcoming him inside. So right. She nestled against him, making a cooing sound.

Chrysalis

Suddenly, she began wriggling in his arms, pushing herself away. She landed on the pier, took two awkward steps, and dived into the lake, leaving rings advancing out across the surface. He knew this was what she was meant to do. Aileen, happy at last.

He knelt, watching her move joyfully a few feet beneath the water's surface, as if the lake had always been her home. The reeds, rising from the lake bottom fifteen feet below, roiled around her in a delicate ballet, weaving through her long silver hair.

She surfaced, her mermaid's body undulating, allowing her to keep her head above water. Dan reached out to pull her back in his arms. Her hand came from the water and grasped his wrist. It wasn't a gentle gesture. More of a clamp. Then she pulled, hard, drawing Dan into the water with her, not letting go, swimming furiously away with him. Deep, into the very cold, dark abyss, water enveloping them both in its wet cocoon.

Nickelback Ned

Maria Alexander

Nickelback Ned lived in a shed
Where his mother had left him for slaughter
But she lost her luck
When lightning struck
And he held her down in the water

It felt like someone had ripped open my chest and knuckle-punched my heart. Two days had passed since I'd moved out and I'd barely stirred from my intense stupor of grief. Depressed by the breakup, all I could do was lie on the floor like a starfish, an anchor planted in my stomach. Three years of my life—most of them in bliss—blown away like candle smoke.

And I couldn't understand why.

My cell phone bleated. I lifted the cell to glance at a number that rarely appeared on my Caller I.D. "Rory?"

"Lilla, baby." Rory's voice purred with a soft southern accent. Coffee grinders whirred in the background over the chatter of patrons. "Ned's killed again."

An alarm clanged in my head. "How? And where?" I sat up and leaned on an elbow. Ned hadn't been seen in twenty-five years. Not since he'd killed Scotty ...

"Where we last saw him. Got an old man this time. Maybe he's slowing down. Squeezed the poor bastard so hard, his ribs snapped in two and perforated his torso before the lightning came." Rory paused as a passing siren howled over the connection. "I'm going to go get him, Lilla. Bring him to justice. You promised you'd help."

I took a few steady breaths as I tugged at the barb of my ill-placed promise. I couldn't stand the thought of blood on my hands, no matter whose it was. "Killing him isn't going to bring back Scotty or our childhoods."

I didn't think Rory had it in him, frankly, although he certainly held his own in his business as a personal investigator-cum-celebrity babysitter. And he loved that 9mm, which he packed for "emergencies."

"You backing out?"

"Yeah." I felt only the residue of my punk rock blood. The younger me that would have leathered up and lashed out. My voice cracked as my throat heated. "Rory, Philippe was hit by a midlife meteor and did some very hurtful shit to me. I had to break it off. I just moved into my new place two days ago."

"Oh Christ." His voice softened. "You wanna talk about it?"

"Maybe later. But please don't think I'm reneging. I just can't work myself up, not unless it's a posse to harvest Philippe's balls."

"I thought he liked that shit."

"Hard to punish a masochist, isn't it?"

Rory sighed. "If you change your mind about Ned ... He ruined our lives, Lilla. Don't forget it."

We hung up. I dropped the cell phone as I closed my eyes and, splayed again on the floor, the last few sleepless weeks caught up to me.

Breakup or no, Nickelback Ned still haunted my dreams ...

"Run!"

Scotty shrieked over the wind as it violently raked the summer grasses, the blackened mountains shouldering a gunmetal sky booming with thunder. His athletic yet tender young legs pumped underneath him with a pronounced limp as he ran towards us from the barn, a filthy gash that wept blood widening on his cheek, terror flashing in his eyes.

The misshapen form of Nickelback Ned scuttled at Scotty's heels, lumpy limbs twitching, his one good eye flicking back and forth like an eel on his scarred face, the other eye sewn shut. A pitiful moan escaped his mealy mouth hole, ragged strands of greasy hair falling into his eyes. The black hair on his shaggy arms and chest was matted like an ape's, his misshapen nose upturned like a pig's. His grotesque frame moved with the frightening liquidity of a great white shark as he cut through the grasses towards Scotty.

Lightning scrawled across the clouds before thunder slammed the sky once again.

I ran with Rory to the dark trees that lined the mountainside at the far north end of the field. At eight years old, I was unsure which was more dangerous—tree shrapnel from lightning or getting caught by Nickelback Ned. We shouldn't have been poking around that old barn. I had known something bad would happen.

Nickelback Ned

As we sailed across the field, Scotty's cry drove a spike of panic into my chest. I stopped and looked back just a few yards away. Scotty had fallen and, as he scrambled to get back up, Ned wrapped his hands around Scotty's pale neck. Scotty's lips—the lips that had kissed me in the dandelion patch when we were six—turned purple as he struggled, gasping and flailing.

Caught between loathing and loyalty, I couldn't move. Meanwhile, Ned dove onto Scotty's body, crushing him to the ground. His discolored tongue darted towards the blood on Scotty's cheek.

A white-hot vein of lightning as thick as a fir tree riveted Ned's back. Ned and Scotty convulsed under the blinding column of light.

I felt the scream scratching my throat, but heard nothing as my ears rang. A ball of heat radiated from the two forms locked in the grass. A repulsive burning odor overpowered me. Ned lifted himself, revealing the smoking, charred remains of Scotty. My friend. My first love. Ned leered at me in the haze of that silence, his eel eye flickering, a long horrible moan escaping those malformed, bloodied lips ...

I awoke, chest lifted to the ceiling, my cries pinging the walls of the empty apartment, the loss of Scotty feeding on the loss of Philippe. A sharp wedge drove under my breastbone, the sickening pain snarling my body until I rolled up like a pill bug. I sobbed, thick hot tears burning my cheeks and throat, until the sickness subsided to rage. The police had abused Rory and sent him to reform school because they didn't believe us. Rory was too frail and bookish to have even knocked Scotty down, much less break his arms and burn him to death. I became a delinquent, dismissed from multiple schools. The Ashville courts put my family through hell, dragged me to trial, and tried to make us recant, to say that Nickelback Ned was just a myth. The authorities were mightily skeptical of anything that smelled like a hillbilly fable, even if they privately believed in it. But he was all too real.

What happened with Philippe was done. I could keep crying into my pillow, but I'd not change a thing just by lying there. The business with Scotty and Ned, however, was unfinished. And as long as I could do something—anything—I couldn't sit on my ass and let Scotty's memory fester.

I reached for the cell phone and dialed.

"Yes."

I wiped the tears with my palm. "I'm coming with you."

A long pause. "I went ahead and bought your plane ticket. See you in Asheville, baby."

* * *

Rory was already wedged in his airplane seat as I maneuvered down the narrow aisle on our flight from Los Angeles. I was late, as usual, and had missed seeing him in the terminal, where he'd arrived from San Francisco on an earlier flight. I'd not seen him in three years, and I was totally unprepared for the changes. Rory's sharp features were more pronounced now, veins bulging on his neck. His muscles swelled strangely on his arms. His cerulean eyes stared wetly at me, haunted by far more than the hunt.

"Hey, mister." I ducked down and retracted the handle of my chubby overnight bag. "Long time, no bite."

Rory wriggled out of his seat and grabbed the bag for me, hefting it into the overhead compartment despite my protests. He wobbled a bit as we ducked into our seats and hugged tightly. His patchy red beard scraped my cheek.

Nickelback Ned lived in a shed ...

According to legend and scattered records I'd found over the years, Ned had been born with hundreds of birth defects and needed dozens of surgeries just to survive. Whatever those "defects" were, Ned was certainly born wrong. Born different, anyway. His father had abandoned the family when Ned was very small. Ned's mother took refuge in alcoholic binges. The last surgery Ned received was a metal rod in his back to correct the scoliosis created by his spina bifida. Although the rod was steel, the kids who'd tormented him called him Nickelback Ned. Bankrupt from medical bills and facing foreclosure, his drunken mother had tossed Ned's oozing, barely stitched body into the shed by the barn, locking the door and leaving Ned to die in the darkness.

My obsessive research yielded some revealing local stories. Apparently Ned began to grow into something not entirely human, a nightmare carved from the wreckage of flesh. Driven by an overwhelming will to survive, he scrounged insects, lizards and other crawling things, devouring anything that crept through the shed slats. He captured rainwater in his hands and drank his own piss for

94

weeks.

Then one night, the black sky wept and howled as white-hot light scratched the horizon. Drowning in a bottle of booze, his mother wandered outside, more moonshine in her blood than in the sky, according to neighbors who witnessed the event. They believed Ned could hear her cursing him and that he could no longer take it. He ripped apart the shed slats to break free.

As his mother stumbled under the heavy blanket of insobriety, he caught her. She stared at him slack-jawed for several moments as his meaty arms clamped around her. Her panic sparked a flurry of kicking as she struggled to get free. Lightning needled the sky and Ned lowered her to the ground. Some say he dragged her flailing body to the deepest puddle he could find and held her down in the water. The steel in Ned's back then drew the bolt's deadly discharge like a lightning rod.

But when the white flame riveted Ned's back, he was not the one who was scorched.

The authorities discovered the charred remains of Ned's mother lying in the field after the storm. The newspapers reported that her upper arm bones were cracked.

But they never found Ned.

And the verse was born.

"Are you all right?" Rory asked.

"I was going to ask you the same question." I touched his cheek. "You look kinda frail."

"It's nothin'. Just gettin' old."

"Oh, please. You're thirty-seven. That's not old. Now fifty-seven? That's thinking about getting old. Thirty-seven is just contemplating the possibility of maybe getting old—some day." I flashed a weak smile at him, running my hand over his arm coated in slick, beat-to-hell leather.

"I'm all right." The gruffness in his voice shut the door on more questions. If he was this closed off, it had to be bad. I rested my head on his shoulder as the airline attendants prepped us for takeoff. The plane eventually nosed into the air through a cloudless sky.

"Tell me who we're meeting."

"Name's Anna Deveaux. She's a widow livin' just outside downtown Asheville on Beaucatcher."

"Fuck. Did she have to be French?"

Tales of Genetic Mishaps, Monsters, and Madness

* * *

Do you know what that is? he asked. His French accent, thick as a baguette, mauled his nearly flawless English.

Of course, I replied, hefting the buzzing antique medical device. It's a violet wand.

We were in a kinky decorating class where dominant women such as myself were dressing our submissives like Christmas trees for the holidays. Philippe stood naked save for a thin leather thong cupping his scrotum, his short hairy legs taut from years of playing soccer. I tied his hands behind his back and wrapped tinsel around his hirsute torso and arms, placing the metallic stars over his nipples. We were so in love, even after two years, that I could have picked up a chainsaw and he wouldn't have flinched. His trust was that deep. We had just come back from living in France for a year because of his job.

We were now heady from moving in together here in the States. I'd returned to my old job. We wanted to buy a house.

I placed kisses down the hump of his large nose until I reached his lips. We kissed passionately.

I clutched the wand's handle like Glinda the Good Witch and touched the purplish glowing tube attachment to the tinsel star I'd draped over Philippe's left nipple.

A tiny arc of light leapt between the glass tubing of the wand, the tinsel and the pinkish nubs of his tits. He squeezed his eyes shut, shoulders raising to his ears as he yelped, Ah-AAAAH!

Although the other female dommes laughed with delight, the sight of the brief electrical storm, for me, stirred a stew of conflicting emotions. The splinter of electricity struck more fear in me than in him, yet the heat swelled between my legs to see my beloved's cock thickening in the leather jock. Play pain. The sort of exquisite agony I could never inflict on a human being who didn't love it. I withdrew the wand. Had enough? I asked.

Whatever Mistress wants, he replied, panting. I knew he wanted more. Much more.

So, with joy, I gave it to him.

* * *

My hate for Philippe now wound itself around my love for him like a muscular boa constrictor on a bony branch. Any minute the latter would snap. Rory didn't ask questions, not even during our layover in Atlanta as we drank margaritas in an airport restaurant. Nobody ever pushed me for details, no matter how much they wanted to know what had prompted the surprising breakup.

Instead, Rory regaled me with anecdotes about rock stars he'd escorted for the record labels, making sure they didn't get sidetracked with drug dealers. Despite my eventful year in France, my artistic life as flash designer for a film studio paled against his. He'd managed to roll his few years in the Army into a lifelong gig either hunting down deadbeat dads or babysitting these musical baboons. Seldom any stories these days about girlfriends. Those had dissipated five years ago.

"You carry that gun all the time, don't you?"

Rory nodded, licking the salt from his lips. "I've hunted him for years now. Whenever there's a sighting, I go out if I can afford it."

Shock stung my chest. "I didn't think Ned had been seen for decades! Why didn't you tell me?"

"I didn't think you'd approve."

"No, I wouldn't approve. You barely escaped trouble once. Why on earth would you court it again over and over? Besides, how'd you know? Who told you? I haven't seen a thing on the Net in years."

"I got a contact."

"Who?"

He looked guilty. "An old enemy. That's all I can say."

The beehive in my head swarmed. "So if you've got this so-called 'contact'—and a fucking gun—what am I doing here? Why did you bring me into all this trouble?"

"Because I need you, Lilla." His eyes glistened as they looked into mine. "I just ... need you."

I hugged him, heart heavy, and finished my drink.

A heavy storm delayed our flight into Asheville but we eventually landed at the bite-size Asheville Regional Airport. After Rory retrieved an overnight case and an impressive suit bag from the baggage belt, we picked up our white Pontiac rental. Rory's eyes jittered as he reached up to adjust the rearview mirror.

"What's wrong with your eyes?"

"Nothin'. Just tired."

I doubted that. "Lemme drive. I'm less tired."

Rory relented.

Tales of Genetic Mishaps, Monsters, and Madness

With the clatter of heavy raindrops on our windshield, we made the long ride up Highway 25 to our tiny motel, which sat across the road from one of the many Waffle House restaurants. The Blue Ridge Mountains loomed in the mists, the lush hillsides climbing up and around us. I hadn't stepped foot in North Carolina since my family fled to Los Angeles. The place was far more beautiful than I remembered, but the residue of childhood trauma smudged the scenery.

Still, things had changed.

The East Indian woman who checked us into our rooms initially seemed like a bona fide, saucer-riding extraterrestrial. I couldn't remember ever seeing anyone who wasn't white in these parts as a child. Asheville was now the Santa Cruz of the South: liberal, hippy-hugging, ridiculously nice. I started to feel a bit hopeful and definitely more comfortable. The woman handed us keys to adjoining rooms that Rory paid for with cash.

As I washed and dressed in my room, a sedan pulled up and someone banged on Rory's door. I heard an older man's voice. Rory answered. I froze, ears pricking as I tried to make out what they were saying. The door shut behind the man who entered Rory's room. I tiptoed to the cold wall in my bra and panties and listened. My skin tingled when I heard the words "special bullets." The mysterious visitor then left. I crouched on the natty carpeting and ever so slightly nudged the drape aside with my index finger.

The elderly man who limped back out to the parked sedan was none other than Scotty's father—frail, silver haired, deep grief carved into his face as he got behind the wheel and drove away. He must have been Rory's "contact." How the two had reconciled and formed this posse, I couldn't imagine. I wanted to call out, "I'm sorry! I'm still sorry!" but didn't.

I knelt beneath the window, wishing I had never agreed to this madness.

The storm had gathered strength by the time Rory and I met outside. Rory's expensive gray pinstriped suit hung on him like a half-empty garbage bag as he held the umbrella over me in what was now a downpour of biblical proportions. When his step faltered, I worried more and cursed as water seeped into my silky flat shoes. I'd forgotten that late summer in Asheville was so rainy.

I got into the car. "Saw Scotty's dad."

Rory said nothing and shut the door. When he slid into the driver's seat, I continued.

"Wanna tell me how you two reconciled?"

"He saw Ned."

"He's your contact, isn't he? God, Rory! Why so many god-damned secrets?"

"Like I said, you wouldn't approve."

"Why wouldn't I approve of you making peace with someone?"

"Because *you* couldn't."

He was right.

We took off at a slow pace on the 240, through the city outskirts, up onto the lush Blue Ridge Parkway, to the 694 towards Beaucatcher Mountain. If North Carolina had a hell gate, this was it. The area was rife with tales of the supernatural, such as the ghost of Helen's Bridge, where a distraught mother had hanged herself.

Anna Deveaux lived on the other side of the mountain, where the roads flattened, leading to open slopes between thick patches of trees. A century ago, on these roads that circled the mountain, young suitors used to "court" girls they wanted to marry. That was how the mountain had got its name.

Lilla, we need to talk. Philippe walked me to the couch, his clammy hand holding mine, and we sat. His face was tight and ruddy. Lilla, I applied for a job in France.

My stomach ached with betrayal and my head whirred with panic: I'd said no to permanent relocation in the past because it meant leaving everything—my career, my family—forever. But now, on the verge of losing the man I loved more than life, I said, Okay, we'll go. We'll have to get married so I can be a French citizen and work.

He put up a hand. There's something else: I want children.

I said: Okay, okay. We'll get married and try to have a baby.

But you don't want children badly enough.

I don't understand. I'm willing. We can try naturally and if that doesn't work, we can adopt—

He looked away.

We just have to get married is all.

I don't know if I want to get married, he said. I don't want to make a promise I cannot keep.

My heart shattered.

Sometimes I would close my eyes and I'd be there, just a week before that conversation. My life full of love, lust and laughter. Then I'd remember how it all changed in a night. But I couldn't believe it. Was I crazy? Things don't change overnight.

Or do they?

The rental car pulled into a long drive lit up by the headlights and lined by towering black trees. Anna Deveaux and her late husband had owned a successful French restaurant in town and another up in Chapel Hill for many years. Their mountainside home showed it. While specific details drowned in the darkness, the broad driveway brought us to the elegant face of a red-bricked Georgian Colonial home with a single light sitting on a front windowsill. Everything else inside was dark.

"It's late. Are you sure she's in?"

"Oh, she's in, all right." Rory stopped the car.

"She took a bite out of him. He's looking for her."

"How'd she do that?"

"She picked up loose board by the barn and hit him in the head to make him let go of her man. She made Ned bleed, but he didn't let go. So she ran."

"So what? Sounds like she got away. How would he know where she was?"

"By her smell. It won't be long before he finds her."

"Does she know that?"

"I dunno. Maybe."

"Won't he smell us, too?"

"That's what I'm hoping."

It was a little late to get mad.

Rory got out of the car, motioning for me to wait until he came around with the umbrella. Never known for his chivalry, he was being unusually considerate. He offered me his elbow. I hooked my hand around it and we walked up the immaculate white steps to the door. Rory rang the bell and, after a few moments of suspense, the door opened. A petite woman in her sixties peered out, pale skin wrinkled, shoulder-length hair frayed, salty blue eyes haunted and watery with grief as they scanned the darkness beyond us.

"Mrs. Deveaux, I'm Rory Cox. This is my associate, Lilla Argyros."

"Hello." Her heavy French accent stepped on the "h." "Please

100

come in."

She led us into the sparsely lit house, using a Maglite to illuminate the way. She wore a thick coat against the chill. "I am sorry. I do not have lights or heat. The storm took them two hours ago."

Lit barrel candles sat on a small table in the hallway. Mrs. Deveaux led us into a bourgeois sitting room near the entryway, where the faint glow of more barrel candles bobbed and wavered on the table. We sat on her comfortable couch with its printed rose pattern while she sat beside us in a matching high-backed chair.

"I hope this is okay." The candlelight made her face more ghastly.

"*Merci beaucoup, madame. Ça marche bien assez.*" I replied reflexively in that beautiful language that Philippe had taught me, although each syllable stabbed my heart.

Mrs. Deveaux's face brightened a bit. "*Vous parlez français? C'est bien.*"

I glanced sidelong at Rory. He'd wanted me with him to put the old lady at ease.

"Mrs. Deveaux, I hope you'll forgive me for being abrupt," Rory said, "but could you tell me exactly where you saw Ned kill your husband? And has there been another sighting since?"

"It was in the pasture ..." Her face quavered, eyes glistening. "Just a couple miles from here. My husband and I, we were wanting to buy an old farm house. This one was empty for many years. It was rumored to be haunted, but we don't believe such things. We went there to see it and ... it was raining ... and then ... the lightning ..." She trailed off, painful memories choking her.

"The farm house just off of Hope Lane, about a mile down the dirt road?"

She nodded, then started shaking as if she sat on a block of ice. I knew the French liked their personal space, but I couldn't help reaching for her hand and saying in French, *I understand perfectly.*

Lilla, I need to know for sure that you can even get pregnant, since you're against IVF treatments. Philippe buried his fist in his cheek, leaning on the dinner table. It will help me make my decision.

What do you mean? What decision?

I need a fertility test, he said. And then I will know if I should stay here and marry you or pursue the position in Brittany.

My world stopped, our happy life suddenly destroyed by the shocking revelation of his misogyny. Who was this narcissistic ogre? I'd been not only willing to have a baby, but to adopt if necessary. What he meant was he wanted out of this relationship and he wanted to blame me for the breakup. He wanted to make it my fault, to blame it on my uterus when he was being the most selfish sonuvabitch on the planet.

Tears scalded my eyes and cheeks. How could you? I said, more from heartbreak than outrage, although that tidal wave of fury would come when I found out how quickly he'd replace me. How could you treat me like chattel? I wept, the humiliation tearing my heart. I hoped he would see his cruelty. Don't you love me for who I am?

Instead he looked at me as if he'd merely asked for my half of the rent.

"*Merci.*" Mrs. Deveaux pulled a hanky from her pocket and dabbed at her tears. She squeezed my hand. "It is very hard. Our daughter died three years ago from breast cancer. Our family in Lyon is sick. And I cannot go to them until I finish this business. I've got to prove to the police he is real, *cette monstre.* If only the police believed me. But they think he is some vagrant. That he has moved on and that they cannot catch him. But ... you should have seen him!" Tears ran down her cheeks. "He was so terrifying. I tried to hit him, like I said to you on the phone, but ... oh ... and I saw him *smell* me. He sniffed the air like an animal ..."

The wind shrieked and rattled the windowpanes. We looked around, startled by the fury of the building storm.

My ears pricked at the sound of a pitiful moaning and my blood chilled. This was not the wind slipping under the eaves. Not an animal loose in the maelstrom. Not anything that normally happens in storms. I would never forget that sound as long as I lived ...

It was Ned.

Mrs. Deveaux's breath sucked in and out rapidly. Ned's monstrous shadow appeared in the windows just before he hit the glass with a horrendous crash.

Rory pulled the Colt from his jacket and leveled a deafening shot at Ned, who stumbled away from the window and scuttled off into the night. Mrs. Deveaux screamed. Rory herded her out of her chair, deeper into the house. I grabbed the dropped Maglite and followed, head twisted back as I watched for the horror from my childhood. We hustled down the hallway and disappeared into the guest bedroom.

Rory pushed Mrs. Deveaux inside. He then tried to shove me, as well. "Lock the door. I'll take care of him."

"Fuck that shit! I'm coming with you."

"Take care of Mrs. Deveaux."

"I gotta take care of YOU!"

His eyes jittered. He loped off down the hallway towards the sitting room.

"*Madame Deveaux, fermez la porte! Vite!*"

She found a scrap of sanity and shoved the door closed. The lock snapped shut from inside.

I ran into the sitting room, brandishing the Maglite. Scattered glass on the hardwood floor threw back tiny knives of light beneath the billowing drapery sheers. The front door stood open to the howl of a brutal storm, thunder ripping the sky.

I breathed deeply and dove into the darkness.

The fragrant scent of rain bloomed around me, the mists rising in thick veils against the mountainside. Freezing rain sprayed my bare face and hands, soaking my legs as I stood on the porch. I dragged the enormous beam of light across the darkness. My breaths came short and hard. Legs quaking with cold and fear, I stepped down the slick porch steps. I passed the rental car, which rested like a sarcophagus in the driveway. I moved onto the grounds of the house. My ears pricked at every noise. I couldn't see Rory or Ned anywhere.

Shots rang out.

I froze. I dropped and crawled to one side of the rental car. My knees shrieked as they scraped the wet pavement, heavy rain pelting my back. I heard nothing but the wail of rain and winds. Maybe Rory had shot Ned. Maybe it was over …

My flashlight beam spilled across the driveway and over the edge of the hillside, bordered by majestic firs that flanked the stately house. At the light's weak perimeter, a thin black figure struggled to his feet. Then it fell again. A flare of lightning lit up the hillside, revealing Rory's pained, panicked face.

I watched. Nothing was following him. I launched myself from the protection of the rental car. Rain blinded me as I ran. "Rory! It's me!"

I knelt beside him in the soggy forest grass. He strained to sit up. Instead, he fell back to the ground, arms dangling. The gun lay in his open hand.

"Take the gun!" His eyes jittered more wildly as he looked into mine. It reminded me of Ned's eye, the flickering eels. The aching look of a diseased man.

"Did he hurt you?"

Rory said nothing.

"Fucking tell me what's wrong, Rory!" Storm winds almost stole my breath.

"I—I've got MS."

"What?"

"Multiple sclerosis. I can't feel my goddamned arms. I can't walk right. I feel goddamned pins and needles." His face twisted with anguish as the secret poured out. "The drugs've stopped working."

My whole body shivered hard. Thunder rumbled above us. "Fuck you for not telling me! FUCK—YOU!" I slapped Rory's arm repeatedly.

Rory managed a weak smile. "Lilla? I can't feel that."

"Awww, Jesus!"

Rory's eyes moved from mine to the gun. "He's hit, not dead. Finish him."

I stared at the gun. That awful moan spiked the storm in the distance. *Fuck this.* I could never again let this bastard ruin my life or anyone else's.

Time to leather up and lash out.

I picked up the gun. It was heavier than I expected, slick and chill. I squinted in the wind. My eyes stung badly as the mascara and eyeliner bled into them. I blinked hard, wiped my eyes with my arm. That eased the pain a little. I scanned the horizon with the Maglite. The beam tore open pockets of flora flailing in the wind. The nearby copse of trees bent dangerously under the bluster.

The moaning rose to a sickening bellow. I struggled to my feet, heart throwing its shoulder against my sternum. I leaned into the blinding spray. A glorious needle of lightning scrawled across the sky, lighting up the hillside ...

... and the malefic form of Ned.

He hunched between the trees. A troll from a childhood fairytale, brutish and frightening. Long strands of greasy hair matted to his cheek.

And then he disappeared.

Arms shaking, I strode down the hillside, swinging the gun and Maglite in an arc around me.

Moments later, muffled screams escaped somewhere behind the house. I was torn for three heartbeats: Should I stay with Rory or chase down that hulking bastard before he killed Mrs. Deveaux?

I chose the beast.

Sliding on the slick grass, I hurried towards the cries. The downpour chilled my skin. I felt numb to everything except the gun. At the back of the house, a grand terrace loomed above me. The woman's screams grew louder. I spotted Ned dragging Mrs. Deveaux down the terrace stairs that landed elegantly in a Provençal garden splayed around the house. He lugged her across the garden onto the grassy slope. Another hot white scrawl lit up the sky.

I trained the weapon and the light on him as he continued to drag the screeching, grasping old woman. *"Ned! Put her down! NOW!"*

He turned in slow motion. That hideous eye acknowledged me. He threw Mrs. Deveaux down the hillside hard. Her limbs splayed as she tumbled and scrambled away.

And then he turned towards me.

In the shaky light, that eye flicked back and forth, its partner swollen and scarred. He looked a lot older now, yet more monstrous with age. He'd probably been in his late teens when he killed Scotty, but now he had to be close to fifty. His lips were melted together where the stitches had been on one side of his mouth, his withered lips curled back. The few strands of greasy grey hair he had left were stuck to his lumpy head. The rain pasted a torn T-shirt to his crumpled chest and his hoary arms bulged where there shouldn't have been muscles.

Terror bolted me to the spot. I was that eight-year-old girl again, incapacitated by the sight. Although terrified for my life, I also felt a surge of triumph. I wasn't crazy. Ned was real. Those asshole sheriffs and townspeople who called me a liar had destroyed my belief in myself. Just as Philippe had tried.

Lilla and I are just on different paths, he told his friends who used to be "our" friends. She didn't want a baby and I did. That's why she left me ...

Fucking liar.

Ned took a step towards me. I trembled. My neck and shoulders ached from tilting my head forward to keep the rain from sluicing into my eyes. I clutched the gun and light, hyperventilating. An icy worm of fright slipped through my bowels.

"I'll shoot!"

Another step.

Nickelback Ned lived in a shed where his mother had left him for slaughter ...

It wasn't that Philippe had robbed me of my last few fertile years. If I'd had a biological clock, the power cord had been unplugged my whole life. But to be treated like meat—like a disposable baby-making machine when I'd busted my ass to beat back the delinquent and be the best person I could possibly be, both lovable and available—that cruelty bludgeoned my heart. How could anyone do that to another human being? Especially a supposed loved one?

How could it have happened to poor Ned?

Ned lunged at me. My fingers lost their feeling, my heart its nerve. I tore away and ran with all my might up the hillside. Ned tackled me. The stench of rotten breath and bed sweat gagged me as I crashed. I dropped the light and the gun. I screamed, my arms and ribcage constricted in the agony of his powerful, repulsive stranglehold. The gritty smell of mud and grass penetrated the stench. My cheek sank into the ground.

Thunder boomed above us. The voice of God.

And then, despite my imminent death, a perverse yet profound compassion overcame me. Perhaps because I'd been called monstrous for my sexuality. Perhaps because I, too, had been rejected for my body. Or because, despite the tremendous heartache, I'd still had more love the last three years than Ned had ever felt in his life ...

"Ned, if I'd been your Momma, I woulda never done what she did to you. Never in a million years."

Because no one deserved to be treated like that. Like meat. And then the world exploded in blinding white light, riveting us to the ground—

silence
a thousand blades scraping my skin

heartbeats

the only sound in my ears

revved to an impossible speed
{gratitude}

silky warmth

(I am you
we are the same
take
the power of death)

blackness

The storm subsided to a dusting of droplets. I curled up on the soaking ground, ears ringing, ozone stinging my nostrils. I unwound slowly and sat up, every nerve screaming in my arms, legs and temples. Still, I sensed that Ned had insulated me, taking the bulk of the trauma. And I felt this intense connection to him. He'd drawn down the bolt to himself, but not to kill me. To give me something.

Oh, God.

I dragged myself to my knees, the mother in me awakened. I had to check on him.

Ned was sprawled beside me, blood oozing from Rory's bullet wounds. He wasn't nearly as frightening up close, but rather more like the big ugly bully kid knocked flat on the grass. His head lolled towards me, grayish tongue sweeping his mealy lips. He said something I couldn't quite make out because of my deafness from the lightning strike and the gunshot. But Nickelback Ned's mouth formed the splintered words, his one eye drowning in pathos as he regarded me. He spoke.

"You hah wuh bowt."

And then he died.

* * *

Rory stayed a while in Asheville to deal with the police. This time, although there was trouble, things went down much differently because Mrs. Deveaux vehemently defended us both. We spent time with Scotty's father, who apologized for calling me a liar.

"Scotty was your first love, wasn't he?" his father said.

I nodded, teary.

After a few days of rest and doctor's tests—I felt bruised everywhere, but miraculously I wasn't hurt—I drove myself to the Asheville Airport, ditched the rental car, and boarded my plane. I sat buckled in my seat by the window, the commuter plane nosing the air, and tried to figure out both what the hell Ned had said and why I had lived when others had died. Had my compassionate words saved me?

Lights flashed outside, bright and erratic. I pressed my forehead to the open window lid. I loved the strong hum and rumble of the plane, the breezy hiss of the air circulation. I watched breathlessly as my little plane slowly flew past an enormous, pyramid-shaped thunderhead that rolled out its black, undulating arms before us. Like a many-faced deity, the smaller clots of cloud were suspended in the monolithic darkness by nothing more than grey mist. And then, they shouted to one another in cataclysmic bursts of lavender light, those angry heads, needles of electricity sputtering from god mouth to god mouth.

I felt a needle stabbing the pad of my right middle finger. I stared in disbelief as a spark of electricity leapt up and down, a pulse quickening. I willed the pulse to calm. And it did.

That's when I understood what Ned had said.

You have one bolt.

I stared out the window at the thunderhead, remembering the words that floated into my head while Ned and I were bonded with the lightning bolt. As I replayed Scotty's death in my mind, for the first time I realized Ned wasn't just a conduit for the lightning. He must have been intentionally drawing down the lightning bolt *into the other person.*

I stared out the window at the thunderhead and wondered if Ned had felt my need to punish like he did, to cause pain and death to those who'd broken my heart. It was a gift—maybe because of my compassion towards him or because he wanted something of himself to survive. But instead of using the bolt to kill me as the bullet drained his life, it seemed that he'd just transferred it *to* me.

The power coursing through me, I wondered if I could trade play pain for lethal pain. I wondered if I could, after all these years of caution and care, deliver a death sentence with the sovereignty and savagery of a Greek god ...

108

The little window reflected my cruel, thin smile. Philippe dancing under the deadly stab of an excruciating, white-hot bolt, begging for mercy—true mercy, not play mercy—that would never come.

No. I wouldn't use it—unless it was self defense, of course. If I ran into Philippe, I might be tempted, but in truth the relationship was behind me now, way on the other side of the post-Ned divide. I knew I would never again suffer from those monsters of ill reason who'd seized my better judgment and filled me with self-doubt. Even if I never became a mother, I had all the qualities to be a great one. And more.

That fight had already been fought.

I'd won.

American Mutant: The Hands of Dominion
Barbie Wilde

As humans dance their merry, destructive way through time, they pretend to know the difference between Good and Evil. They think of Good and Evil as intoxicating outpourings from deities that are as crazed as they are. God or the Devil, whatever they believe in, lives on in their minds. But I am the physical manifestation of both. Good and Evil live within me and are separate from any ruling divinity.

I have now been reborn in the light from the darkness. I will carry on the work of my father and it will be good.

— The Gospel According to Mikey (aged thirteen and a half)

* * *

The Reverend Billy Bob Bannon was smooth all over: smooth talking, smooth looking; even his outfits were … well … smooth. He dressed smart casual in gleaming white: white jeans, white long-sleeved shirt, white tie (decorated with discreet little silver teardrops symbolizing the suffering of Our Lord), white linen jacket, white leather belt with a silver buckle, white patent leather loafers with little silver chains and white socks—all of which matched his pearly (and not so natural) white teeth and glowing bleached-blond hair. All this gleaming whiteness set off his tan perfectly. No orange, sun-bedded, George Hamilton skin tones for Billy Bob: His tan was real honest-to-goodness (no pun intended) exposure to the sun.

Billy Bob was a dauntingly charismatic individual. He rose from revival-tent poverty to owning his own TV company in just over five years—admittedly, not a major one, but "big oaks from little acorns grow," as Billy Bob was fond of saying in his fake southern accent. His views, religious, political or otherwise, were ridiculous and overblown, but his flock adored him as much as liberals avoided him. His weekly Sunday morning TV show, *Billy Bob on the Box!* was a modest hit in southern and midwestern states, and gullible viewers would send him their crumpled, grimy dollar bills in smudged envelopes whenever he demanded it of them, which was on a day-to-day basis.

111

(And don't forget Billy Bob's daily radio show, *On the Air with Billy Bob!*)

Billy Bob was a success, but it was lonely at the top. His wife Susanne had left him for a vacuum cleaner salesman during the lean years, and it was tough to find a woman who wasn't either: (a) a religious maniac, (b) a rabid fan, or (c) a prostitute. Not that he had an aversion to fallen women. On the contrary, he had a great appreciation for working gals, but he had to keep his distance. After all, he didn't want to go the way of the Swaggarts and the Bakkers—having it all and then blowing it all to kingdom come just because he couldn't keep his pecker in his pants.

Of course, deep down, in his shriveled, blasted, hockey puck of a soul, Billy Bob was about as religious as a mongoose. It was all showmanship to him, and if his parents had had any real money, he would have gone to Juilliard, studied to be an actor, and gone on Broadway. But thanks to Jesus & Co., he still got to act a little.

All would have continued going swimmingly if it hadn't been for that one fateful night when Billy Bob was in Biloxi doing a diabetes telethon. The telethon had gone like gangbusters, and he'd pocketed his usual fat fee. After a rewarding stint at the hotel bar with a few ice-cold vodka martinis, he nestled into the nice, cool, cotton-rich sheets of the Holiday Inn's best king-size bed.

Billy Bob closed his eyes and conjured up the last call girl he'd been with. Years ago it was, after Susanne and before the crazy success had kicked in. Her name was Tiffany, and she was a hot little redhead that some hotel concierge in Kansas City had summoned after a desperate 2:00 a.m. plea from Billy Bob. Tiffany had been a nightly guest in Billy Bob's mind ever since, and over the years, her boobs had grown bigger and her juicy smile wider. Man, she was sweet, and Billy Bob imagined her diving under those cotton-rich sheets and enthusiastically gobbling up his johnson. A little groan escaped Billy Bob's lips and he grabbed said johnson, fully intent on rubbing his chubby into acquiescence and himself into a sound sleep.

Then he heard a little noise, like a dry cough. One eye squinted open and all activity under his sheets ceased. A woman was standing at the foot of his bed.

Holy Roller levitation was not Billy Bob's speciality, but it almost looked like it as he leapt out of the bed.

"Who the hell are you and what are you doing in my room," he sputtered, before noticing the boy standing next to the woman.

"Language, Billy Bob, language. There is a child present," the woman gently scolded.

Billy Bob, his mind befuddled by the martinis, tried to take in the scene. There was something familiar about the woman. She was as redheaded as his dream girl Tiffany, but she looked plumb worn out. Attractive, but frumpy at the edges, not like the hard-bodied little number of years past. He looked at the boy, who was ginger-haired, blue-eyed, and freckled, obviously her son. The kid smiled at him and he felt a chill. He knew that smile, having seen it too many times in the mirror. Oh yes, a smile of infinite charm and absolutely zero sincerity. Billy Bob felt trouble brewing: child support payments, scandal, his wonderful, cushy life draining down the plughole. Damn it to hell.

"What do you want?" Billy Bob demanded.

"What do you think I want?" Tiffany replied. "I saw the look in your eyes. You know who I am and you know the boy is yours. Easy enough to prove nowadays with all that DNA stuff."

"Thought you were on the pill, girl. You were a professional."

"Oh yeah? And you should have worn a condom, like I asked you," she shot back.

"Why now? It must have been over twelve years ago, Tiffany."

"Thirteen, actually. Well, I stuck it out as long as I could—all this parenting shit—but I've had enough of this kid. He's yours now. I don't want anything to do with the demonic little fucker. Maybe you can exorcise him in the bargain."

"Whoa, momma," Billy Bob protested. "If we do the test, and he is mine, I might consider child support, especially if we can keep this on the sly, but I'll be goddamned if I'm going to keep and raise the boy. I don't do kids."

"That's what nannies are for, numb nuts," Tiffany spat back. "Send him to an island, bustle him off to some hoity-toity English public school. I don't give a damn. I don't want a dime. I just want him off my hands."

"That's not very maternal of you, Tiffany."

"Excuse me, may I have a say in this discussion?"

Billy Bob and Tiffany turned to look at the boy, who was regarding them with what Billy Bob could only describe as scorn.

"Mother, why would you think that I'd want to live with this insincere, Bible-bashing moron? He's an embarrassment, not only to himself, but to his religion."

Tiffany turned to speak to the boy: "Mikey, listen to Momma. This so-called moron makes at least two mill a year from the other morons who believe his trash."

"Oh, I see." Mikey turned away from his mother, walked over to Billy Bob, and said, "Hi Dad, when can we go home?"

Billy Bob was flummoxed. This woman could make big trouble for him. His whole empire could vanish if she made a fuss. Maybe there was some way to make his unexpected son work to his advantage.

* * *

On the flight home, Billy Bob and Mikey sat together without saying much, enjoying the perks and comforts of first class. The kid seemed happy enough just to stare out the window. With all the other things on his mind, Billy Bob hadn't noticed before this moment that Mikey was wearing fine leather, flesh-colored gloves, at odds with the rest of his outfit, which was pure JC Penney. *Oh, great,* he thought. *The kid's got some kind of skin complaint. What do you want to bet that it's an expensive one?* He asked Mikey what the problem was with his hands, and the boy smiled that spooky smile again.

"I have to wear them because if I don't, people might get hurt."

"Hunh?" Billy Bob was astounded. "What do you mean 'might get hurt'? What are you talking about, boy?" On top of the skin complaint, did the kid have mental problems as well? Fabulous.

"I channel things from other things. If something bad wants to come out, then a person could get hurt, is all I'm saying. It happened when we were living in Kansas City. They nearly put me away in some prison for nutty kids. If Mom and I hadn't done a midnight flit, we'd both be in the hoosegow."

"Jesus save me, you mean you're a fugitive from justice?" Billy Bob hissed.

"Nah, they eventually dropped the charges. They couldn't prove anything. The autopsy results were inconclusive, but not every nine-year-old dies from a heart attack, so you can understand their concern."

Billy Bob couldn't help but pull back a bit, which was difficult, considering he was strapped into an airplane seat. "What do you mean by 'channel,' anyway? Who's channeling what?"

Mikey sighed and spoke slowly, as if he were talking to a retarded child. "I don't know who or what is doing this through me. Could be aliens, angels, demons, the government, the French—it's a crapshoot. All I know is that from the moment that I could string two sentences together, I had the power of what I call 'The Touch.' Do you want to see?"

Billy Bob pulled back again, straining his seat belt and almost wishing he hadn't started the conversation. But his curiosity got the better of him. Just as Mikey was in the process of peeling off one of his gloves, the stewardess came over to ask them if they wanted any complimentary drinks or snacks. They both answered in the negative, and Billy Bob waited impatiently until she moved out of earshot.

Mikey asked, "Do you want to see the 'Good Hand,' or the 'Bad Hand' first?"

"Your choice, kid," Billy Bob replied.

Mikey smiled and slowly took off the glove from his left hand, his "Bad Hand," as he called it. Billy Bob had seen some messed-up people in his time on the road, when his revival-tent tour would dredge up some of God's more unfortunate-looking believers, who hobbled into his tent praying that Billy Bob might cure their hideous afflictions. Unfortunately, all he was really good at was giving them a smidgen of hope and taking their money. But the hand on this kid, it was something. It was evil. (Not that Billy Bob believed in evil, or even in the devil, but if anything could be described as evil, it was his son's hand.) It was nasty, shiny bluey black and satanically insectile. Just looking at it gave Billy Bob the creeps and turned his guts to ice water.

Billy Bob told Mikey to put his glove back on his "Bad Hand," *tout de suite*. The kid obeyed, pleased that he'd managed to freak out his dad in such a short space of time.

"Shit, boy, can't the doctors do anything about that? I mean, cutting it off would be better than walking around with that thing on the end of your arm."

"A skin specialist looked at it a couple of years ago. He disobeyed my advice not to touch it and he got a brain embolism. If it hadn't been for my 'Good Hand' and the fact we were in a hospital at the time, he'd be dead. Luckily, he's only paralyzed on his left side now."

115

"Damn." Billy Bob was worried. Now he realized what Tiffany was talking about when she mentioned exorcising the kid.

"Okay, let's see the other one."

Again, Mikey did a slow, smiling striptease with his glove, revealing his "Good Hand." In many ways, Billy Bob was more frightened of this appendage. It reminded him of one of da Vinci's drawings of the hand of God, or Jesus maybe. He had a strange sensation in his stomach, like you feel when you see a beautiful woman for the first time. The hand—and even as he was experiencing the sensations, he knew how weird it was—the hand was so perfect, so beautiful, so golden, so fine, that Billy Bob felt like he was falling in love with it. He reached out to touch it, and Mikey snatched it away.

"You got to be careful. This one's more dangerous than the other one." Mikey hurriedly put his glove back on.

"Why?" Billy Bob asked. The pain of the "Good Hand" being withdrawn was palpable. The loss was heartbreaking.

"Whatever evil the 'Bad Hand' reveals about a person's soul, the 'Good Hand' seems to have the power to put right, but sometimes it doesn't work out the way that person wants it to," Mikey said.

"Just one touch, please."

"You don't know what you're asking. I don't want to hurt you. When I figure it out, I'll let you touch it."

"Has your Momma touched it?" Billy Bob said, trying, unsuccessfully it turned out, not to sound jealous.

"Of course," Mikey replied. Billy Bob's face flushed with a quick anger and a covetousness that he could not understand. "But Mom is immune. She doesn't get hurt by the 'Bad Hand' and she can't receive any benefits from the 'Good Hand.' She's lucky."

Billy Bob gazed into his son's clear blue, guileless (or were they?) eyes. The wave of rage and jealousy had passed. This child, preternaturally intelligent, well spoken, and mature, had a gift. An idea came to Billy Bob. An idea that could make him—and his son, of course—very rich. Very, very rich, indeed.

* * *

As Billy Bob tossed and turned that night—the very same night that he and his son returned from Biloxi and settled into his mansion in the smug suburban backwater of Opportunity, Washington—he wondered how this could have happened. How could a child of his turn out this way? Maybe he should have some kind of DNA test done, but what would it show on his side: that he shouldn't have gone to work as a janitor in the nuclear power plant at Hanford all those years ago? Or that he should have bypassed that stint slaving away in that pissant little gift shop in Love Canal, New York? Of course, Billy Bob's experimentation with certain prohibited substances in his college years probably hadn't helped his overstimulated genes either. As for Tiffany's share of the blame, anything was possible there. Whatever had happened, whether it was drugs, toxic waste or an overdose of radiation, he'd fathered some kind of mutant kid.

On the other hand, who's to say that it wasn't an "Act of God"? Not that Billy Bob believed any of that horseshit, but his devoted, deluded followers didn't need to know that. Yes, little Mikey, born of the Reverend Billy Bob Bannon, out of an illicit relationship with a fallen, Mary Magdalenesque, red-haired stripper called Tiffany—well, that sounded a hell of a lot better. And little Mikey was blessed with a talent that needed to be nurtured into something BIG. The Church of Michael the Young Redeemer and Healer. That had a nice ring to it.

* * *

It took a few months to set everything up. Billy Bob's business advisors, Deke and Stevo Highdecker, were hot for the idea, although he could tell that neither of them personally warmed to Mikey. But what did they care, as long as the cash rolled in? And shark-souled as Deke and Stevo were, they could size up the kid and scent his potential like their fishy kindred could scent blood in the water.

So the Church of Michael the Young Redeemer and Healer opened up in a converted TV studio on Main Street in Spokane, Washington, just down from the Jehovah's Witnesses and across the way from the Buddhists' storefront temple. Billy Bob had a conference with his TV people, and when he revealed Mikey's "Hands of Good and Evil," they freaked out for two minutes and then immediately started to figure out how they could get enough footage for an Easter Special.

The only problem was—and Billy Bob guessed he should have known this—the young man himself. Mikey didn't want to show his

117

hands off to a bunch of "crazies in a church," as he put it, and he certainly didn't want to "perform like a monkey" in front of TV-viewing millions. As far as Mikey was concerned, the Bible was for the birds, written by amateurs—just like Wikipedia, but without the fact checkers. However, Billy Bob wore him down eventually, feeding his ego and intelligence, telling him that he, Mikey, could hoodwink hundreds of thousands of people into sending him money, and it would all be legal. Nobody could touch them, because in America, all sorts of religious stupidity was allowed.

The first *Michael the Young Redeemer and Healer Show* went out on Good Friday, and Billy Bob spent days beforehand with his advisors working on his sermon. It had to be worded carefully, as Billy Bob's claims were, as far as he knew, completely without foundation. But he worked the sermon, shaped it, contorted his words, snaked around the issues, and generally made up the biggest load of tosh-filled, Bible-referenced windage in the world. He was very proud. He showed the sermon to Mikey and was pleased to see that, after his initial hilarity, even the kid had to admit it was a masterpiece.

On his end, Mikey rehearsed with a few well-chosen subjects, mostly street people gathered from alongside the railway tracks and the riverfront park. There were a few glitches along the way, but nothing that showed up in the news, or that couldn't be cured by the generous donation of a bottle of Jack Daniels.

* * *

Lights. Camera. Action. Billy Bob walked out to welcome the folks in the studio audience, who were sitting comfortably in the gleaming Church-TV Studio oak-hewn pews. He spoke and his followers saw that it was good:

"My friends, if you are watching me today, you know the tenets of my ministry well. You know that I abhor all adulterers, all sinners, all fraudsters, all fakes, all bankers, all politicians, all abortionists, all gays and lesbians, all liberals, all journalists and especially all those God-denying atheists out there propagating like flies. All those who spit in the face of Our Lord. Unless they repent. Yes, if only they would be penitent. We would forgive them if they gave up their heathen wicked ways and atoned for their sins," Billy Bob said.

"My friends, you all know that for many years, I've been a lone man, fighting a losing battle against the transgressions and corruption that are infesting this nation. I've had my dark nights of the soul, as you all have. When my wife left me all those years ago, although she broke my heart, I knew that it had to be for a good reason. God's reason. For we were without issue; we could not have children. Not that I'd blame my poor, benighted, adulterous wife for that, but she did leave me for greener pastures." Billy Bob allowed a manly little sob to escape his lips.

"But I know now that it was God's will," he continued. "For I also found a green pasture to lie down in, to give me comfort unto the Lord. 'He maketh me to lie down in green pastures: he leadeth me beside the still waters.' Psalm 23:2. That soothing green pasture was a beautiful woman named Tiffany."

The audience buzzed with this new revelation.

"My friends, she was a fallen woman, as Mary Magdalene was, but remember, our Lord loved Mary as he loved himself and he said: 'He that is without sin amongst you, let him cast the first stone at her.' John 8:7. Jesus forgave Mary Magdalene and I forgave Tiffany her sinful life, for underneath her surface corruption I could see that her soul was pure. We lay together as a married couple, even though we were not married, but through the darkness of sin, came a light. A light of divinity, a light so bright that it blinded me when I first saw it." Billy Bob shielded his eyes dramatically as the studio audience leaned forward with anticipation.

"My son, Michael, he of the light, named after the Angel of Light, entered my life a short time ago and I now know that God saw fit to make my one night of sinfulness into something so powerful and so good, that it nearly struck me dumb. 'Fear not, for you will not be ashamed; be not confounded, for you will not be disgraced; for you will forget the shame of your youth ...' Isaiah 54:4.

"For Michael, in whose name I have christened this new church, has been blessed through our union by God and hence he has been given a great gift directly from God. A gift that passeth all understanding. A gift that only angels could comprehend.

"Michael has the power of life and death, of good and evil, in his hands, my friends. His touch will either redeem you—or it will send you straight to the bowels of hell to burn for all time. It is not his decision, for his power comes directly from God. But take comfort in the fact that Michael is your ally in the fight against eternal evil. 'And

119

there was war in heaven: Michael and his angels fought against the dragon.' Revelation 12:7.

"Michael's sole purpose in life is to be here for you. Each and every one of you. Yes, my friends, my son is prepared to sacrifice the normal, everyday life of a normal, everyday child to become your savior. Remember Daniel 12:1: 'And at that time shall Michael stand up, the great prince which standeth for the children of thy people: and there shall be a time of trouble, such as never was since there was a nation *even* to that same time: and at that time thy people shall be delivered, every one that shall be found written in the book.'" Billy Bob paused dramatically, just before the last sprint to the end.

"Now, prepare to witness the miracle, the miracle of my son, the miracle of Michael the Young Redeemer and Healer!" Billy Bob shouted. "Michael is here for all those who want to be healed. All those who want to be saved. All those who seek the truth.

"Now, we just happen to have here today some willing volunteers who will be happy to test Michael's power—his God-given power. Yes, every one of these brave and strong believers in the faith will give themselves up to Michael and allow his 'Hands of Good and Evil' to decide their fate. They will literally put themselves in Michael's— and God's—'Hands.' And remember, God moves in mysterious ways. Hallelujah!"

To thunderous applause, Mikey walked out on the stage, wearing a startling white outfit that was a carbon copy of his father's, with the addition of a pair of bejeweled gloves: one decorated with black crystals, and the other one with silver. They were so blingful that Michael Jackson himself (if he'd been alive, that is) would have coveted them. The lights picked up on the crystals and reflections danced across the studio floor, as if they were coming from two miniature mirror balls, like God's own disco.

People gasped at the sight, as both Billy Bob and Mikey had calculated his appearance very carefully for maximum effect. Mikey did look almost divine, in an over-freckly, Billy-Mummy-from-the-TV-series-*Lost-in-Space* kind of way.

Mikey mounted a specially-built podium, so he appeared to be taller than his father. He took in a long, shaky breath, unaccustomed to public speaking as he was. But deep in his heart, Mikey knew he was up to the task. Showmanship was as thoroughly ingrained in his DNA as his mutated hands were. Mikey raised his arms up and spoke.

120

The crowd and the TV audience listened with rapt attention.

"'And let the beauty of the Lord our God be upon us: and establish thou the work of our HANDS upon us; yea, the work of our HANDS establish thou it.' Psalm 90:17," Mikey intoned.

He reached over his head and ripped off the glittering silver glove from the "Good Hand," which Mikey then dramatically pointed up to the heavens. Everyone in the studio audience and all those watching on the box at home gasped as one. People cried and prostrated themselves in front of their television sets. It was truly the most beautiful hand in the world, especially as it was set off so artistically by the studio lighting.

Mikey continued: "Our Lord Jesus Christ said, 'Behold my HANDS, that it is I myself ...' Luke 24:39." People in close proximity fell to their knees. The phones started ringing off the hook. Mikey was instantly hooked on the adulation.

In another dramatic gesture, he ripped off the black crystal glove covering his "Bad Hand," and then lifted both hands up to the ceiling, while he shouted (backed up with impressive reverb effects from the sound technician), "'Now therefore, O God, strengthen my HANDS.' Nehemiah 6:9."

A woman fainted and was almost trampled by the crowd as the audience surged forward towards Mikey. Luckily, Billy Bob had anticipated this and had some hunky bodyguards move in to contain the mob.

"Please, my friends," Billy Bob pleaded. "Stay back. Return to your seats. Everyone will have a chance to see."

The bodyguards brutally pushed the crowd back to the pews. When things had quieted down, Mikey gestured for the guinea pigs to be shepherded over to him.

One man stepped forward and said, "Michael, my name is Brian, and I'm a bad man. I've spent time in prison for rape. I'm no good, but I want to change, honest. Will you help me?" Mikey looked at Brian closely. He looked like a "bad 'un," as his mother used to say: squinty-eyed, shabbily clothed, dirty, and smelly. Mikey didn't like him, so he thought that this was the ideal man upon which to test his powers for the first time in front of the TV cameras. Mikey quietly directed Brian to turn around so he faced the audience.

Mikey raised both arms heavenwards again: "O God, strengthen my hands. Search out the evil in this man!" and then he clapped his

121

"Bad Hand" on the top of Brian's head.

Brian shrieked with pain and surprise. Blood squirted out of his eyeballs. His knees buckled, but PorkChop and Duffle, two of the heftiest bodyguards, were on hand to catch him and prop him up.

Mikey hollered: "'And when ye spread forth your HANDS, I will hide mine eyes from you: yea, when ye make many prayers, I will not hear: your HANDS are full of blood.' Isaiah 1:15."

Brian juddered as if he were getting a massive electric shock. Blood spouted from his nose, dribbled from his open, silently screaming mouth and his ears. The audience was stunned into silence, some even noticing that blood was seeping through Brian's pants in his nether regions. They had thought they were going to experience a ceremony of healing, not witness a horror show.

In his previous encounters, Mikey had never felt anything untowards with his (what he truly considered) accidental victims, just a rushing, "channeling" feeling, as he called it. But this time, everything seemed to work in reverse. He was receiving a barrage of images from Brian's brain: countless women being raped and murdered, their naked, brutalized bodies being disposed of like garbage, carelessly dumped in rivers and forest thickets. Mikey realized that not only was Brian a convicted rapist; he was a murderer as well, a serial killer. Mikey felt like throwing up, but he continued on:

"May the power of God compel the malicious spirits out of this corruption that is your body!" Mikey shouted.

Slumped between PorkChop and Duffle, a stinky, drooling Brian looked a goner at this point, and the same woman who had fainted earlier stood up and vomited spectacularly over the man seated in front of her.

Mikey whipped away his left hand and placed his right hand on top of Brian's head, at the same time yelling, "Brian, go forth and sin no more!" Heavenly lighting and sound effects accompanied his movements as Brian jerked upright and his mouth opened in an enormous "O" of surprise, uncannily mimicking the expression of a blow-up sex doll. Now, with a little help from the special effects technician, myriad lights were swirling around Brian, making him look like a refugee from an ancient Jefferson Airplane video. Brian gurgled some very disturbing sounds, a combination of whale song and great ape calls: "Whoooo, whoooo, whoooop!"

Mikey removed his "Good Hand," and Brian shook himself free

from PorkChop and Duffle. He boogied a crazy, hopping–on–hot–coals kind of dance and hollered, "I'm saved!"

The audience went nuts, applauding frantically. Brian collapsed in a heap. PorkChop and Duffle swiftly dragged him off to an ambulance that was waiting in the wings. White-coated janitors leapt into action, cleaning up the slug-like trail of blood on the studio floor. Billy Bob felt the teensiest little swirl of jealousy. This was truly spectacular. Billy Bob moved forward to take over the proceedings. Everyone on the production staff had agreed that the first show should only have one "Purification Rite," or whatever they were going to call it.

Mikey slowly knelt down on the podium on one knee, his arms crossed over his chest in a Knights Templar pose, trying to compute the murderous show-reel that was playing over and over in his head. He stood up and looked straight at the camera and announced, "Brian has revealed his sins to me. Brian is not only a rapist, but he is a murderer as well. I witnessed his crimes. I saw his victims. Hidden away for years, they cry to me for justice. I will speak for them now."

Billy Bob's jaw dropped. This hadn't happened during rehearsals. The other guinea pigs looked uncomfortable. What hidden miserable secrets could Michael winnow out from their hearts? Michael raised his arms again, and this time a woman frantically ran towards him. "My name is Eileen and I've been told over and over that I am a sinner. Michael, can you seek out the truth within me?" she cried.

Mikey was tired, drained, with the thoughts of a serial killer rampaging through his brain, but, in spite of his mental exhaustion, he gestured to PorkChop and Duffle, who moved into position. Billy Bob felt like his show was being hijacked, but the crowd was baying for more, and he might cause more of a ruckus by stopping the proceedings than by letting them continue.

Mikey's left hand descended upon the woman's head, and images of Eileen's sad and pathetic life flooded into his consciousness. Mikey didn't know much, or even care, about the reasons why women have abortions. In his mother's more cruelly drunken moments, she'd told him straight out how she wished she'd gotten rid of Mikey before he'd grown into the problem child that he was. But Eileen's carelessness and ignorance had caused her to have three abortions. Yet all her regret at terminating her children hadn't stopped her from having yet another unfortunate, unprotected liaison with some no-hope, pizza-brained guy who'd left her in the lurch.

123

However, Mikey's true feelings about abortion and their moral convolutions did not concern him, because what was flowing from Eileen was not her remorse, or sadness, but the angry, howling, unbearable screams of the unborn fetuses, demanding retribution. The rage flooded Mikey's brain, and he was almost knocked backwards with the force of it.

Between the furious fetuses, the naked dead women, and the twisted faces of Brian and Eileen filling his head, Mikey was feeling pretty wretched.

He opened his eyes, and that's when he noticed the noise. He looked down from the podium at Eileen, her head lolling back, her bleeding eyes looking into his, pleading for him to make it stop. He whipped his left hand off the top of her head and then laid on his right hand, hoping to channel some good into this wretched woman. Eileen jerked and jumped straight up into the air as soon as Mikey made contact, then fell down on the ground in a steaming heap. PorkChop whisked her up in his arms and hurried for the ambulance.

The audience was again dumbstruck. What was this kid doing to these people, cooking their brains like popcorn? Was he a healer, or just a dangerous freak?

Mikey looked into the camera again: "The sad truth about Eileen is that although she is a good person, her ignorance put her at odds with the new hopeful lives that grew within her. Her lost children scream to me. I speak for them. I speak for the dead. They are crying in the wilderness."

Mikey raised his arms again, and Billy Bob noticed with a stab of horror that the insectile blackness of Mikey's "Bad Hand" was creeping up his arm almost to his elbow. The attractiveness of his "Good Hand" was diminishing: not so golden, not so compelling. The evil (and now Billy Bob believed in it, oh yes) was growing and the good retreating. And at what cost to his son?

Mikey had sunk back down into his Knights Templar pose. The woman who had fainted and vomited before now began to scream, and Billy Bob decided that the insanity must cease. He signaled the bodyguards to slowly clear the audience out of the studio.

Billy Bob walked to the front of the podium and said, "My friends, today you saw two miracles. I must admit, I didn't know what to expect today, certainly not this. But Michael is compelled to do the Lord's work and that is what he has done. He has transmogrified the evil in people's souls into something good.

"Michael needs your help, so please send five dollars or more for his ministry today without delay to the address that you can see right now on your TV screen, so he can help more sinners. Thank you and God bless."

Billy Bob didn't see Mikey rise up behind him. He had removed his white linen jacket and ripped off his shirt, showing his thin boyish freckled chest. Mikey raised his arms again. The creeping darkness was now visibly slithering up Mikey's left arm and across his upper torso. Thin tendrils curled up his neck, creating a Maori-like tattoo effect, which soon took over his face. This was no CGI, no magic from the lighting guy. This was really happening.

Mikey opened his mouth and stuck his tongue out: a pointed, lizard-like, bile-green horror. It was at this precise moment that Billy Bob turned around to take in the sight of his blackened, wasted, ruined son, whose frail body now contained the evil remnants of Brian's crimes and the wrath of Eileen's unborn children. Mikey's bloodshot eyes met Billy Bob's baby blues and Billy Bob realized too late that his fabulous idea of capitalizing on his son's "talent" was a big mistake.

But Mikey was a survivor. Deep down in the reptilian part of his brain (the eat-shit-fight-fuck part), something was stirring. He needed to live on, to continue his work. So Mikey did what most animals do when they ingest something poisonous: he vomited. But it wasn't just a polite little retch; it was a colossal projectile vomit that would have entered the Guinness World Records, if there were an entry for such a thing. And Mikey's power-puke was so vile, so noxious, so putrid, that the flow, when it hit the unfortunate Billy Bob full in the face, was a lethal cocktail that burned and blinded him in an instant.

Billy Bob dropped to the floor, writhing and howling in agony. Everyone in the studio was screaming, but Mikey didn't stop. The rancid turgid blackness continued to gush from his mouth, and other people were hit. They also fell shrieking to the ground as if burned by acid. Pandemonium and fear gripped the crowd.

If it hadn't been for the bravery of PorkChop and Duffle, the show would have been an even bigger bloodbath than it actually turned out to be. From either side of the soundstage, the bodyguards sprinted up to the podium, tackled Mikey, and brought him down to the floor. However, Mikey continued to spew out his evil vomit of death. Pork-

Chop—having served in the Special Forces—instantly assessed the danger and took action, realizing that it was a "him or us" situation. He put Mikey's noggin in a headlock and then wrenched it sharply to the right, hearing the telltale "click" of a neck being broken. The geyser of horror stopped, but PorkChop could have sworn he heard a child's voice whispering in his ear, "You can't kill me."

"Did you hear that?" a startled PorkChop said to Duffle, but Duffle was already up on his feet and moving to Billy Bob's side. Pork-Chop turned back to look into Mikey's staring, glassy eyes. He knew the kid had to be dead. The evil darkness was already fading from Mikey's face.

Duffle turned Billy Bob over. His face was burned beyond recognition, and the insufferable pain had caused a massive coronary. Billy Bob was well on his way to meet his Maker.

Duffle was a man of few words, but he knew his Bible. He turned to the jostling crowd and the TV cameras, and announced: "'But of the tree of the knowledge of good and evil, thou shalt not eat of it: for in the day that thou eatest thereof thou shalt surely die.' Genesis 2:17."

The remaining people in the audience dropped to their knees as one and cried, "Amen!" Duffle was a bit surprised and gratified. What power do words possess!

* * *

After he recovered, Brian the serial killer happily confessed to all his crimes. He was extradited to a red state and summarily executed. He had a smile on his face when the lethal injection finally hit his bloodstream. Eileen joined a convent and became renowned as a talented singer-songwriter in the "Singing Nun" mode.

PorkChop and Duffle managed to avoid any charges in the Mikey affair, starting up a ministry of their own.

* * *

Billy Bob and Mikey were buried in Spokane's Riverside Memorial Cemetery side by side. Tiffany came to pay her respects and wept, wondering, if she'd only kept her mouth shut, whether both her boys would still be alive. But being a hard-bitten broad, she was soon over it and bellying up to the bar at the nearby Riverside Tavern for a few comforting margaritas.

Late that night, after all the grave diggers had gone home, the dirt shifted above Mikey's grave, as if some powerful creature were trying to free himself from his boxy prison. The next day, Harvey Mention, the cemetery gardener, was astounded to see that Mikey's grave had been opened and desecrated: the coffin empty, the body gone.

Harvey thought he could hear a boyish voice murmuring from the shadows: "'And the Lord God said, "Behold, the man is become as one of us, to know good and evil; and ... he put forth his HAND, and taketh also of the tree of life, and eat, and liveth for ever ..."' Genesis 3:22."

Menagerie of the Maladapted

Stephen Woodworth

The glare off the bone-gray asphalt of the I-5 was so bright that, even with my dark glasses, I had to squint to make out the broken black lines that marked the lane I was in. I concentrated so hard just on seeing the road that I almost missed the exit to the I-10.

I grunted and shook my head. And to think some idiots in Sacramento had actually proposed paving the highways in bright white to reflect a few more degrees of heat back into space. Who were they kidding? Did they want to blind us all?

I was just barely old enough to remember when the roads were black and the stripes down the middle were white, back before the asphalt in L.A. got hot enough on an August afternoon to melt the soles of your sneakers. Back before the cops had to scrape up the sunstroked remains of the homeless as if they were fried eggs in a pan. Back when L.A. didn't look like Phoenix. Back when human beings could still live in Phoenix.

With relief, I veered my truck onto the 405 freeway. The sooner I made the delivery, the sooner I could get out of this hellhole. The route took me past the new desalination plant they'd built where Santa Monica was now submerged. *Water, water everywhere . . .*

Southern California was such a mess now, I sometimes wondered why I ever bothered to come back. Most of my customers were rich enough to live up north—Minnesota, Canada, places like that—where they could let the "pets" I brought them roam among real trees and green grass. Nowadays, you'd be lucky to find a living cactus growing wild in Los Angeles.

I knew perfectly well why I kept coming back, though: Jules. She paid me less than any of my other clients, yet she was worth more than the rest of the lot put together. And she was the only one who didn't make me feel like a common criminal.

Like the rest of the buildings on campus, the exterior of UCLA's Terasaki Life Sciences Building was tiled in solar panels, most of them devoted to powering the central air conditioning that ran almost continuously year-round. Out front, the facility featured a Japanese-style rock garden of raked gravel and serene stones of the sort

129

that had become fashionable since California freshwater conservation regulations had outlawed grass lawns. But I drove the truck around back, where large loading bays made the rear wall resemble an industrial warehouse more than an academic institution.

I needed to make this delivery indoors, and not just because my cargo couldn't take the 114-degree heat outside. If the Feds found out what my shipment was, Customs would have me in jail faster than you could melt a popsicle on the hood of your car.

I stopped in front of one of the roll-up bay doors and videoed Jules with my camera phone. "Here I am!" I flashed a big grin as I held the phone in front of my face. "You miss me?"

As usual, she chose not to let me see her. "Only 'cause my aim is bad," her voice replied. "Gimme a sec to let you in."

A moment later, the door rose, and I parked the truck in the bay's cool interior. The door rolled back down almost immediately. Yet, as I got out of the truck's cab, I still felt a furnace blast of parched air gust inside before the door closed completely, as if the heat were on a mission to infiltrate the air-conditioned haven.

Perforated with air holes, the polymer cage in the back of the truck was big and heavy enough that I had to use a pallet jack to move it. Even as I rolled it down the ramp, I could see the cage quiver as its contents stirred and slithered within.

I guided the jack down a long corridor of laboratories and classrooms until I came to the pair of double doors at the end with a sign that said "STAFF ONLY—No Admittance." I pushed on through into a barn-sized room that smelled like a pet store but looked like a pharmaceutical testing lab. Metal cages on every wall rattled as the animals within them pressed up against the grating to see and sniff me.

But these weren't the usual rhesus monkeys or white rats. A three-tailed cat hissed from my left, while an albino fox peered down at me with its unearthly pink eyes from high on my right. Other creatures—ones whose deformities were too severe to allow them to survive—floated, almost unrecognizable, in jars of formaldehyde. Jules fondly referred to the collection as her "Menagerie of the Maladapted."

Her long brown hair knotted in lazy bun, Jules wore her usual blue jeans and black tank top. When no one was around, she walked around the lab barefoot, and her skin had the moonlight pallor of

130

someone who seldom went outside. She didn't look up as I entered, but continued to stroke the shell of a two-headed tortoise that scrabbled across her desk.

"Is he a new addition?" I asked.

"You mean 'they.' Conjoined *females*, in case you're interested." She let the left head drag the body a few inches to one side, then pulled the shell back so the right head could take the waddle in the opposite direction. "And they're so *pretty*, aren't you?"

I leaned on the cage in front of me and grinned. "That's one of the things I love about you, Jules. Always the champion of the evolutionary underdog."

She didn't crack a smile, nor did she call me "Ray," as I'd been trying to get her to do for the last ten years.

"In natural selection, you learn about the winners by studying the losers," she remarked softly, and her expression became even more glum than usual. That was one of things that got me about her, I think: pretty as hell, but she always had this sad, worried look that made me want to tickle her until she forgot about the fate of the earth for a few seconds.

"So, Mr. Gaynor, you finally bring me my dodo bird?" A dodo would have been the *pièce de résistance* in her exhibit of extinction, so she always asked, even though she knew perfectly well there were only a handful of dodo skeletons in the entire world, each of which would fetch exorbitant sums at auction.

"If only," I sighed. "Maybe then I could retire."

"What about a quagga?" she asked. The rather goofy-looking African herd animal, striped like a zebra in front, brown like a horse in back, had died out in the late 1800s.

"Nope."

"Tasmanian tiger?" Jules always had to run down the entire list of the failed species she coveted. It was her way of building rapport.

"Sorry," I said. "But my supplier assures me he's got something very special for you in here." I rapped on the lid of the cage and felt an answering thump from within.

Jules eyed me skeptically, then set aside her conjoined tortoises and came over to inspect the merchandise. A flap on the side of the cage opened to reveal a clear plastic window, and Jules peeped through it. She rolled her eyes. "You brought me an *anaconda*? It's not even albino."

"That's just the wrapping." I pointed to a large lump in the snake's body. "The real prize is inside."

She frowned. "You mean I have to—?"

"Afraid so, Dr. Pierce."

"This better be worth it, or you don't get paid." Although Jules had dissected hundreds of animals during her career, she clearly didn't relish having to kill one. Nevertheless, she plugged all but one of the air-holes in the cage, then gassed the reptile with chloroform.

Even I had to admit that Cazador's security measures were extreme this time. Emulating drug couriers who seal their heroin in plastic bags and swallow them, the poacher had sealed a dead specimen in plastic and placed it within the body of a dead dog, then fed the dog to the anaconda. The snake had gulped the shipment whole, but the double protection of the plastic and the dog's body kept the snake from digesting the merchandise. Cazador nurtured many well-paid connections within the ranks of Customs agents, and the chance of anyone examining the snake's stomach contents via X-ray had been remote, I was sure. Still, whatever Cazador had wrapped in that package must be special, indeed, for he'd gone to great lengths to keep anyone from discovering it.

Jules not only put on shoes; she donned an entire set of scrubs, latex gloves, and a surgical mask before arranging the dead anaconda on a dissection table. As she slit the snake's abdomen with a scalpel, the lump split open like an egg sac, disgorging what had once been a dog. Hidden in the dog's remains, she found a blue bundle. Jules removed the anaconda and the dog and cleaned the steel table before slicing open the azure plastic package as delicately as if incising skin. Inside, chemical ice clustered around the dead specimen to keep it from decomposing.

When Jules plucked the blue bricks from around the specimen, I took it for another reptile. It curled in a shriveled ball, its leathery hide a mosaic of large, scaly diamonds and trapezoids. Its stubby, withered-looking appendages were folded close at its sides as if used to scrabbling, lizard-like, over the ground. Even when Jules rolled the thing on its back, the mere stub of a nose and nonexistent ears gave it the flattened, featureless visage of a salamander.

Then I saw the navel on its belly, which still dangled an inch of a carelessly-cut umbilical cord. Below that, hairless pubes peeked from the crux of its stubby legs. The thing was a girl—a *human* baby girl.

132

My face went cold, my stomach sour. I'd trafficked in hundreds of species, both dead and alive, but never a human being. It was a new level of crime that made me dizzy with dread.

"I swear, Jules," I babbled, "I didn't know—"

"Hush." She bent over the dead infant, exploring it with her latex-sheathed fingers, her eyes aglow with fascination.

Her enthusiasm made me squirm. "What happened to her?" I asked.

"I'm not sure. It *looks* like ichthyosis."

"Which is?"

"Alligator skin. It's a congenital condition. But this doesn't seem to be a buildup of dead skin cells as in ichthyosis. The thick skin tissue seems to have been alive and had a normal, healthy lipid layer underneath. I've never seen anything like it—in humans, at least. Nor this."

She lifted one of the infant's arms. A gelatinous film of what I took to be pus appeared to cling to the baby's side. As it fanned out, however, I saw that it was actually a translucent membrane finely threaded with veins and capillaries. The network of vessels had blackened with congealed blood.

"Wings?" I lamely suggested.

Jules shook her head. "Too thin, too fragile."

Peeling off the gloves, she hastened to her desk and pawed among the hanging file folders in a lower drawer. She yanked out a dog-eared college composition book and leafed through it. I read over her shoulder as she selected a page and ran a pen down a scribbled two-column list:

Environ. Change	*Possible Adapt.*
rising sea levels	amphib.?
lack of fresh water	higher saline content in blood?
excessive heat	nocturnal?

There were many other entries, but the pen stopped at "excessive heat." Below "nocturnal," she scrawled the word "thermoregulation," circled and starred it.

"Not a very successful adaptation if it killed her," I remarked.

"The mutations didn't kill her." Jules gently lifted the baby's chin with the tip of the pen. The wrinkled red line that ran between the

133

scales on her neck suddenly gapped open to reveal the rictus of a knife slit. "Your supplier do that?"

Jules awaited my response with the patience of a prosecutor during cross-examination. I thought of Cazador and found I couldn't answer right away.

"No," I said without conviction.

"In that case," she replied, "I need you to take me where he got this. Now."

* * *

Manaus, Brazil, had become a ghost metropolis. Overlooking the dry bed of the Rio Negro, the city's high-rises jutted from the earth like fossilized saurian bones. Their corporate tenants had all fled, vacating offices as commerce collapsed. Supermarkets had given way to a handful of ramshackle street vendors. With no running water, sanitation consisted of any patch of unused pavement in the fetid back alleys. Only those residents too poor to relocate had remained, and from our seats in the helicopter we could see them speckling the empty streets like dust motes. A few trudged on listless errands, but most clung to the shadows, unwilling to move in the daytime heat. It was late August—midwinter in the Southern Hemisphere—and a quarter-to-nine in the morning, yet the temperature was already 112 degrees Fahrenheit.

"This is exactly the kind of environment that sparks adaptation," Jules commented, shouting to be heard over the swooping of the rotor blades.

We'd hired the chopper because the local airport had shut down more than five years ago. Besides, flying in the small craft made it easier to land at our appointed rendezvous location, right in the middle of what had once been one of the largest tributaries of the Amazon.

The skids barely sank into the hard, cracked soil as the copter touched down beside four custom-made off-road vehicles parked in the dry riverbed. Five men awaited us beneath a makeshift canopy stretched between two of the vehicles. As we alighted, four of the men came forward to help us with our gear. I immediately knew who the fifth man was, dressed in loose-fitting linen clothes and calmly waiting for us in the awning's shade.

134

"So you finally come to visit me, eh, my friend?" Cazador grinned as we approached, his teeth wide and white beneath his thick black mustache.

A compact man, he made up in bravado what he lacked in height. His nationality and ethnicity were almost impossible to place; his olive skin and glossy, jet-black hair might have been *mestizo,* or Italian, or Arabic, or Sikh. He'd trapped rare animals on every continent on the planet and spoke so many languages with smug fluency that his accent had smoothed into a polyglot gentility. He freely admitted that Cazador was no more his real name than any of the others on his many passports. But he was the best poacher in the business. We'd made a lot of money together, he and I, but I did not like him, and he was *not* my friend.

"This is business, not a social call," I reminded him.

"But, of course, my friend! That last one, it was special, just as I told you, no? And you have brought me this lovely creature in trade."

He extended his hand to Jules. She didn't take it. "Did you kill it?" she asked.

Cazador laughed. "Dr. Pierce, isn't it? Tell me, doctor . . . why would I slaughter my own profit? The living beast would have been worth a thousand times what you paid for it."

She crossed her arms. "Then I can assume that, if we ever find another one, you won't slit its throat?"

"I promise you, doctor—I will kill only the person who tries to keep me from taking the creature alive." He smiled to let Jules know that his statement included her.

She nodded coolly. "Then let's do it."

Cazador's men barely had time to take down the canopy before we climbed into the off-road vehicles and tore off up the dry riverbed, the oversized tires pluming dust in our wake. The size of armored personnel carriers, the vehicles were equipped with air-cooled engines to avoid overheating. One of the four vehicles contained our gear and food. One contained Cazador's tranquilizer guns, traps, nets, and collapsed cages. The other two were filled with nothing but plastic jugs, tanks, and bottles of water.

The journey up the Rio Negro was surreal, for the cracked soil on which we drove was at least twenty feet below the river's former water line. Fourteen years of unrelenting drought had reduced once mighty tributary to a trickle of mud. Nevertheless, slack-limbed men and women crowded the bottom of the enormous gully, attempting to scoop what sludge they could into buckets and pails in hopes of filtering a few gallons of drinkable water from the contents. At either side of us, the abandoned derelicts of boats from the once-thriving fishing industry lined the inlet, their spars jutting over the dry shores like the tusks of beached narwhals.

As we made our way upriver from Manaus, the banks became littered with the detritus of the dying Amazon rainforest. The thin layer of fertile topsoil had mostly dried up and blown away, denuding the jungle vegetation's shallow roots. Fallen samauma trees that once wove the forest's canopy lay in jackstraw heaps, their trunks either bleached gray by sun or blackened by wildfires.

After passing through this wasted landscape for miles and hours, Cazador abruptly ordered the vehicles to stop. Jules and I scanned the wreckage of deadwood along the river's edge, but could find little life of any kind, much less human habitation.

Jules frowned at Cazador. "You said there'd be a village."

He checked his satellite GPS. "There is."

Stepping out of the climate-controlled vehicle felt like walking into a convection oven. "At least it's a dry heat," I quipped, but even I didn't laugh. The brutal air thickened around us like hot pitch, clinging to us, resisting every movement of our muscles, so that even shouldering our backpacks seemed an exhausting burden. Even before we had crested the modest slope of the nearest riverbank, we oozed perspiration, but it brought no relief. The ambient temperature cooked our bodies faster than evaporation could carry the heat away, and the sweat only made our skins itchy and miserable while leeching the moisture from our mouths. Already, I craved a swig of the coffee-warm liquid in my canteen, but Cazador had set a strict rationing regimen for our water supply.

As we ascended over the Rio Negro's parched lip, Cazador and his men in the lead, I saw the corrugated tin roofs of what might once have been shanties strewn about like scattered playing cards, but still no inhabitants. Yet the air reeked of humanity, the stench of people who could no longer afford to squander water to wash away their own filth. And there was a worse smell underlying the sewage and sweat, a curdling odor of putrefaction and decay.

I gagged and tried to hold every breath as long as I could. Jules took out a jar of Vicks VapoRub and dabbed a bit of the mentholated ointment under each of her nostrils, a trick she'd learned to deal with the decomposing animal cadavers that she had to dissect.

Cazador stalked ahead of us and shouted down into a pit that resembled a giant mole's burrow. A gaunt man in a broad-brimmed hat, his brown skin and ragged beard greasy with grime, thrust his head and shoulders out of the hole, which made him look as if he stood inside an open grave. Most likely, he was a *caboclo*, a rubber harvester from back when there were living rubber trees to tap. I realized then that this hole and the others I saw around it were in fact hovels that the villagers had dug in the ground, seeking the coolness of the earth's natural insulation. The whole town had been buried alive.

Cazador and the man exchanged rapid conversation in Portuguese, a language I don't speak. I knew enough Spanish, however, to understand why the local man's eyes widened when Cazador inquired about the *cidade de crianças mortas*. The City of Dead Children.

The man waved his arms and yelled, attempting to shoo Cazador away. He fell silent, though, the instant the poacher took a gallon jug of fresh water from his backpack. Cazador dangled the jug from one crooked finger, and the man rubbed his mouth with the back of his hand and nodded.

He climbed from the pit and motioned for us to follow him on a path among the logs of the ruined forest. Along the way, we passed one of the wells that either the Peace Corps or the Brazilian government had drilled in the wilderness in order to tap ground water for the natives. Their clothes stained yellow like our guide's, a long queue of people with pails awaited their turn at the single faucet with the joyless determination of panhandlers in a Depression-era breadline.

As it turned out, we didn't need the local man to show us how to find the City of Dead Children. We could simply have traced that terrible stink of ripening meat to its source, for it grew more rank with each stride we took. Finally, our guide halted, as if he refused to get any closer. He simply made a slicing motion across his throat and pointed ahead of us. Cazador held out the jug of water as payment, and the guide snatched it from his hand, greedily hugging it to his chest.

The spot he'd indicated was another earthen pit, as wide and deep as a swimming pool. The putrid hole had attracted the most wildlife we'd yet seen in the Amazon. A haze of flies as thick as coal smoke

137

churned above the cavity, so many that I was afraid to open my mouth for fear of swallowing some. Perversely beautiful dung beetles jeweled the forest floor with an undulating carpet of iridescent blue and purple carapaces, all trundling towards the pit. King vultures swirled and dove and swooped up again with unidentifiable scraps caught in their orange beaks. Enterprising villagers threw rocks at the birds, hoping to land an easy meal.

As we got close enough to peer over the rim, I saw that the villagers would soon need to dig another hole, for this one was nearly full. Tiny corpses flopped on top of one another in a heap, like fish spilled from a net. Some had already been reduced to skeletons with little toothless skulls, indistinguishable from those of normal human infants. But others still retained enough ripped and ragged skin to show the distinctive diamond-shaped scales we'd seen on the specimen I'd brought to Jules—and the grinning slashes at every child's throat. Gas bloated their little bellies, and their complexions ranged from gray to blue to black depending on how long they'd been left to rot.

Cazador's mercenary game hunters made the sign of the cross at first sight of the mass grave. It was Auschwitz in miniature.

"No," Jules said aloud. Then again, her voice rising to a shout. *"No!"*

I assumed she was aghast at the carnage. But, no—she gaped straight across the pit at something on the other side. A local woman approached the opposite rim, clutching a caterwauling infant. From the way the baby clung at her breast, it was obvious the woman must have been its mother, yet she pried it loose with revulsion as if it were a giant leech. I could now see the bald head, earless and nose-less, etched with interlocking scales like jigsaw puzzle pieces. The child bawled louder, its wail rising to a scream. It kicked and flailed in its mother's grasp as she drew a machete from a belt around her waist. With the stoic ruthlessness of the women in ancient Sparta who hurled malformed newborns off cliffs onto the rocks below, she slashed the baby's throat, nearly severing the head, and cast it into the *cidade de crianças mortas* as if tossing garbage into a landfill. The child flopped onto the other infant cadavers, gouting blood, and before it had ceased twitching, the vultures flocked to pick at its puny carcass.

Cazador had whipped out the Desert Eagle .45 that he wore as a

138

sidearm and leveled it at the woman, seemingly intent on carrying out his threat to kill anyone who prevented him from obtaining a live specimen. But in the end he simply cursed in Hindi and holstered the weapon again. He'd always prided himself on mastering the profanity of every country he'd ever been to.

"*Why?*" Jules yelled at the mother who'd just butchered her own offspring, as if the woman could understand her. When the woman simply walked away, Jules stalked back to our guide, who took miniscule sips from his water jug as if savoring a fine Bordeaux. "You!" she commanded Cazador. "Ask him why they do this."

The poacher snorted with annoyance, but repeated her inquiry in Portuguese. The guide responded with an angry outburst, spitting words and gesticulating fanatically as Cazador translated.

"What do you expect us to do? This land . . . she is cursed. We have nothing . . . no work, no food or drink . . . and our women only give birth to devils. Are we . . . supposed to feed these monsters . . . when we can't even feed ourselves?"

I didn't realize until then that I hadn't seen a single child since we arrived. Not in the village, nor in line at the well. There didn't seem to be anyone under the age of twenty in the vicinity, and I began to wonder just how deep the *cidade de crianças mortas* went, how long the villagers had given birth to nothing but monsters.

"Why don't you leave?" Jules demanded of the guide, gesturing for Cazador to pass on the question.

The *caboclo* gave her an incredulous look. "And go where?" he retorted through Cazador. He spread his arms to indicate the wasteland of the Amazon, but he might just as well have meant the entire planet.

* * *

Cazador exchanged words of his own with the guide, negotiations I couldn't understand, but which involved the exchange of several more gallons of water. As a result, we secured lodging for the night in the dugout hovels of our guide and his extended family. Cazador put Jules and me together in one of the underground shelters, more because we were the only gringos in the group than because we were longtime acquaintances.

I could hardly call the place a room, for it was little more than a crawlspace, ten-by-ten, with a ceiling so low I had to squat to keep from hitting my head. Rough branches from fallen trees were bound together and used to reinforce the hard-packed dirt walls. The place stank, but by then so did we, so the smell didn't bother us as much.

The setting of the sun and the insulation provided by the soil around us had cooled the interior temperature from intolerable to merely uncomfortable, so we sat cross-legged on the dirt floor to wolf down our dinner of dry sausage and trail mix, which we washed down with extravagant gulps from our canteens. Jules stripped down to a tank top and boy shorts, and the light of our fluorescent lantern glossed the sweat-dewed skin of her lean legs and pale shoulders with silver. It was like a wet dream come true, except that I was too exhausted and malodorous to do anything about it.

"Ordinarily, I don't pry into my customers' business," I said, for the sake of making conversation, "but what exactly is going on here? Some weird disease? Pollution?"

"No. Evolution." Jules looked straight at me for the first time since leaving the mass grave that afternoon. She seemed as grim as if that pit brimmed with her own fetuses. "We're seeing what may well be our species' only hope of survival."

I jerked a thumb over my shoulder. "You mean those things? You've gotta be kidding me. And, anyway, isn't evolution supposed to take, like, a zillion years?"

"That's the prevailing wisdom, yes. But back in the eighteenth century, a French naturalist named Jean-Baptiste Lamarck suggested that species mutate in order to better adapt to their environment. Giraffes need to reach the leaves on tall trees, so giraffes develop long necks.

"Then Darwin came along and said, no, mutation is random. It was just a happy accident that some giraffes happened to be born with long necks, allowing them to thrive while all the short-necked giraffes died off."

"You don't believe in natural selection?" I eyed her with mild surprise; she'd always seemed like one of those hard-nosed, no-nonsense science types. "Do think it was—gasp!—*intelligent design*?" I whistled the *Twilight Zone* theme.

She frowned and fidgeted. "Look, all I'm saying is that, in some sense, Lamarck must have been right. When a comet hits your planet and causes an Ice Age in less than ten thousand years—or when greenhouse gases raise the average temperature by a dozen degrees in only a century—you don't have time to roll the dice. You need an adaptive mutation, and you need it *now*. I think there's some unknown biological mechanism in our DNA that senses changes in the environment and alters us to survive in that environment."

I leaned back against the wall and crossed my ankles. "You think those dead kids are *homo superior*? Please!"

Jules started to get mad. "*If they were allowed to live*, they'd be way more suited to this climate than you and I. I mean, look at us!" She tugged on the straps of her perspiration-soaked tank top. "Sweat is a great way to cool off, but look at how much water it uses up. Not good if you're going to be living on a desert planet in the near future.

"Rather than waste precious moisture on evaporative cooling, those children circulate their blood through that thin, wing-like membrane beneath their arms. The tiny capillaries release heat into the surrounding air before returning the blood to lower the body's internal temperature. All without losing a drop of water."

I chuckled. "Like Cazador's air-cooled car engines." Her ideas were incredible, but they made a crazy kind of sense. "But if these kids are the future of the human race, why worry about them? Why not just kick back and wait for them to take over?"

"Because, as we saw today, humans are the only species that can choose *not* to adapt. They're afraid of change, even if that change is necessary for their existence. That's why we have to protect these new mutants before they're all exterminated by their own parents or penned up in zoos by humanitarians like your friend Cazador."

"Okay, for the last time, Cazador is *not* my friend—"

Speak of the devil. Cazador chose that very moment to jump down into the hollow of our underground shanty and stick his head inside. I don't know if he heard me disavow him, but he made a harsh gesture for silence as he entered, then motioned for us to follow him. He carried his dart rifle in the crook of one arm.

We scrabbled out of the dirt hovel and onto the level ground of the village. The night was clear but still hot, the air as thick as sorghum around us. The rays from a low, full moon made the crisscrossing lattice of dead and dying trees into a black-and-silver bas-relief of shadow and light. We trailed Cazador as he soundlessly zigzagged from one pool of darkness to the next. From behind another tree about ten yards ahead, I saw the *caboclo* who'd served as our guide

141

that afternoon. He beckoned and pointed excitedly at the incline of a tilted samauma.

A small silhouette, about the size of a Doberman pinscher, scaled the trunk's diagonal on all fours. When it reached a height almost level with our view of the moon, it stood on two feet. Now it appeared to have the proportions of a five-year-old boy. Then the figure raised its arms to pull taut the translucent membranes on its sides. Illuminated by the moonlight shining through the rubbery skin of the wings, the delicate tracery of veins pulsed with liquid life.

At least one of us gasped. It might even have been me. I remembered one of the other notations in Jules's list of possible adaptations: *Nocturnal.*

Cazador raised the barrel of his rifle to eye level, angled up at the strange prodigy perched on the tree trunk. Just as he squeezed off his shot, however, Jules let out a shout. The creature leapt off into darkness as the dart whistled into oblivion.

Cazador expended only a split second to glare at Jules with murderous fury before charging up to the spot where the thing had disappeared. With a small LED flashlight, he scanned the ground until he located a set of small, human-like footprints. We didn't have to track the prints far to see that they looped back towards the village.

For a minute, Cazador appeared to be muttering to himself in Portuguese. Then I saw him adjust the earpiece of his headset and realized he must be communicating with his men via shortwave. Next, he questioned the *caboclo*, whom he'd evidently recruited as his personal ferret. I caught enough to glean the gist of their exchange.

Was there anyone in the village without a family? Cazador wanted to know. Someone who could hide such a monster from the neighbors?

Yes, the *caboclo* replied, there was a widow who lived alone, whose husband had died about four years earlier.

Take me to her, Cazador commanded.

A few minutes later, we were all arrayed outside one of the village's dugout shanties. Cazador's four hired thugs had already stationed themselves around the hole. Each of them held a tranquilizer gun. Despite their stolid stance, they betrayed a restless anxiety I'd noted ever since they'd seen the mutant creatures in the pit that afternoon.

"*You* stay here," Cazador said to Jules when she tried to accompany him into the widow's home.

He nodded for me to join him, however, so together we descended into the hovel without bothering to announce ourselves. Almost immediately, a panicked woman appeared in the beam of Cazador's flashlight as he ducked through the threshold. She shook her head frantically, pleading in a barrage of syllables and flailing her hands this way and that to indicate the empty floor and vacant corners.

Cazador ignored her. Advancing in a crouch, he swept his flashlight beam around the perimeter of the room. A few filthy rags of clothing, some meager piles of food in wooden bowls—nothing more. Struck by a sudden impulse, he shone the light straight up at the low roof above him.

In a recessed cubbyhole, a small face patched with large scales flinched at the sudden glare.

Cazador fumbled to aim his rifle into the cramped space, but the creature pounced right on top of his head. He floundered and fell to the floor as the thing scurried out the door.

"Foge tu, Nando, foge tu!" the woman shrieked.

Nando, she called it. Short for Fernando. Unlike the mothers who had cast their offspring into the waste heap of the *cidade de crianças mortas*, she had named her extraordinary child and nurtured it as her son.

Cazador clambered out of the widow's hovel and tried to make angry eye contact with each of his men. When they finally looked back at him with dumb, abashed expressions, he exploded, berating them for allowing their quarry to escape. Then, with frightening ease, he reassumed his affable swagger.

"Well, my *friend*," he said to me, stressing the word, "it seems we may bring back our live specimen after all, eh? We begin the hunt at first light." He gave an ingratiating bow to Jules. "Dr. Pierce, I can have one of my assistants drive you back to Manaus—"

"I'm coming with you." She crossed her arms to cut off debate.

A hint of menace sharpened Cazador's tone. "I do not think that would be a good idea. Out in the woods, with no one around for miles—almost anything could happen. I would hate for any harm to come to you."

"I paid for this expedition," she retorted. "And I'll top any fee you're getting from someone else."

I doubted she had that kind of money, but she didn't blink as she

Tales of Genetic Mishaps, Monsters, and Madness

said it.

Cazador silently sized her up. "Very well, then," he concluded, as if accepting a challenge to a duel. "Tomorrow, at dawn."

While the rest of us went to grab a few hours of fitful sleep, Cazador's four thugs lingered behind, whispering to each other with worried faces and nodding. I should have known something was up. They were ne'er-do-wells that Cazador had most likely pulled from the streets of Sao Paulo. Deeply superstitious, they had taken the job thinking they would be hunting an animal, not a chimera that resembled a demon from a Hieronymus Bosch painting.

In the blood-orange light of morning, when Cazador returned to the dry gulch of the Rio Negro to ready his gear, he found that all four off-road vehicles were gone. No doubt, they would fetch a good price for the mutinous henchmen—as would the water they contained.

Cazador gaped at the empty gully in a state of strangled outrage, then called the thieves bastards in Swahili, Farsi, Afrikaans, and Quechua—and those were just the languages I recognized. Although he was a master at anticipating the wiles of animals, the actions of human beings often confounded him.

"We can probably make it back to Manaus on foot," I suggested when he calmed down.

"*You* go to Manaus." Cazador shouldered his backpack. "I will capture the creature."

"But you have no traps. And no water."

He patted the canteen strapped to his pack. "I have more water than *it* has."

I turned to Jules, hoping she would listen to reason.

"If he's going, I have to go," she said. She waggled her half-empty water bottle. "Maybe we can top off at the well."

I groaned. If she went, then I had to go.

We set out sleep-deprived and dehydrated, muscles screaming with every step, and I knew it would only get worse. As it turned out, Jules and I didn't get a chance to top off at the well, because Cazador hiked at such a relentless pace we had to keep up or lose him entirely.

For a while, I nursed the vain hope that Nando had so much of a head start that Cazador would lose the trail and give up. But the poacher was as keen and tenacious as a bloodhound, and every time the dotted line of small footsteps petered out, Cazador would scour

144

the vicinity until he found some telltale droppings or a papery peeling of sloughed-off skin. We traveled during the heat of the day because Cazador needed the light to check for signs of his quarry. Since he believed Nando to be nocturnal, the poacher planned to catch the mutant asleep during sunlit hours.

Nando's path led inland from the dried-up river, and the farther we followed it, the more arid the environment became. There were no wells here, for there were no longer any people to need them.

"It will work to our advantage," Cazador assured us with unshakable hubris. "We are herding it to where it must come to us for water or die."

In retrospect, I think the truth was just the opposite: Nando was instinctively luring us onto *his* turf, where his natural adaptation would give him the edge against us.

Our rations of water diminished from a capful an hour to one every four hours, to one every six hours. Even when we got a drink, it seemed as if we didn't swallow the mouthful of liquid so much as absorb it directly through our cotton-numb tongues. Our need for more water than we had slowed us down considerably. Nando eluded us that day. And the next.

By the end of the second day, Jules had drained her water bottle, and I shared what little I had left with her. We licked sweat off our unwashed forearms to reclaim what moisture we could and hobbled along, leaning on each other like contestants in a demented three-legged race.

Cazador marched on in front of us with the implacability of a machine. But by the third day, I could see him falter. His gaze lost its focus at times, and he would stagger a step out of line. On those rare occasions when he permitted himself a sip from his canteen, he took a drunken swig as if from a flagon of whisky. Hours passed without any of us saying a word, our mouths too raw for speech.

With our water exhausted, I thought Cazador would have no choice but to turn back. Even if he didn't, I urged Jules to leave him to his fate. The mutant child was most likely already dead, I told her as we talked every night before dropping into unconsciousness. Even if the creature were still alive, Cazador would die looking for it, and there was no reason we should perish with him. I think she was about to relent when Cazador gave a rusty but triumphant shout.

Before us, the tiny footprints we'd been tracking veered into a niche formed by the canted trunk of another collapsed samauma tree. For a hunt, it was an anticlimactic ending, for no cornered monster with gnashing fangs lay in wait there. Only the forlorn figure of a small, naked boy, his legs and arms drawn up to his chest, his eyes shut in the sweet blankness of innocent sleep. He may have had strangely-veined membranes under his arms and a thick, reptilian hide, but he was simply a little boy for all that.

Nando.

Cazador laid down his dart rifle, for he could tell that he would have no need of it. The child remained a petrified lump as the poacher dragged the immobile form out of its crevice and onto the bare, parched ground. The body looked desiccated, gray and stiff with dehydration, as if mummified.

Cazador muttered something in Mandarin Chinese that I knew must be an obscenity. Then he rasped a laugh and turned to me, wearing a wan semblance of his usual cocksure grin.

"I guess we do not bring the creature back alive this time, my friend," he croaked. "But we do not leave empty-handed, eh? A nice specimen here, and not too heavy to carry. I think it might even fit in my pack, no?"

Jules hung her head, her face in her hands. If she'd had enough water in her for tears, I think she would have wept. Cazador calmly started emptying his pack to make room for his consolation prize. I just stood there, knees quivering as I struggled to remain upright, too wrung out to feel much of anything except thirst. Maybe that was why I was the first to see the forest move, as if it were stirring back to life.

At first, it seemed like a heat mirage—a slight wavering of the moribund landscape around us. Then pieces of the dried wood and parched ground detached themselves and unfolded to full height, the earth tones of their skin shifting tint, chameleon-like, to visibility. Yet another advantageous adaptation: camouflage.

Cazador had made a crucial miscalculation. He was not hunting a lone animal, as he thought, but rather one member of an entirely new race.

More than two dozen of them surrounded us. All of them were fully grown, the broad chests of the males and the full breasts of the females all plated with the rough but supple diamond-shaped scales. Obviously, Nando hadn't been the only—or even the first—mutant child to survive and escape to freedom. Perhaps their stunted noses had scented some pheromone signal that one of their kind was in distress, or perhaps Nando had called to them in some private tongue that we would never understand. Whichever it was, they had come to his aid.

As one, they raised their arms and fanned out their veined membranes, panting in unison. Whether it was a gesture of greeting or of warning was impossible to tell from their smooth, expressionless faces. Many of them held weapons: wooden spears and large machetes that they had either fashioned themselves or stolen from the scattered conclaves of humans in the area. The peculiar grandeur of the sight inspired such awe that, for a moment, Cazador himself could only gawk in dumb amazement.

Then he must have sensed either overwhelming danger or a perverse opportunity to bag a live specimen, for despite the fact we were grossly outnumbered, he dove to retrieve his tranquilizer dart rifle. Jules moved faster, though, kicking the gun out of his reach.

Cazador howled and drew his .45. If they had been alone, I'm sure he would have shot her. But the circle of mutants contracted around us, spear- and knife-points raised, and he had no time. He wheeled on them and fired, his unerring aim sending a bullet smack into the ridged chest of one of the young males. The thing reeled and dropped.

I knew Cazador would take down another creature for every cartridge left in his pistol. I also knew he didn't have enough bullets left to shoot them all, and that he would get us all killed in the process. With the last of my strength, I sprang on him, grabbing hold of his gun arm and letting my overbalanced weight slam us both down to the ground.

We'd barely hit the dust when I felt scaly palms seize my biceps, tugging me off Cazador. *Well, that's it*, I thought with some relief, expecting the sting of a machete across my Adam's apple. A fitting punishment, really, given how many of their throats we humans had slit.

Instead, they merely dragged me back a few feet and left me sitting in the dirt. Their mercy did not extend to Cazador. As the poacher thrashed and cursed them in a dozen different languages, four of the beings took hold of one of his limbs each and held him, supine and spread-eagled, on the ground. A fifth, the largest and beefiest of the males, raised his machete over his head and arced it down on Cazador's neck in a crisp chop. It took two more hacks before the head finally came off.

Before too much of the blood jetted out of straggling arteries of the severed neck, the creatures picked the decapitated corpse up by its ankles and inverted it over the papery bundle of skin and bones that had been Nando. The instant the first spatters rained upon the crinkled hide, capillary action within the skin absorbed the moisture. A stain spread out from around the expanding puddle of liquid as the pallid gray scales darkened to a healthier brown hue. Shriveled wattles filled and rounded to smoothness, and the curled limbs stretched out as if released from the confines of a chrysalis. It was then that I remembered the African lungfish—how it can remain in a state of suspended animation for up to four years during a time of drought, then revive as soon as it comes into contact with water.

Nando soaked up every drop of Cazador's blood so thoroughly that, by the time the boy opened his tight-lidded eyes, his hide was not even damp. He jumped to his feet, his gaze as bright and restless as any preschooler who has just awakened from a nap. A female extended her hand to him, and he scampered to embrace her thigh.

The mutant warriors carried Cazador's carcass away on their shoulders, for what purpose I hesitated to speculate; no doubt, such fresh meat would not go to waste. The large, stocky one picked up the head and held it out to me, neck tipped up, as if offering a cold beer.

Jules doubled over, dry-heaving. She clapped both her hands over her mouth to keep herself from retching, however. Good girl. We couldn't afford to lose a drop of fluid under these conditions. How far was it back to the nearest well? Two days' journey?

Getting up on my knees, I peered at the head. Cazador's eyes had rolled up under the open lids, and I imagined that his mouth still bobbed for breath. I tried to swallow, but my throat felt like sandpaper all the way down to my gut. Refusing this token of goodwill would not only be a bad move diplomatically—it might deprive us of our only source of water for the return trip. Recalling stories of shipwrecked sailors who survived by drinking their dead comrades' blood, I scrambled to grab the empty canteen from my pack. I'm ashamed to admit that, as the creature decanted the head's blood into my flask, I couldn't help but lick my chapped lips.

Still clutching Cazador's scalp by the hair, the creature gave my shoulder an indulgent pat with his free hand and walked off beside his fellows. Only little Nando lagged behind, cocking his head to peer at Jules and me in our sweaty, thirsting exhaustion. Not with fear, for we were no longer a threat. Rather, with curiosity and a little puzzlement, the way we would look at a quagga or a dodo, clucking our tongues and shaking our heads, wondering how such ungainly, hapless creatures ever came into existence. The newest exhibit in the Menagerie of the Maladapted.

Then Nando ran off to be with his own kind in the world they would one day inherit.

The Dream In A Box

Wendy Rathbone

The thing in the other room has just finished its breakfast of fried eggs and beets. It bellows for me to come clean up after it.

I go into the bedroom, smell the stink of sweat on sheets I haven't changed for three days. It begs for more pills.

"Not until eleven," I say.

It moans that it hates me. "Oh I hurt. I hurt." Its lips are stained purple from the beets. It looks like a cruel clown, an old child.

I turn on the TV news. It groans, says over and over, "Fuck you. Fuck you."

I ignore it as well as I can. Some days are easier than others to endure. Some days the thing can blubber and yell, spit and fart, and I am unmoved. Other days the scent, the suffering, the words of the thing are shards, and cut me deep, and the house becomes a jail, and I am imprisoned for something I haven't done.

I am innocent of all charges.

"I am innocent of all charges," I say aloud.

"Fuck you and get me my pills," it says. "It hurts!"

I turn, my composure exceedingly patient for a Saturday, and go into the hall. There I find clean sheets folded by my own hands, fluffed with softener, and I think, *You don't have it so bad,* "you" referring to the thing.

I go back into the bedroom. The thing is moaning, its reddish-stained mouth parting to reveal yellow teeth, a dark blot of tongue. It coughs and spits at me.

"Now I'm going to change the sheets," I say.

"Be gentle. Be gentle." It starts to cry.

I roll my eyes. Pull down the covers.

The thing has one arm and no legs. It is naked. It has red smears on its side, rose-shaped. These are its blister scars from when it was very sick. I rub oil into them every night. The hollow sockets of its hips dip into scars where legs used to be. I oil those as well. From the lump of its torso, genitals, withered and red, dangle. Sometimes, with its good hand, it strokes them, not even caring if I'm in the room.

The thing's hair is silver and long because I haven't cut it in

151

awhile. Though I try to comb it every day, it remains tangled.

I gently roll the thing onto its side, despite its loud protests, and pull the sheet free from the mattress. The news babbles in the background about smog, war, new viruses, the environment we can conquer and rebuild through intellect and preservation. Strange, new diseases appear every day. Nothing changes. Nothing will ever change.

I go to the other side of the bed, roll the thing onto the scarred lump of what is left of its bad arm. It wails. I pull the whole sheet loose, ball it up.

The thing falls to its back again, looking up with dark, cold eyes. "You have no soul," it says.

"Ah, but I do have clean sheets." I repeat the process, putting on the clean bottom sheet. As I do so, the thing urinates, soiling the sheet. The plastic beneath catches most of it.

"You're supposed to ask for the bottle," I say. "Now we'll have to go through this all over again."

It whimpers, but it's smiling.

When I finish cleaning the thing, the morning is only half-gone. I have an hour before it'll demand lunch. I leave the thing dozing in front of the TV and head for my room, where the closet waits with the secret I have hidden there.

I keep my secret in a cardboard box on the top shelf behind my old photo albums of Mom and Dad and me when I was happy. I push aside the albums and slide the box into my arms. Cradling the package, I go to the bed and place it on the bedspread beside me.

Many people break the law. It's not even considered abnormal anymore to exist above the law, or below. But I still have some respect, instilled by my parents, perhaps, for rules that make life more pleasant on the whole, and for the legal process, which attempts to protect those who, by no fault of their own, become victims.

Therefore, every time I lift the lid on the box, I experience a twinge of doubt, a hesitation of fear. I cannot help but feel unclean, perhaps a little insane, for that first moment when the contents of the box are revealed.

Soon, however, I relax, and know that no amount of guilt can cause me to resist this piece of illegal magic, this pure form of desire.

The contents of the box are difficult to describe. What exists within is a kind of mist rainbowed with an oily sheen. The mist is home to a dozen or more pulsing amber lights. Like fireflies, they play along the circuits of the rainbow, never repeating the same pattern twice. The scent of Christmas fills the room.

This is The Dream, a little piece of electric magic, captured dark matter, invisible except when mixed with warped, inside-out, gravity-light puffs of energy. It is a self-contained piece of another reality. The stuff of creation, so some say; what the universe was formed from when nothing became something. No one knows who actually discovered it or invented it, or where it originated. In fact, officially, it does not exist. The rumor is that The Dream was destroyed by the government. Even now that all traces of it have supposedly been "eradicated," The Dream is considered so dangerous that to possess it or anything like it could get you twenty years in prison. It is a legend. A dark street fairy tale. I came upon it by luck. I would never find another one in a thousand years. The seller I bought it from, an old school friend, denies any association with reality pirates or products. He'd come upon a cache of The Dream by accident and just wanted to get rid of it fast. The one I got was the last of his supply. I spent everything I had to buy it.

All forms of reality-altering drugs and devices are illegal. Anything that goes into the brain and changes it, and is not a simple prescription for pain or a cure for disease, is illegal.

But this is different. It isn't a drug. It isn't a brain-controlling device. This, which I call The Dream, is unlike any of that stuff, completely unique. You have complete control over it. You can relive memories. And no new reality it shows you actually exists unless you decide, finally, to remain there and leave all other realities behind. You decide where it can take you, what to create.

I place my hands in the box and The Dream rushes to meet my body warmth with the soft snapping sound of static electricity. The energy seems intelligent, almost alive. I might go so far as to call it a creature, except that I have never noticed any independent reaction from it, other than the patternless flashing of lights and an aurora-pulsing of the mist, which gives the impression that The Dream is animate. The Christmas scent is a reflection of my own mind. Every time I open the box, I'm reminded of the enchantment of childhood Decembers; evergreens surrounded by brightly colored packages, the aroma of sugar cookies.

The nature of The Dream is to absorb thoughts and moods, and create out of that whatever the person holding The Dream wills it to create. Will is important, the seller told me. Will is like "soul." You infuse your will with the stuff of The Dream and you can go anywhere you wish, experiencing anything you desire. It is more than even a lucid dream. You are there. With The Dream, I can have Christmas as often as I want, or birthdays, or travel trips, or adventure limited only by my rustic imagination.

The Dream coats my hand with soft tingles. It is weightless. A breeze. A cloud.

The scent changes from Christmas to rain. I grin as the mist flows over my palms and wrists. The amber lights make the purples and greens and yellows of the moving rainbows look hot, fluorescent. Now the scents are of flame and smoke.

"Henrick!"

Startled, I almost drop the box. The Dream twists; the edges wither as an ochre hue edges the rainbows, the fog.

"Henrick! The pain! The pain! Pills! Now!"

The call of the thing in the other room causes The Dream to squirm even more. The inner program that touches my hands and absorbs my will gives off scents of shit and steam. I hate when this happens more than anything, for this is the purity of life, of goodness, and to see The Dream, *my* dream, tainted in any way, makes me sick to the very center of myself. I need to keep it away from the thing.

If I dared enter The Dream now, with the thing's distraction and interruption, I'd simply relive a cruel reality exactly, or near to exactly, as wretched as the one I find myself caught in now.

I cannot stand to see The Dream respond like this. The sooner I settle The Dream back in the box, the sooner its healing can begin. I can try it again later.

Carefully, my hands lower the gossamer form to the cardboard container. Now that I am not in contact with its energy, the revolting ochre sheen in the mist turns to pink, then angel white. I smell freshly baked sugar cookies.

"Henrick!"

I drop the lid onto the box. "I'm coming!"

Into the closet, behind the photos, sequestered in darkness where nothing can touch the magic until I'm ready, I hide The Dream.

"Henrick!" The voice is agonized.

154

The Dream In A Box

***

The thing is having a particularly bad day. It screams when I medicate and moisturize its scars. It spits food at me. It blubbers and assaults me with pornographic words. I try to ignore it as best as I can. I tell myself the thing is not really angry with me, but is frustrated by pain and suffering, by the condition of its warped form that causes the evil within to erupt uncontrolled.

If the thing gets worse, I know I can always call the doctor to come in earlier than her regularly scheduled visit. Sometimes, though, I think the thing needs an exorcist instead of an M.D. The thought offers me some much-needed amusement.

"What are you grinning at? Are you laughing at me?" the thing demands. With its good arm, it swings at me.

I easily duck and shake my head.

"You're nothing! You'll amount to nothing. You're too stupid to do anything worthwhile! You should never have been born!"

I finish tying back its hank of gray hair with a twisty and set the comb aside. I really should cut the mess, but when it was younger, the thing liked to wear its hair in the fashionable ponytail of its lost era. A strange nostalgia keeps me from cutting it.

I reach for the electric shaver. It spits at me. "You are ugly and no good. Who wants you? Not me!"

"Then who'll take care of you?" I ask calmly, wiping the spittle from my arm.

"Edith."

"Edith isn't here."

"You lie! You're an abomination. You keep her from me. You've raped her. You've killed her. I know. And I'll turn you in to the police, you fat, ugly ..." The rest is too horrible to repeat.

Sometimes my inner calm is truly tried by the thing's vehemence. I understand that pain and misunderstanding cause hatred. And the hatred is almost always misdirected. But I am overly sensitive about my weight and my less-than-average looks. And I am overly sensitive about Edith.

I cannot shave it when I am shaking, so I set the razor back on the table and turn away.

"You get Edith in here now! I want Edith!"

"Edith isn't here." I keep my back to it.

155

"That's because you killed her. You killed her!" It repeats its allegation over and over. I can hear a cry in its voice. Desperation. Mourning.

It is right about one thing. Edith is dead. But I am not the one who killed her.

* * *

The Dream is blue-tinted in my hands, scented with salt. The lights flicker sluggishly along muddy rainbows. Without another second's hesitation, I bring my hands up and press The Dream to my wet face.

Immediately, I am in the thing's room. It is bellowing and cursing. It has stained the bed with its eliminations.

I breathe through my mouth, short, timed puffs. It grins at me, yellow teeth caked with the mucus of dried spit. "You are a murderer," it says.

"This time," I say, "you are right." I take the carving knife from behind my back and plunge it into its quivering throat. Blood squirts into my eyes. I pull the knife out and watch the stream of red fountain onto the thing's chest. Its body twitches. Its mouth works silently, as though it wants to, but cannot, scream. It seems to take a long time for the thing to die. When it finally stops moving, I set to work carving what's left of its body into little pieces. These I dispose of down the kitchen garbage disposal. The bones I burn in the fireplace.

When I am finished, I take a hot shower. As I come out of the shower stall, I wipe the misted mirrors and stare at myself. In the mirrors, I am tall and broad-shouldered, muscular and lean. My nut-brown hair, slicked back from the water, shines. My eyes are clear and brown, with dark lashes forming an exotic line about the edges of the lids.

This is The Dream. I'm free of the thing at last. And I'm handsome, strong, manly. Because of The Dream, this reality is no less real than the default reality I was born into. With a little more will, I could choose to stay. The Dream would suffuse itself into my brain. My original body would die. But this reality isn't my choice. I have many dreams that are so much better. I can take my time to choose.

When I am finished with The Dream, I awaken in my room. The mist snakes about my shoulders, flashing, smelling of sunlight and roses. I reach up, grasp it—like grasping a cloud—and settle the device in the box. I shove the box gently into the back of the closet, then go to check on the thing.

It is sleeping, a soft snore escaping its chapped lips. I lean over it and press my palm to its warm forehead. "I'm sorry," I say softly.

It doesn't stir.

* * *

When I use The Dream again, Edith is alive. She is too beautiful for me to accept; blue eyes, creamy golden skin, slim waist, blonde curls that fall like sunlight about her shoulders. She has the scent of wildflowers. That I am related to her seems impossible. I am flabby and dull next to her. I am awkward and clumsy.

But Edith doesn't think so. She loves me.

"You can be anything, do anything, Ricky," she says. Her smile is reflected inside me. "You're intelligent and compassionate. That combination is rare these days. Beauty can be bought. A tender soul, a gentle conscience, cannot. In that, you are more beautiful than anyone in the world."

"You're supposed to say those things to me," I say. "It's your job."

"I wouldn't say them if they weren't true."

"I love you, Mom."

Her slim hand cups the side of my head.

The Dream allows me to experience a whole day condensed to an hour with my mother.

I wake up rested and smiling.

When the thing yells, I go to it with a new strength.

* * *

The day the doctor comes, the thing is listless and inattentive. It keeps falling asleep, even while she pokes it.

"What's wrong?" I ask.

"Nothing physical that wasn't there already," she answers.

"I've done everything you told me to do, every day. I never leave the house."

She puts a hand on my shoulder to stop me. "I know. You take very good care of him. It's not for lack of care that he's having a bad day. I can see that. Clean sheets, clean house. His hair is combed; he's

157

getting his proper amounts of medication. How has he been otherwise?"

For a moment it's difficult to answer. I have trouble thinking of the thing as "he" or "him." "Depressed," I finally reply. "Irritable. Angry. Usually violent."

The doctor writes on a notepad. She rips off a page. "I'm going to change his medication dosage a little. Here's a new prescription. It's the same thing, but the pills will be more potent."

I nod, taking the paper.

"It should make him more receptive to you, and less violent. Let me know how he does in the next couple of weeks. I may want to change my schedule to fit him in for another examination before the end of the month."

"Thank you," I say.

She looks at me, with her black eyes soft and glimmering, for a long moment. Then she says, "You're doing a great job, Rick."

I shrug.

"A lot of people would turn their backs on a situation like this," she continues. "Turn the case over to the state."

"It … it's not what I want to do," I stammer, glancing sidelong at the thing.

"I know." She smiles with only her eyes and turns away. "If you have any problems, you call. And you still have that list of other numbers I gave you? Just in case you want assistance, or someone to talk to."

I nod.

"Good." She picks up her medical bag, grabs her coat from the chair by the door. "No fee, as usual. And I'll see you again soon. Are you okay?"

"Yes," I say, touching the side of the bed where the thing lies, feeling the stiff press of clean cotton. "Yes."

"All right, then."

I snatch my hand up and step forward. "I'll see you to the door."

* * *

In The Dream I can relive any situation I want, or create new scenarios to star in. I can be slim, good looking, and desirable to any woman. I can relive old holidays, or create new ones. I can save the Earth

158

from alien invasion, heal the sick, bring back the dead ... I can experience anything, and when I am ready to choose, I can remain there forever. My favorite situation to dream is one in which Mom and Dad are still alive, having narrowly avoided death from the new, unheard-of virus that, in real life, consumed them both like a sudden fever, eating flesh and bone, withering them painfully from the inside out. And I am their son again, not necessarily handsome, not perfect, but well loved.

Tonight The Dream gives off my father's old scent: English Leather and rose wine, printer's ink and Borax. Because this is The Dream, the magazine and newspaper business still flourishes despite laptops and electronic book readers. In the past, in his prime, my father made a good living at his print shop.

The Dream's lights flicker amber, rare lime green and gray. As I hold The Dream, staring into the mist and ever-swirling rainbows, it pulses against my palms, tickling them with what feels like faint electrical charges. I raise my hands to my face. The Dream presses into my nose, eyes, mouth.

I inhale. I am fourteen.

Dad comes into my room, fresh from work, his hands and fingernails gray from too much ink and too much soap. My mood goes from sour to hopeful to ashamed.

"What's this I hear about a fight at school?" he asks me.

I've been crying, so I don't look at him.

"Well?" he prompts.

"Sean called me 'Tubbo' again."

"That all?"

I shrug.

"So, what have I told you in the past? That names don't matter, right? It's what's inside that counts."

I look at him, at his slicked-back black hair caught in a tight tail, at his smooth face and honey skin. I don't look a thing like him. It's hard to believe, sometimes, he's my father, my true, blood father.

"Dad, don't you see how easy that is for you to say? You don't look like me. You've never looked like me. You *don't* know what it's like!"

He sits beside me on the bed. "So you have to hit to defend yourself," he says softly. "You have to lash out, hurt, until the inside and the outside match your view of yourself."

159

I blink, look down at my lap. My chubby fingers fold together. I hate myself.

"You're not ugly," he continues. "So you don't have to be ugly."

"You don't understand," I repeat, whispering.

"No," he answers. His hand touches the top of my head. I can feel his fingers curve in my hair. "You're right. I don't understand. Because when I look at you, I see what's good and right. I see what's beautiful about human beings. Something rare amid all the destruction of our world. Something different. You've never done me wrong before. Don't start." His hand moves to my shoulder, squeezes.

For a moment I am all he says I am.

For a moment.

I wake on my back. The Dream puddles on my chest, oily, shifting in light and mist.

The thing down the hall is calling. "Food! Food!"

I close my eyes tightly and force myself to take deep breaths.

* * *

Its one good arm throws its food on the wall. I clean it up.

It urinates on the sheets. I clean it up.

It spits its medicine at me. I clean it up.

"Get me Edith," it demands.

"She's not here."

"I know you're keeping her from me, you idiot, you fat toad, good for nothing ..." The thing thrashes, crying out. It pushes off its covers with its flailing arm. It's cool in the room. I grab the sheet and blanket and cover the thing back up as it screams.

"Get out," it yells. "If you can't bring me Edith, then just get out. And never come back!"

I leave the room as it continues to spit at and curse me.

In my room I remove The Dream from its box.

The Dream remains my only escape from this madness. My chest is tight, my eyes swollen. Reflecting my mood, The Dream in my hands twists and bends. The center becomes devoid of rainbows. A dark tornado appears in the mist. The scent is acrid, like burnt tar.

This isn't what I want.

Even in the privacy of my own room, I can still hear the thing down the hall. It moans and howls for Edith. Wincing, I start to raise

160

The Dream In A Box

my hands and The Dream to my face.

The thing screams in a horrible, high-pitched voice. "Edith!"

My hands stop. I'm breathing hard, trying not to cry. I've had enough. I jump up, balancing The Dream on one hand, and yank open the door.

The hall is dark, but The Dream gutters like a candle lighting the way.

At the end of the hall is the thing's room. With my free hand, I turn the cold metal doorknob.

"Edith?" questions a sobbing voice from within.

I enter the room. The only light is from a lamp by the bed. The thing lies in a mess of covers, its face scarred with tears, its eyes pained, terrified. This is what the virus left me after it killed my mother and father. My mother is dust now. But my father ... Before it left his system—still barely breathing, still pumping blood—it had taken most of his body, most of his mind. The virus changed him from my father to the thing.

"Not Edith!" he says, seeing me come into the room. His chapped lips grimace.

"No, you're wrong." Resigned, I walk slowly towards the bed. Even though the virus took away the father I knew, still, I have never been able to deny him anything. "I've brought her."

"Edith? Here?" he whispers.

"Yes." I move my hand forward and show him the slowly darkening miniature electrical storm that is The Dream. "Edith is here."

Treasure

Jim Schoen

The hooded eyes wink closed, then open again on the white cold falling out of the darkness. A mewl of drowsy approval as the beast thinks the sound of a word.

"*Beau-dy ...*"

This is how it remembers, when it remembers. The white cold is "Beauty." "Beauty" is the white cold.

The hooded eyes wink heavily, jaws sagging ajar, then snapping shut again on a grunt. Jewels of ice rattle in the thick crest of fur as a shudder chases down its spine. It has gone up into the high wood in search of food, and has only just returned. Now, in its head, the sound of the word from before: "Un-ga ..."

Yes, and from before that to a time beyond remembering, a word it can sink its teeth into. It chews the sound with a soft growling, "Un-gaa ..." And then, with a massive upheaval of blood and muscle and bone, a deafening roar into the winter stillness:

"Un-gaaaa!"

Hunger is a word it knows. In the season of white cold, creatures are few, hungers many. In the season of hunger, sleep is the only reprieve. And even in sleep:

"*Un –gaaa ...*"

From the surrounding trees, the creaking of heavy limbs mortally burdened under snow. The small, cracked voices of birds and the fierce chittering of squirrels have fallen silent. To the ceaseless whisperings of mice, the beast shakes its great head as at the buzzing of flies. To its interminable hunger, such creatures are more taunt than answer. Rather, it listens for the sounds larger and more promising, listens and listens.

The white cold falls and falls in a slow, mesmerizing descent. Behind the timber wall, the hooded eyes flicker and close. The massive head slowly nods, down and down, before dropping all at once, like an anchor slipped from its chain, with an audible thud and a soft eruption of dirt. Dust rises to hover in the frozen dark.

It is some time later that another sound intrudes, the sound of a fat bee buzzing among spring flowers. Asleep, the beast groans and champs its teeth. Its tongue curls out, tasting the air, returns with a

163

hyphen of the fine-churned, ancient silt that serves as its pillow. A second flick of the tongue retrieves another small measure of dirt, and with it, a morsel blindly scented and then feverishly sought, a tattered relic of black silk pressed deep in the loam.

Mother ...?

The scent of Mother; and now the scent enfolds. A deep and contented murmuring as her jagged smile makes itself heard, and thin fingers begin to gnaw with a soft scratching noise at the beast's scar-twisted hump. The beast mewls its pleasure, the fat bee noise forgotten as it fades beneath the soft keening of the night wind.

"With my black dress?" Mother asks.

In the dream, the beast raises its head, blinking dream-eyes against the light slanting down. Mother sits on one of the lower stairs, a blood-red stone depending by two delicate fingers from the lobe of one ear, a pendant doubly as large suspended across the milk-pale hollow at the base of her throat.

"No?" she asks, brightly, and it is as if she has been there all the while.

The beast watches intently, its surprise of a moment giving way to anticipation as Mother bends, softly humming over the heavy wooden chest on the stair below. All at once her humming stops, and she lifts something out, shows him as she showed him the others a moment before.

"An emerald night, then?"

The beast's smile at her eagerness is an easily mistakable rendition of pleasure, monstrified. Emerald, yes, like Mother's eyes, beneath hair the white of snow.

Now, in the dream, the Good Doctor appears, hypodermic in hand. But no longer are they Below. Here, sunlight streams through a bay of mullioned windows, gleams on polished wood. The air tastes of silk and lemon. And Mother has—

"Tom?"

Mother?

The Good Doctor raises the hypodermic, his pale eyes narrowing as light flickers from the tip of the needle in a golden barb. "This will fix you, Tom," he says, one fingernail tick- ticking against the glass wall of the tube. "This will— "

In sleep, the monstrified grin returns with a baring of teeth as the Good Doctor finishes, "—make you Better."

Better, yes; and before this the word had been *"Normal."* And before that: *"Like any other little boy."* Which it had always imagined it was; like Brother. Like Mother in many ways. Like Father himself when he was not the Good Doctor.

All of this while it was still a boy, of sorts, although not as pitifully small as Brother, who comes now rarely, and only in the Red Dream.

In the Red Dream, the beast is searching the woods frantically, calling and calling. "Ba-ru! Ba-ruuu!" Arriving at the Pit, guided by the smell, to find Brother lying motionless at the bottom, the beast leaps down to help. Instantly a great caterwauling goes up as children encircle the rim of the Pit and begin throwing down rocks. It is all the beast can do to cover Brother against their barrage. But one of them has a long stick, sharpened on one end, plunging and plunging. Each bright, searing pain driven deep and then wrenched away is punctuated by a rabid outburst of laughter. Everywhere there is Red.

Mercifully, the Red Dream comes only seldom now.

Following this encounter in the woods, Brother had been sent away. The beast had been led back Below to suffer the Good Doctor's further ministrations. "Father," it seemed, had gone away, never to return. And Mother—

In the end, after she had seen, Mother had not allowed it. In the end she had descended in the cold and dark to turn the key and kick loose the frost from the iron door. When the Good Doctor had awakened and come to them, like an offering, there had been a great feeding, after which the Good Doctor was no more. There had been fire then, which had swiftly crumbled the big house into Below while the two of them looked on from the frozen riverbank.

The beast remembers still following the red lights in a riotous gallop through the cold, moonless night, running and running as it had never run, until they reached the island.

Now, in the dream, the Good Doctor says, "Are you ready, Tom?"

The beast opens its throat wide, but no sound comes. Its lips peel back in a snarl, in answer to which the Good Doctor only smiles. Raising the terrible instrument in his hand, he turns towards the window. From the tip of the needle, a sudden glint, like a flash of sunlight across sweet spring air, where a fat bee buzzes and buzzes and—

Opening its eyes, at once fully aware, the beast rises to scuff the well-worn undersides of the beams overhead. Across teeth far too long, save for the massive jaws grown deep to accommodate them, it hangs its tongue, panting, to taste the frigid air.

Mother?

Padding ahead to peer out at the winter night, it tenses, back bristling, and begins kneading the cold-stiffened earth in heedless anticipation, churning up rocks with its heavy claws, tearing out root ends of the ancient trees that once grew here.

Lights! Mother is—

Yes, Mother had come down to scratch its hump and whisper its name aloud. She had taken her place on the stair above the open chest, as before every hunt, to ask that it choose from among the pretty stones.

Mother would be beginning her preparations.

The beast raises its head to await in utter stillness the near-silent tread from above. Anticipation is like the wing beats of startled birds. And it begins to pant with a soft keening, its gaze riveted on that place to which a pale outline of rough-hewn stairs rises to the floor planks an arm's reach away.

But the footsteps do not come, and the wing beats slow, and then fall still as the beast remembers.

Yes ... And no longer the faint, razoring scream of wheels across the floorboards overhead. The hooded eyes rise to look again, the keening reduced now to a soft piping note that finishes every frost-rimed expulsion of breath. Its eyes glance away, then return, utterly still.

From above, from Mother's house: silence.

Abruptly, the keening ends. With a huff and a disconsolate grunt, the beast drops heavily to its haunches, remembers the round, hollow sound of yet another word: "Lone ..."

Turning back to the view between the timbers, it observes the lights far off, sweeping through the long curve where the white cold does not gather, towards that place where it does again, where intruders might continue their crossing.

How many had Mother brought in this way? How many since she had stopped those arriving uninvited because they had seen, because they had heard?

Of Mother's Things ...

Treasure's Things ...?

For, about the pretty stones, Mother had offered this assurance:

166

"When I can no longer bring them to you, when I have gone and you are alone, you must stay, my Treasure; you must wait." She had dipped one delicate hand deep into the chest and lifted it out, then again, the pretty stones cascading. "For they will come, my Treasure. They will come—to you ..."

The lights seem to float far off in the darkness. Now they turn away, fade to a distant glow, and disappear. But the sounds of Mother's words are indelible, only the sounds, their intonation like scrawls deeply carved into the cold stone of the beast's heart. *For they will come, my Treasure ...*"

Every bit as memorable had been Mother's next visit, following a considerable time of scarcity and ever-increasing hunger, memorable because she had not descended to her place upon the stairs, had instead leaned ahead from the peculiar wheeled chair to peer down into the darkness, sorrow-eyed, utterly silent.

And, yes; afraid.

The beast softly mewls and turns away for another upward glance, expectant, unsure; no thread of light defines the hatchway above. And yet it can smell her here, her scent powerful where its muzzle grazes the one step worn with sitting, and then the contents of the chest sprawled open on the stair below, as if she has only just left.

Its stomach growls. An answering grunt is mere acknowledgement; the smell of Mother nearby means food, the tearing of hot flesh and the crunching of bone. Its mouth fills at the thought; its jaws begin to drip. There comes an instant of leaden dread at an image from the Red Dream, of Brother lying broken in the pit, and the remembered smell of Brother's blood mixed with its own, still warm. And now, as dread blossoms in its mind's eye, rage.

The beast growls in a panting rhythm and begins to toss its head, as if this might shake loose the terrible remembrance of voices shrieking above, from the rim of the Pit, of the horrible sharpness plunging and plunging.

With a soft keening, the beast lowers its muzzle to the earthen floor, where the pretty stones glow with muted fires of blood and wine, the green of damp moss in the cold, shadowed places, the crystalline blue of this moonless winter night.

It thinks the sound of a word from before: *"Beau-dy ..."* And then two others, its favorites, yes: *"Treasure's Things ..."*

167

The hooded eyes, as it remembers, shine with the yellow of sunlight glimpsed through a film of river mud. It thinks these sounds again: *"Treasure's Things!"*

Now the fat bee sound returns, nearer and more grating. Through the spaces in the timber wall, the beast sees only the lights of the distant town. And then nearer, drawn by an indistinct tumble of motion, its gaze leaps to the foreground, where a plume of snow tracks swift passage through the frozen night.

The sight unsettles. Not with fear, an emotion ancient in its history. For as its size had continued to increase under the Good Doctor's ministrations, as its arsenal had refined beyond useful purpose, in a region where bears and wolves were the most formidable prey it might encounter, those receptors by which it might know fear had atrophied.

Curiosity, however, remains within its capacity.

Also puzzlement. Because absent here is Mother's voice, which had always stayed the urgings of hunger until their current guest had arrived in the room above, and still further, steeling the patience of its ravenous hungers, while she and their guest talked for a time. Always, the talk would turn to "Her Treasure." The beast would wait in the darkness below, claws churning the earth while it listened to the word sounds from above. Its jaws would begin to drip with anticipation for that moment when Mother would speak these particular sounds:

"Oh, my, yes! Would you like to see?"

The great, terrible thing inside its chest would begin to hammer and pound. And as the hatch was lifted, as light spilled down warm into the cold, clotted dark of "Their Secret Place," as Mother called it, all of time before and all that must follow would be reduced to that moment just ahead when the lavish urgings of hunger would have their way.

Now, the thing in its chest drums steadily. Beyond the timber wall, the skirling of the wind across the ice fades, while the bee sound sharpens to an urgent bray. All at once the great plume tumbles up the shore, and out of it, a single figure emerges in a clumsy, headlong sprawl: one, and then a second, who delivers a savage kick to the first.

The second man is angry, his sounds cruel, fierce. Another savage kick and the first man sprawls again, groaning as it struggles away with a crippled effort. The other turns to look back where the plume

168

has faded into the dark; he looks as if he is expecting others, as if he fears the arrival of others. In the darkness behind the timber wall, the beast's growl is a desultory acknowledgment of this symptom, a disagreeable symptom, recognizable from others who have come, as Mother had promised they would, to take Treasure's Things. Perhaps twice as large as the first, there is about the second man the vicious manner of the wild dogs that sometimes found their way to the island. These, too, preyed upon the crippled, the sick. The beast, in its forays into the high wood, has come upon creatures savaged for reasons other than to feed, creatures it would dispatch and eat, with little pleasure.

There is about this second one another feature that disturbs. Its every sound is a sharpness plunged deep where the beast cannot reach, plunging and plunging.

"Wherever she kept it, Ted," the man cackles, "you'd best get a clue!"

"Don't know, Mick," answers the smaller man. "I don't, really, 'cuz I never—"

Another kick and the larger man makes these sounds, bright, happy, savage. He only stops to say, "You just think you don't know, Ted. But I'm here—" he kicks him again, "I'm here ta help ya, Ted! You used to come here alla time, hey, remember? You and Mom and Dad and the Monster? You hadda seen something, sometime! Am I right?"

He kicks the small man again and again, asking between moments of ferocious exertion, "Is 'iss helping any, Ted?" All at once, he stops.

"Hey, you remember this one? *DUMB TOMMY-TOMSTER, BIG, BAD MONSTER!*"

Memory stirs. A whine rises in the beast's chest, escapes across pulsing tongue and glistening teeth bared in a bleating, the sound inaudible across the distance beneath the soft shrieking of the wind across the ice. The wind cools an ever-reddening heat as the beast drinks of it, panting now, drinking deeply of the smells it delivers, then deeper still.

That smell ...

"So, Ted?" asks the big man, delivering another kick before reaching into his coat pocket. "Anything coming to you? I mean is 'iss working, or—"

He pulls the hand from his coat pocket, flicks open something

169

long and glinting, hooked at its end. "'Cuz I can sure's hell boost your motivation here if that's what it's gonna—"

He stops in mid-motion, turns, the cruel grin flattening as his gaze cuts sharply to the abandoned timber-built cottage set back into the hill, within the darkness of the woods.

"The hell was 'at?"

The small man lying in the snow lowers a shielding arm, lowers it some more, listening.

"For Chrissake!" says the other. "You din't hear that? Sounds like— the fuck izat?"

The smell, burnt, Bully-bitter, is more ancient in the beast's brain than the terrible fear it had first inspired. It is a smell from the Red Dream, of a long stick turned and turned as it was whittled to wicked sharpness.

Out from among the trees and hard down the rubble track, the beast launches itself at full gallop, lands like a boulder plummeting, with an agonized roar. Its momentum as it strikes tumbles them far out onto the ice, its claws raking to bone.

At the hunt its instinct is to swiftly dispatch and eat its prey. Now, the smell alone fuels an impulse towards utter destruction. Although its hunger surpasses anything its animal brain can recall, it is the Bully's screams as its jaws envelop the flailing head that nourish it first.

The struggle does not last, cannot. Brute strength, coupled with so prodigious an arsenal for destruction, is far too great. At a flicker of motion from one of the torn pieces, the beast falls upon the thing with a deep-throated snarl, savages it once more before flinging it away, its bloodlust hardly sated.

But there is another; there is a second. And there is—

The beast is already moving as it gives voice to the thought, huffing and grunting with the sudden vigor of its exertions: There is "Ung-aa! Ung-aaa!"

Its claws carve the ice beside the straggling, wounded trail through fresh snow, where it lowers its muzzle into one smell that mirrors another, an ancient smell, lodged deep in its brain. Seasons have passed, summers and winters beyond number. Memory is a groaning, rust-creaking thing that all at once looses a juddering barrage of images, sounds, smells.

The beast gallops faster, bloodlust giving way as abruptly as it has come, to an avid, if nameless, curiosity.

Abruptly, too, the wounded trail turns, muddied here by a fall, a roll, a burrowing beneath crystalline snow. It glimpses the burrowing as it passes, claws carving deep in an effort to redirect its rushing hulk. Sudden alarm looses the hammer in its chest as a great "BOOM!" resonates from somewhere below. It turns its head to see how frighteningly near is that place where the white cold does not gather.

Too late, the ice gives way.

Water rushes up, in, engulfing. The beast gasps, flailing at the frigid water, at the jagged ice, tearing down great heavy slabs, now from below, which the current carries swiftly away. It feels itself swept along a fissure of its own making, the voice of the waters all around, everywhere, hungry sounds.

The waters will eat it. Yes! It will rip the waters and tear them and still they will eat. It! This is fear. It remembers now the fear of a boy as the waters gathered to swallow it down into the cold, dark place, and someone had—

"Stand up!"

Yes, Brother had called out.

"Shallow here! Shallow, do you understand?"

It does not understand. Because Brother has gone away forever, save for the numbing terror of the Red Dream. And yet the smell, and those sounds, too, are—

"Push your feet down! Stand up!"

This as the thin ice breaks yet again under its frantic bludgeoning, as the waters tear it easily down and away into the cold, dark, airless place.

Spinning and turning between the mud and rock below and the ice above, the beast stretches out its arms, its powerful legs, claws screeling over rocks to find purchase in the cold-stiffened mud eight feet below. Now the current pushes and pushes, a tremendous force turning it upright, bending it taut beneath the heavy ice.

It tries to stand, the water rushing past, rushing and rushing as it adds the immense strength of its legs to the columns like malleable iron up its back, driving the gnarled and unfeeling scar of its hump against the cruel underbelly of the ice.

The ice tents with a slow, sucking sound, collapses with a crash and a tremendous rushing of the waters. Hungry waters!

The beast churns ahead, bludgeoning its way through the ice to waters that might eat only the smaller half of it now, alarmed at the small, anxious noises that emerge from its yawning jaws. Where the heavier ice resumes, it bends across, clawing for purchase as it pulls itself ahead.

"That's it! There you go!"

Another pull as it raises its massive head to regard the speaker, watches him abruptly cease his approach, then retire a step, this other who would take Treasure's Things. With one leg free of the suck of the waters, the beast coils it under, fur dripping as the second follows. Its growl expels a mucous of brackish water, rekindling fury as if it had never left.

Mother's Things!

Another growl from deep in its chest, and the beast commences panting, its tongue laving the frigid air. The air tells of many things. Fear is there. Yes, fear and—

It champs its jaws repeatedly, suddenly distrustful of what the air tells, gnawing the growl that shudders to garbled bits between its teeth. Steam plumes from its muzzle into the cold.

Fear and—

The smell is there now with every intake of breath. The beast rises and shakes itself, flinging water in generous arcs, dropping heavily to the ice in an unmistakable threat.

"No, don't! You'll go through again!"

This from the man, the fearful man who does not run as the beast begins its slow, menacing approach. Shambling nearer, and then past, it is jarred once more by the smell, and then the smallness, too, the wounded frailness of this one. Hardly a snack. Another growl, a warning, as it bends its massive head, its mouth lolling open over the wounded track through the snow. Yes, there too. One and the same, one and—

"Tom?" A whisper.

The man shivers violently, speaks again. "I thought you were—"

A sudden lunge and it catches the man by its neck, choking back a growl, its tongue lashing. Squeals and garbled cries from the man as it is carried for some distance across the snow, then tossed in a sprawl. For in the taste is no answer to the conundrum of the smell. No answer. It knows only that it cannot eat—

"Un-gaaaaa!"

172

Yes, but cannot—can-not—

It circles the man once more, warily, hot breath champing plumes into the moonless dark.

"Tom? It's me, Tom. It's—"

"Me ... Tom ... Me ..."

Abruptly, wary with the unaccustomed taste of its own fear, the beast moves off, dropping to all fours in a loping canter.

"Must eat! Must must must eat!"

It finds the other as it had left it, absent the smell of interlopers come to take what is not theirs.

Treasure's Things!

The smaller pieces it eats quickly, with errant glances into the surrounding darkness, and up into the night sky, out of which the thief birds fall. It will share nothing of this hunt, and asserts this, loudly. "Un-gaaa!"

Not with the thief birds, who fall in numbers but take only little and, occasionally, by errors of judgment, add to its repast; nor with the frail man creature approaching now, haltingly, across the disheveled snow.

The beast snarls a warning before crunching through a heavy bone, crunching and growling around the blood-sweet, jagged-edged gobbets.

With the pieces quickly gone, it falls vigorously upon what remains of the haunch. The man watches, without appetite it seems, as the beast makes quick work of what remains, and as it licks at the blood-sodden snow, occasionally eyeing the morsel that it has saved for Mother, to be left on the porch above, before Mother's door. Then it remembers what it is about Mother, and it eats the morsel as well, remembering, too, once more, the round, hollowed sound of that other word: *'Lone ...*

With a wary glance at the man, a final prodding of its muzzle into that unsettling smell, the beast wheels hard and gallops away across the ice. The distance is not far.

Inexplicably, the man follows. Peering back through the spaces between the timbers of the wall, the beast watches with growing unease as the man comes on in its strangely wounded gait. Surely it will stop where the waters lie piled and broken below.

But the man continues on, lurching its way up the rubble track, falling once, and then again, and coming still, until the beast can

173

smell it panting there on the other side of the timber wall.

The beast cocks its massive head, its tongue uncurling to lave the fingers, thin and brittle and cold, that intrude across one of the timbers. At the taste, a shudder treads its spine, raising the hair to bristle across its back and head.

It cannot eat this one, no, cannot break and tear it and—

From deep in the barrel of its chest, the beast growls. The man, heedless of the warning, whispers, "Jeeze, Tom! I can't hardly believe! I thought—I thought you were dead!"

The beast, listening in surprise, begins to rock from side to side. It tosses its great head and snarls, its teeth gnashing around the sound that emerges. Only inches away trembles the meat that might ease its insatiable hunger. It huffs repeatedly and, when this lesser warning, half plea, goes unheeded, growls again from deep in its chest.

The man makes wet coughing, choking noises. It wipes its face with one frail hand, which it then returns to rest across one of the timbers. The beast turns its head to breathe once more, guardedly, of the scent. It snakes out its tongue to taste of cold-brittled flesh, withdraws once more in renewed alarm. The man makes more sounds, entirely different from those of a moment before. When it has finished, with a final "Huh-uh-uh," the man says, "Tom, would you like—more?"

"More?"

At first it imagines that this is Mother speaking, that Mother has returned. But when the man speaks again, it is not to say, as Mother had a single time before she'd gone away, *"We mustn't be greedy, now ..."*

No, what the man says is, "I will bring you more, Tom. I—will bring you more ..."

Now the man has gone, trailing lights red as blood through the frozen dark, that sweep from sight through the long curve where the white cold does not gather. The fat bee sound quickly fades beneath the soft skirling of the night wind across the ice.

In its earthen hollow, beneath the cabin secreted deep among the trees, the beast claws amidst a brittle detritus of sticks and leaves and pretty stones carelessly strewn, turning and turning. It prods with its muzzle among shreds of cloth for a ragged scrap of black silk from which the smell of Mother's blood has nearly faded.

Treasure's Things ...

What remains is an essence very nearly as dear.

And with the smell of Mother everywhere, with the promise of *More* from the frail, wounded man to quiet the ache of an interminable hunger, the beast growls a final warning to any creature foolish enough to range the night within hearing of so terrible a sound. And with a disconsolate grunt when no answer is forthcoming from the darkness beyond, it slumps heavily to the earthen floor to resume its vigil.

In only moments, because the peculiar rigors of this hunt have taken an exceptional toll, its head falls heavily; the hooded eyes slowly wink, and then close. Sleep comes, and with sleep, dreams.

The Transmutation
Charles Austin Muir

On nights like these—*when the dark rises in a seething tide and I dream of cells with teeth*—it's impossible not to think back on my college days with Paul Challas. My roommate for nine months, Paul was a graduate student in microbiology, six-foot-six, with hands like a gorilla's paws. Only twenty-two years old, he was diagnosed with lung cancer and terminated his studies to face the disease with his family. He refused, however, to let this disrupt our ongoing philosophical debates, stopping by as often he could to share his latest theory on the nature of reality.

I never took him literally, knowing my friend's intellectual energy but also the sickness that absorbed his attention. Like the night he flashed his secretive, dark eyes at me and declared:

"Nothing exists but patterns of stuff that behave in ways we don't understand, but seem to revolve around reproduction, death, and the purchase of life at the cost of other life through every cycle of existence."

I smiled, having peeked at some of the reading material in his duffel bag. Moved by influences ranging from mathematics to the occult, he had taken the materialist narrative of physics and applied it to biology with the hyperbole of a horror writer. Melodramatic, I thought, and yet the argument intrigued me. I saw how I could apply it to my creative writing thesis, a collection of vignettes about a group of sex-obsessed intellectuals with exotic-sounding names.

Paul's ruminations so consumed him that he sometimes failed to distinguish between my willingness to understand him and my own investment in the illusions of which he often spoke. This proved to be a maddening character flaw when I found myself one evening—accompanied by Challas—in the emergency room to address a rather worrisome problem with my bowel movements. As I flipped through *The New Yorker* while leaning away from a man in a bloodstained army surplus jacket who reeked of cheap whiskey, Challas abruptly launched into another of his nihilistic rants.

"When we look at existence for what it is," he said, "we have to admit, George, that the wall between health and unhealth, wellness and suffering, seems alarmingly fragile." He was referring to an earlier conversation wherein he argued that humans were reducible to the mysteriously encoded behaviors of microorganisms.

"Some of the ghastliest forms of sickness and suffering," he continued over an infant's wail, "are caused by tiny irritants invading or growing to unacceptable proportions in our bodies. Since we don't understand where or why their behavior is encoded, we can't understand how it is we feel unhealthy, except that we attribute certain behavior patterns at the level of personal action (an illusion, since we don't exist) to higher probabilities of feeling ill or, conversely, free of pathology. To those of us who want to believe that life is what we make of it, that our health and well-being are to a great degree in our hands, this mystery is like the room we try to avoid in our dreams but must face at some point."

The tiny irritant behind us had ceased bawling, so that Challas's discourse perked up ears around the room.

Only when I told him there was nothing mysterious about a bloody toilet bowl did he desist from his lecture and leave me to my magazine.

Still, his ideas seemed to be borne out in as minor a concern as my hemorrhoids. Barely a year his senior, I was forced to admit I had no idea why any of us feels healthy or why the universe seems to turn against us and hand us inflammation within the anal canal or, in my friend's case, a life-threatening tumor.

Challas's health declined to the point where he no longer visited me. I missed his Goliath-like presence, his compulsive handwringing and sleepy grin. But studies went on, and my adviser demanded I rewrite my 150-page manuscript before the winter break; apparently I was unsuccessful in blending my oddly named intellectuals with Challas's biological nihilism.

The last time I saw Challas, I was mulling over a passage in his most recent letter, which I had just read while sitting alone in the café we used to frequent. The handwriting was urgent, in some places stabbing through the sheet:

"Artists, like scientists, must illuminate the grisly truth of existence. The key is to be able to live with this truth in such a way that you can organize your experience, whether in poems, paintings, symphonic compositions or what have you. For those gifted with high intelligence and afflicted with a profound psychological disturbance, the capacity to examine such a universal vision of horror might be maintained through prescribed medications, therapy, and a mysterious ingrained ability to create coherence out of extraordinary intuitions. But for the rest of us we must not only find a way to face the truth of existence, *but allow ourselves to be devoured by it.*"

It puzzled me not only because Paul never explained what this devouring entailed, but because he seemed to categorize himself as an artist. When I saw him outside the café window, I rushed into the snowy streets to ask him what he meant.

It had been months since our last visit. A handsome man—I called him Dorian Gray with gigantism—Challas seemed to have aged twenty years, and he hobbled through the snow as if his feet hurt him immensely. He was bundled up in a pea coat and his head was shaven. He squinted into the flurries, wringing his huge mittened hands and yanking his boots out of the drifts with angry, determined jerks. He was not the sort of man I would have accosted at that moment, but he was my friend and had written me a cryptic letter without once mentioning the progress of his treatments.

When I shouted at him he showed no signs of hearing me. I dashed across the street to the corner where he had turned and disappeared on his apparently urgent errand.

Bone-chilling gusts distracted me from the gradual atrophy of my surroundings as I pursued my ex-roommate. His Sasquatch-like tracks and the occasional glimpse of his barn-door shoulders led me deeper into a maze of white, twisting streets that seemed like a giant Nativity scene set in an abandoned slum. Here, nothing but the snow stirred, the wind walled out by vacant storefronts and the squalid ramparts of tenement buildings. As I passed in their shadow, calling to my friend, I wondered if I had seen Challas after all or if, out of some playful impulse, he was setting me up for an ambush. A sense of unwelcome bled through the derelict calm in which only the snow moved, fluttering on sour breath from the mouths of alleys and smashed windows, its milky circulation strangely beautiful against the mute, decrepit backdrop.

Somewhere ahead I heard a cough.

The gray was deepening in the sky when I gave up my search. The snow had covered my friend's tracks near the landmarks I'd noted. When I came home, I asked my neighbors if they knew anything of the environment where I'd made my wild goose chase; according to them, I'd been wise to abandon my efforts before dark.

That night I went to bed early, sweating despite the cold, watching the shadows of the snow drift down the ceiling and wondering if at that very moment Paul Challas huddled in some filthy alley in a degenerate quarter of the city, shivering in the storm's arctic breath. A week later, when I saw the headline: "RISING ACADEMIC STAR TURNED CANCER VICTIM GONE MISSING," my worst fears were confirmed.

* * *

I'm forty years old now. I'm unmarried, childless, living alone, enjoying the last months of a year I took off to write full time and increase the number of short stories to my credit. None of these involve sex-obsessed intellectuals, though I can't deny the intellectual whiff of Paul Challas's somewhat dubious views. Perhaps because of this I've been labeled a "third-time-around (no one has yet identified the "second-time-around") Chopper-Kovsky," referring to Edward Chopper-Kovsky, the award-winning horror writer. "The Alchymist," as his fans call him, is famous for his Crawl stories, a cycle of Lovecraft/goth-style tales set in a notorious slum that in my mind has always resembled the district where I last saw Paul Challas.

The resemblance is perhaps a little wishful, as subsequent ventures into that area, while teaching me to ignore certain quivering shapes I've glimpsed in the gutters and public parks, have so far failed to fill me with the pangs of alienation I felt when I wandered its snowy labyrinth almost twenty years ago.

Out of nostalgia for the sentimental young man I'd been (and if I thought hemorrhoids were tough back then, I'd have thought twice about making it to forty), I decided to make a day of it wandering the university where we so often debated our cosmic theories. In the student union, I took from a bulletin board a flyer I'd seen posted on kiosks and telephone poles all over campus. In a serif font on plain white paper, it invited all lovers of Edward Chopper-Kovsky to gather for refreshments and discuss the author's latest novel. This intrigued me, firstly, because the meeting was to be held in an elementary school in the part of town where I'd lost Paul Challas; and, secondly, because I'd never heard of Chopper-Kovsky publishing a novel.

It was his affinities with my young friend's dogmas that drew me to the author in the first place. Despite my efforts to break away from the man's style, I couldn't help but devour his largely out-of-print collections, soaking up his Challas-like motifs and shades of voice (one could argue I'd been writing like Chopper-Kovsky before Chopper-Kovsky). I knew the writer's *oeuvre* rather well, and within an hour's research determined that no such novel existed, at least under his own name. Perhaps the author, knowing the totemic power over collectors inspired by the rarity of his works, had released it in a more accessible format, albeit secretly, over an unpublicized website ... With the flyer in my pocket I set out for that rundown part of the city to learn more about this phantom book.

Over the years I've observed few changes in the neighborhood, save that somehow even more condemned tenements seemed to pop their ulcerous faces above the wreckage. This time it was, however, atmospherically different: night had erased all specificity from its streets, all semblance of modern use. It now very much resembled Chopper-Kovsky's Crawl, "a graveyard of illusions couched in high, ugly buildings and twisting, shadow-clotted streets, in which the windows held secrets and you sensed a contiguous relation to the vast hungers at the bottom of the world." This relation, however, again seemed a little wishful, suggested by the novelty of seeing the area in a nocturnal setting (which I'd been warned to avoid), as opposed to my previous sunlit forays.

Three quarters of an hour passed. The school was beginning to prove as elusive as my old friend. I took the crumpled flyer from my pocket and checked the address; it was useless to go by numbers in this place. Still I persisted, starting at my own shadow, taking comfort in the distant hum of traffic even as I regretted that it masked any sounds that might issue from the vicinity. A watchful presence seemed just out of sight, as if a one-way mirror stood between me and the purpose that kept me prowling that desolate district ... a purpose that was beginning to seem like pretext for a deeper mission, given my usual indifference to literary socials.

I almost missed it. The school stood at the end of a cul-de-sac half-hidden behind a willow tree. It was a red-brick edifice, its lower windows, but not its upper windows, boarded in front. All looked dark within. A figure observed me from one of the upper-story windows; in the moonlight from the street it resembled one of the artist DeGrazia's stooped, faceless angels. I waved; it turned and withdrew.

I took one more glance around the cul-de-sac—at the squalid

shacks, all unlit, tumbling towards their own shadows on the deserted street—then climbed the central steps and opened the door.

I'd seen even dingier venues for assemblies of a similar clandestine nature. In college, I sat on a vomit-stained beanbag chair in the catacombs beneath a punk bar to swap manuscripts with a half-dozen would-be Ballards and Vollmans. The organizers of this meeting likewise seemed to derive satisfaction from building anticipation through a convoluted and somewhat paranoid process. A bright red arrow painted on a piece of cardboard sticking past the inner wall assured me I was in the right place. Through the doorway where it pointed, tiers of seats reached high into shadows from the paper-strewn floor of an amphitheater. Scattered throughout those seats, while atmospherically worthy of association, were attendees hardly qualified to discuss the work of Edward Chopper-Kovksy.

They were masks, lifelike but grotesque distortions of the human visage. Uncannily detailed, staring blankly through skewed, flaccid skins from the wig heads on which they were mounted. They represented all ages, from the freckled youth to the goateed matriculant to the puffy-cheeked matriarch. It was as if someone had stolen the heads from Madame Tussaud's waxworks. Spaced along the walls irregularly, torches threw the masks' features into childish semblances of emotion.

I assumed this resulted from some perverse tradition among squatters. It also made me reconsider whether I'd come to the right place. A slip of paper clung to my heel; I disengaged it.

"DISCUSS THE NEW NOVEL BY HORROR MAESTRO EDWARD CHOPPER-KOVSKY," it said, in the same serif font as the flyer in my pocket, "COME TO THE ADDRESS BELOW. WE HOPE YOU FIND US." Somewhat puzzled by this last statement, I discarded the announcement.

I worked my way up the center aisle. Across the projecting wall of the balcony above the entrance, an elaborate mural had been painted. By the ruddy torchlight I recognized the tenements, the gaping storefronts, the winding streets. Throughout, like unearthly visitors in a cave painting, stooped, scaly creatures crouched in alleys or stared from tenement windows, while gigantic, undulating shadows descended upon the rooftops like carnivorous black clouds.

Another red arrow, painted across the right-hand door, directed me across the threshold. The right side dead-ended; the left led down a brief set of stairs and curved out of sight, lost in pitch black. As if there were any doubts as to what route I should take, a sandwich board stood outside the doors with the words

THIS WAY TO THE TRANSMUTATION

painted in the same arterial-red color, the last letter running into an arrowhead aimed down the hall.

For a moment I felt my way through near-total darkness. But around the bend I caught sight of a fire in the distance, dancing in a metal drum. A smell both earthy and metallic carried down the corridor. Upon the walls the firelight improvised wavering patterns based on variations of a deep red. Loose sheets of paper slid and crackled under my feet. Holding up a sheet of wide-ruled loose leaf, I could just discern a child's arithmetic problem. On the other side, a jotted bit of mysticism:

Among the ruins I see my inner pathology, the mechanical business of matter reorganizing itself into lower orders. These orders remind me of my own descent into a similarly less organized state, a malignant Otherness

There was more, but I noticed someone watching me from behind the burn barrel. Whether man or woman, I couldn't tell from the nondescript physique in its bulging sweatshirt. The hood framed a charcoal shadow. A blackened hand drew back from the fire—it was actually *in* the fire—to hook its distended thumb in a vague gesture ahead of me before resuming its self-immolation. This I explained to myself as some sort of artistic stunt accomplished with a fire-resistant glove.

The figure seemed to be neither in pain nor aware anymore of my presence. I dropped the loose-leaf sheet into the blaze. "I'm here … for the book group?" I asked.

The figure nodded over its shoulder. "That way," came the mumbled reply.

Around the corner stood a row of lockers and empty glass cases. At the end, down a wide path littered with more papers, another barrel blazed next to a set of double doors. Inside, other makeshift fires illuminated sections of bleachers and parquet floor. There was no one by the drum. Drawn by the aromatic scents from the smoke, I peered into the flames and saw, embedded in the kindling and ashes, strung about like a broken necklace, what appeared to be human teeth.

Just then my attention turned towards a man disappearing through the doorway. He looked like a biker, his silver hair tied in a

183

ponytail and his tattooed arms bared in a frayed denim vest. I followed him into the gymnasium, stopping at a discreet distance.

We were in a queue reaching from the baseline of the basketball court to the half-court, where it angled towards an arched opening in a giant dome. This was composed of a fibrous, tobacco-colored material riddled with orifices like half-rotted lips. It lost itself among the rafters and, from what I could discern by the glow of barrel fires in the bleachers and around its base, spanned both free-throw lines and nearly both sidelines. In that darkened arena it seemed both monumental and arcane, a larval shelter built to the scale of a circus big top. Shadows quivered along its vaulted roof, chased by ragged illuminations. A dark, acidic residue hung on the air, the breath of burning waste.

I waited some minutes, checked by an impregnation of the air that seemed to immobilize the assembly. It was as if we were listening to the shadows overhead, a murmur of space shifting, making room to accommodate a higher order of space, a more evolved form of darkness. For a moment it seemed that my head lost contact with my body and hung suspended in a spinning abyss …

I focused my eyes on the biker in front of me, and the vertigo subsided. Roused from the communal trance, I felt a sort of connection with this guardian angel of floating heads and leaned over his shoulder to ask:

"Is this … for the book group?"

He cocked his head, as if I'd distracted him from some crucial detail in a public announcement; someone ahead grunted affirmative, in an admonishing tone, cutting off further attempts at conversation.

The line was building behind me. Feigning idle curiosity (even this seemed indecorous), I scanned the faces in the firelight, men and women of all ages and ethnicities, their mouths hardened with concentration. There seemed to be a preponderance of younger people—in their twenties or thirties—tattooed and pierced and sporting retro hairstyles. Oddly, no one looked at the man emerging from the bleachers, a hulking figure dressed in a black suit, wringing his hands … I almost cried out his name. It was the man whose novel we were here to discuss—Edward Chopper-Kovsky!

I recognized him from the few images that had entered the public domain. Sweat glistened on his prodigious bald head; his eyes shone with an excitement that was almost gustatory. Though he was imposing, well over six feet tall, he had such a buoyant air in person that I might have advised him to attend events via a sterner proxy. I guessed him about my age, although he'd gone under the knife too many times or perhaps grown dependent on pain medications. A flaccidity about his face, a rubberiness in the skin brushed over in pictures, aged him grotesquely, so that he resembled a jack-o'-lantern after Halloween when it starts to spoil.

He spread his hands, addressing the line. "Welcome to The Transmutation," he thundered, in a voice so loud even he looked startled by its volume. Then, in a lower tone, he said, "I'm indescribably happy for you all."

No one responded or even glanced at him. Though the inference that I had not, in fact, come to a book group meeting was by now obvious, this indifference to the famed author baffled me. My astonishment caused the writer to single me out from the solemn crowd.

"George," he said, and pulled me from the queue towards one of the burn barrels, "I've admired your work for a long time. How splendid to meet you."

His delivery was awkward, forced. His handshake was limp, his palm like ice. He went on to commend me for the work I'd been doing "in a field suffering from a dearth of artisans willing to particularize their nightmarish ways of thinking."

What did one say to that? I smiled, blurting the thank-you's I'd always wanted to give out from behind a dealer's table at a bookstore or convention. It was ridiculous. We were ignoring the dome-sized elephant in the room.

"This is some book group," I said, taking the initiative.

His pink lips creased. "Yes—it is. And I'm sorry you've made it. I really had hoped I would never see you again."

"Again?"

He let out a deep, portly sigh. "Oh, let's stop it, George. You know who I am."

He was wringing his hands again. They were large even for his frame, interlocked like overgrown crustaceans in either the throes of passion or mortal combat. It seemed hardly possible as he suggested, yet the suspicion had been hovering in back of my mind. Only one person I knew was so equipped to create that manual spectacle of agitation.

"Paul?"

185

"I'll explain," he said, drawing me farther into the shadows, "but quickly—it's almost time."

I started to inquire about The Transmutation, but he cut me off, promising that all would be made clear shortly.

He explained that he had not responded well to treatments during his illness nearly twenty years before. The cancer had spread viciously; he was given less than six months to live. His extremities ached excruciatingly from the failed therapy, and he was told his suffering would only worsen. He contemplated suicide. Then some friends visited him at home, having tracked him down despite his efforts to avoid social contact. They blathered on nervously, meeting his eyes with doleful glances and ignoring his foul disposition until the group's leader, a pretty brunette, whispered in Paul's ear and deposited a slip of paper in his hand. When they left, he read it.

"It was an invitation to a book group meeting. To discuss a novel by an unknown writer named Edward Chopper-Kovsky."

"But who is—"

"No one," my old friend shrugged. "Not that I knew it at the time. It was what the girl whispered in my ear that intrigued me: *The Transmutation.* An alchemical term, maybe. But what did it have to do with a book group meeting? What could she have meant? There'd been such urgency in her voice—and what a voice. She was a blues singer. I'd dated her once; all her friends were artists of some sort."

At this point he diverged from his story. Nowadays, he stated, in an age of instant communication, one needn't whisper and pass off slips of paper to spread the word; I was a rare attendee in coming here uninformed.

The flyer was meant as a coded message for the less tech-savvy initiates, he explained. But since I chanced upon it, and succeeded in finding the location, it was obvious that I'd become part of a society no one, at least at first, opts to join.

"Have you had a biopsy, George?" Challas asked.

"What? No. Why would I?"

"Have you had headaches?"

"Well—I stare at a screen all day. Of course."

He frowned. "Don't take it from me. But Pamela knows. There are dogs that are said to sniff certain kinds of cancer; think of Pamela as a sort of otherworldly cancer dog, though the analogy is imprecise. Why do you think you lost me the night you followed me? You were

186

cancer-free then. But don't think it's the end," he added. "It's really a new beginning, as horrid as that sounds. But Pamela's coming, George. I'd better let you go. You won't want to miss it."

"That's not fair," I said, grabbing his sleeve as he nudged me back towards the line. "You still haven't explained anything. What happened after I lost you? Who is Pamela? Who are these people?"

"They're like you. They're like me when I came here, close to death. They have something inside them. Something that naturally occurs in all of us, but has grown out of control, feeding off everything around them. *Cells with teeth.* These cells don't know how to die, they just spread and spread. We demonize them. But who are we to say our bodies are not properly *their* domain? Perhaps *we* are the mutants, the unwanted material, suffering because we won't embrace what we really are, which is to say are not: 'patterns of stuff that behave in ways we don't understand, but seem to revolve around reproduction, death, and the purchase of life at the cost of other life through every cycle of existence.'

"I had no idea just how true this was when I said it," Challas continued. "Nor how right I was in writing to you that the difference between certain troubled minds and the rest of us is the ability to plumb the truth of an existence without meaning but predicated, essentially, on carnage. For some of us help is needed, and then only under unique conditions: cancer. It is the ultimate pattern of cellular matter behaving in ways we can describe but don't understand, may never understand ... *because it's stronger.* It is the highest form of what we call life. But I've rambled enough, George—" He prodded me towards the line, which had begun moving. "—Go. She can help you. You're an artist, correct? Your duty is to tell the truth. First you must become that truth."

"Sure," I said, lacking the sarcasm I had intended, and shrugged him off, leaving him in the shadows.

Yet despite my astonishment at my friend's words, I watched the scene unfold with a growing admiration. Calmly, almost in step, the congregants marched into the dome, like disciples of a hidden Messiah welcoming a revelation.

One by one they slipped through the arched opening. I wondered how many could fit inside. Still the procession continued, until I estimated that those inside the dome must be standing elbow to elbow, breathing next to each other in the dark. The slow tempo created a feeling of unreality. The dream quality lulled me into a state of detached vigilance as the last in line were swallowed into the door's dark gullet.

The gymnasium swelled in size, opened by the relocation of some hundred people. The dome, too, seemed to have expanded, an immense pregnant belly in the light of the barrel fires, recumbent beneath a dense black fog.

It struck me, in the mood of that gymnasium, a repository of almost mystical anticipations, that what emerged from the roof was not only momentous, but logical. This time, however, it was irrefutably present, not as a peripheral impression of shifting space, but as a black membrane that detached itself from the shadows and seeped down the porous exterior of the dome. It flowed over the structure like a sentient syrup, to be slurped up by the orifices on the dome's surface, puckering around the oozing substance. A chill invaded the gymnasium, despite the lingering body heat and blazing fires.

The dome shuddered as though an engine had started inside it. It lit up from within, a luminous silver haze, exposing the silhouettes of those inside. Or rather the one silhouette, for no individual form was distinguishable in the lump of shadow shapes, an amorphous curdled mass filling the inner chamber. The surface of this coagulant bulged and twitched as things suggesting fingers—and faces—attempted to push through it. These animations grew sluggish and then ceased as the blob slid up the sides of the chamber. The silver light went dark, and the dome's exterior became opaque once more.

A heavy hand fell on my shoulder. "You should've gone in," Challas said.

"What just happened?"

"The opportunity of a lifetime."

He said something more, but I didn't hear him. I was watching the top of the dome. The dark thing pushed through the apex and buried itself in the shadows of the rafters like a giant, roving, alien tumor.

* * *

Despite my facility for mimicking Chopper-Kovskian description (or perhaps because of it), I know I can never fully evoke the loathsomeness of that surreal scene. Nor the aftermath of that protean abomination's exit when the fated ones in the queue, my fellow supplicants, emerged from the dome. You must see it yourself, as I do in flash-backs triggered by the everyday sight of human beings plodding wea-rily along the street—though I'm not so sure the ones I saw in the gymnasium could be called human anymore after encountering "Pam-ela" that night.

See them move off in all directions, dragging themselves towards the exits. See the man I knew as Paul Challas remove his crumpled jack-o'-lantern face, revealing the blackened skull beneath. His pink tongue rolls in a groove of ash, the syllables fluting into the air with-out a trace of impediment, despite the twisted ribbons of his lips.

You mustn't be prejudiced, he says, nodding at the sluggish crea-tures. What you see is a transition stage, the old and new cellular ma-terial struggling to integrate within the altered membrane. Within days they'll walk upright again, shedding the gray, silken material that envelops them, regaining some of their former stature. A few won't even require a disguise, assuming they wish to re-assimilate into the outside world.

How long will they survive, I ask.

Flaps like walnut flesh close and open on his bulging eye whites. His pupils hold me like water reflections on their lambent black disks. You're looking at it from the wrong paradigm, he explains. They're not diseased; they're *transmuted*. The metamorphosis for which they were born and are conditioned to deny or fight all their lives is com-plete. Pamela—my nickname for it, though its name, in truth, is Le-gion—has consolidated the darkness inside them. Now they go forth as artists and give this darkness back to the world, either disguised among the outsiders or unveiled among their own, in here, among this beautiful proliferating spoilage. It's what every artist wants: to explore the truth free of social baggage and exigency.

They have all the supplies they need. As for food, they're cellular omnivores—they feed on everything. The world nourishes them through every pore of their skins. You could've been one of them, George. *Now you're all alone.*

The memory—an epiphany born of nightmare—ends there. I have no recollection of how I got home that night. Fortunately though, I remembered Chopper-Kovsky's shocking remarks about my headaches, prompting me to seek medical attention. The cancer was treated early on.

Charles Austin Muir

Eighteen months have passed since my discovery of that unearthly laboratory. I'm back at a desk job during the days, while nights I continue with my "third-time-around" prose regurgitations of one of my favorite writers (who would've thought Paul had such a literary gift?). Life has resumed its humdrum rhythms.

But I wonder.

The other day I had a dream, a vision apart from the impossible occurrences I've mentioned. A dream that, despite its imagery, binds me to a future of cells with teeth. On the surface it was a tidal wave dream, a recurring dream I've had since college. I always outrun the wave in these dreams, but this one was the Mother Wave, and I woke with the feeling I would not escape. All the world's oceans were gathered in that apocalypse of water blotting out the sky, rushing with such immensity that it froze all sense of relative motion. I could see inside it, and it was black and seething.

It was the Cancer Wave—*is* the Cancer Wave—building inside me, rising over me.

Most of the time I dismiss this as a hypochondriac's fancy. But when the panic overwhelms me I set out for that rundown part of the city where I lost Paul Challas and found Edward Chopper-Kovsky. I walk and walk until I can no longer feel my feet; these excursions save me the trouble of waiting for a biopsy report.

Someday I'm going to find that cul-de-sac again. And when I do, with the smile of an old friend telling me my fate, I will stand in line and join the faceless angels who wait beyond the dome.

190

About the Contributors

Ed Kurtz: "Angel and Grace"

Ed Kurtz is the author of a novel, *Bleed*, and his short fiction has appeared in *Dark Moon Digest*, *Deadlines*, *Shotgun Honey*, and *Needle: A Magazine of Noir*. A lifelong denizen of the American South, he spent his formative years in Arkansas and has lived in Texas since the turn of the century. Kurtz can be visited online at www.edkurtzbleeds.wordpress.com

"Angel and Grace" derives from his fascination with the all the things that go bump in the South's backwoods at night.

Helen E. Davis: "Queen of Hearts"

Helen E. Davis, a current resident of Ohio, is a transplant from Louisiana, the Bayou State. She enjoys knitting, building with LEGO building blocks, and creating stories. Her fiction has appeared in print in *Sword and Sorceress* anthologies, and online at *Abyss* and *Apex*. She is currently working on *Past Future Present 2011*, an e-book anthology of short fiction.

"Queen of Hearts" mutated from an idea about how to solve the world's need for suitable transplant organs—and the question, so what could go wrong?

Jarret Keene: "Swanson"

Jarret Keene earned a Ph.D. in creative writing from Florida State University before moving to Las Vegas, where he documents the underground metal scene for *Vegas Seven* magazine. His Pushcart-nominated stories appear in many literary journals and anthologies, and he has edited several fiction collections, including the forthcoming *Casinonomicon: 13 Tales of Las Vegas Horror*. His post-apocalyptic sludge-rock band Dead Neon terrorizes the dive bars of Sin City.

"I wrote 'Swanson' after reading the wonderful book *Howard Hughes: Power, Paranoia & Palace Intrigue* by Geoff Shumacher, to whom the story is dedicated," says Keene. "Schumacher's book, which examines the reclusive billionaire's Vegas years, inspired me to situate Hughes within an alternate-history narrative involving mutants, robots and, scariest of all, humans."

JT Rowland: "Compatible Donor"

JT Rowland had a thought one day while reading a random issue of the *X-Men*. What if someone who had the healing ability of Wolverine donated a kidney? This inspired the premise of "Compatible Donor," Rowland's professional debut. A former member of the air force, JT Rowland lives on the island of Oahu in Hawaii. He spends his days writing and acting. He can be seen in local film productions and television commercials.

Roberta Lannes: "Chrysalis"

Roberta Lannes began publishing with a story she wrote while in her high school Senior Advanced Exposition class. She didn't write again until she entered the UCLA Writer's Extension Program in 1983. She found her milieu in Dennis Etchison's Writing Horror class. In her second term in the class, Etchison bought her story "Goodbye, Dark Love," written for a class assignment, for his award-winning anthology *Cutting Edge*. Over the last twenty-six years, she has continued to publish stories in science fiction, fantasy, and horror, much of her work with editors Stephen Jones in the UK and Ellen Datlow in the USA. Her stories have been published in more than a dozen languages. Her bibliography is available at www.lannes-sealey.com/author.

She lives in a suburban, alternate universe outside of Los Angeles called the Santa Clarita Valley. She's married to Mark Keynton Sealey, British poet, journalist, and classical music critic.

Regarding "Chrysalis," Lannes shares this story behind the story: "I

192

met Emmett Anderson around 1970. He was a kind, very funny, good man who was self-conscious about having been born with one arm. In 1976, his skin began to get extremely dry and scaly, and he was diagnosed with Ichthyosis vulgaris. It seemed no normal girl would become interested in him. But he met someone at a friend's wedding who seemed to see past his deformity and the condition of his skin, which covered 85 percent of his body in scales and rough red patches. Sadly, she turned out to be emotionally and physically abusive to him. It took years for him to leave her because his condition worsened, and he felt no one else would want him. With a lot of help from his friends, he finally left her. Within a year, his condition spontaneously cleared up, and he met his future wife. He married and, with his wife, was raising their two-year-old son when the disease returned, this time to the point that he was bedridden. His family continued to care for him until he died of complications from other immune system disorders in 1989. I wrote this story idea then, for Emmett, although the genders of the characters are reversed. The story grew from that early draft for this anthology. I always wanted him to live the life he wanted, and imagining him released from a body that tortured him gave birth to the transmutation of Aileen."

Maria Alexander: "Nickelback Ned"

Maria Alexander has committed a number of literary crimes as an author of humor, suspense, and horror. Her deeds have appeared in award-winning anthologies and magazines beside greats such as Chuck Palahniuk and David Morrell. Praised by disreputable rags like *Rue Morgue* and *Fangoria*, she atones for her vices by being an award-winning copywriter for Disney's websites. For the full literary rap sheet, visit her website: www.mariaalexander.net.

The opening verse for "Nickelback Ned" came to her in a dream she has happily forgotten.

Barbie Wilde: "American Mutant: The Hands of Dominion"

Barbie Wilde is best known as the Female Cenobite in Clive Barker's classic cult horror movie *Hellbound: Hellraiser II*. She has performed in cabaret in Bangkok; robotically danced in the Bollywood blockbuster,

193

Janbazz; played a vicious mugger in *Death Wish III*; appeared as a robotic drummer for an electronica band in the so-called "Holy Grail of unfinished and unreleased 80's horror": *Grizzly II: The Predator (AKA Grizzly II: The Concert)*, and was a founding member of the 1980s mime/dance/music group, SHOCK, which supported such artists as Gary Numan, Ultravox, Depeche Mode and Adam & the Ants. In the 1980s and 1990s, Wilde hosted and wrote eight different music and film review TV programs in the UK, interviewing such pop personalities as Cliff Richard and Iggy Pop, as well as actors Nicholas Cage and Hugh Grant.

In 2009, Wilde contributed a well-received short story, "Sister Cilice," to *Hellbound Hearts*, an anthology of stories edited by Paul Kane and Marie O'Regan, and based on Clive Barker's mythology from his novella, *The Hellbound Heart*. Wilde also co-wrote the book for a musical called *Sailor* with composer-lyricist-writer Georg Kajanus and screenwriter-playwright Roberto Trippini. Containing a unique perspective on life, violence, vengeance and love, *Sailor* has been conceived as both a stage and film musical drama. Wilde is now working on her second book, a horror story, after completing her first novel, *The Venus Complex*, a fictionalized journal of a serial killer. She has a short story appearing in the horror anthology *Phobophobia* in 2011, and another short story to be published in *The Mammoth Book of Body Horror* in 2012.

Of "American Mutant: The Hands of Dominion," Wilde confesses, "I've always been fascinated by the way religions can mutate into something rather distant from their origin sources of belief. I decided to take this mutation and push the process into something even further in "American Mutant: Hands of Dominion," which explores the shadowy world of American TV evangelism and twists the normal perceptions of what healing and forgiveness really are."

Stephen Woodworth: "Menagerie of the Maladapted"

Stephen Woodworth is a graduate of the Clarion West Writers Workshop and a First Place winner in the Writers of the Future Contest. His "Violet Series" of paranormal suspense novels includes

194

the *New York Times* bestsellers *Through Violet Eyes* and *With Red Hands*, as well as the most recent volumes *In Golden Blood* and *From Black Rooms*, and his short fiction has appeared in such venues as *The Magazine of Fantasy & Science Fiction, Year's Best Fantasy, Weird Tales, Aboriginal Science Fiction,* and *Realms of Fantasy.* He is currently at work on a new novel.

"When most of us hear the word 'mutant,' we think of deformity, aberration, monstrosity," Woodworth observes. "But the fact is, we are all products of mutation. Without the ability to adapt to a mutable environment, a species cannot survive and progress. Ultimately, we must either accept our place in the Mutation Nation ... or end up in the Menagerie of the Maladapted."

Wendy Rathbone: "The Dream In A Box"

Wendy Rathbone has had over 400 poems published in various magazines and anthologies, and dozens of stories published in anthologies such as: *Hot Blood, Writers of the Future, Bending the Landscape, Air Fish,* and more. The book, *Dreams of Decadence Presents: Wendy Rathbone and Tippi Blevins,* contains a large collection of her vampire stories and poems. She won first place in the Anamnesis Press poetry chapbook contest with her book, *Scrying the River Styx.* Her most recent poetry chapbook is *Dancing In the Haunted Woodlands,* from Yellow Bat Press. She lives in Yucca Valley, California, with her partner of thirty years, Della Van Hise.

Regarding "The Dream In A Box," Rathbone explains, "The whole point is that the main character, miserable as he is, not handsome and basically having no life, is to the core a very good person with heart. I love stories, especially horror stories, where humanity wins out, and love wins even in its darkest hour."

Jim Schoen: "Treasure"

About his childhood, Schoen vividly remembers sleeping four to a bed and warring with his ten siblings for the best food. College educated, he earned his degree as a carpenter and a mason. He has always enjoyed humor, as demonstrated in his story "Ice Cream," available soon

195

in *Structo 7*. But just as dear, when he can get his hooks into it, is the nasty creature gnawing at its chains in the dark.

"Treasure," Schoen assures us, will be best read in deep silence, under a dim light.

Charles Austin Muir: "The Transmutation"

Charles Austin Muir's fiction has appeared in several small-press magazines and e-zines, including *Cthulhu Sex Magazine, Whispers of Wickedness, Microhorror.com* (under the pseudonym George Kuato), and *Morpheus Tales.* His story, "Ding-Dong-Ditch," received an honorable mention in *The Year's Best Fantasy and Horror.* Forthcoming publications include *Title Goes Here* and *Hell Comes to Hollywood,* an anthology of horror relating to the motion-picture industry.

A morbid fear of disease following his cousin's death inspired Muir to write "The Transmutation," a story of cellular alchemy offering a new vision of what it means to create "outsider art."

About the Editor

Kelly Dunn started her writing career in journalism, churning out copy and editing trade magazines covering subjects from human resources to infotainment. *Mutation Nation* marks first stint as editor of a fiction anthology. She has worked as a university instructor, a stage actress, and a hearse dealer. These experiences inform her short fiction, which has appeared in e-zines and anthologies such as *Necrotic Tissue*, *Aberrant Dreams*, *The Dead That Walk*, *Midnight Walk*, and *The Undead that Saved Christmas*. Her alter ego, Savannah Kline, recently published her first novel, *Beloved of the Fallen*. She lives in Southern California.

29784616R00114

Made in the USA
Middletown, DE
06 March 2016